MURDER BY NUMBERS

A Langham and Dupré mystery

Eric Brown

SEVERN
HOUSE

First world edition published 2020
in Great Britain and the USA by
SEVERN HOUSE PUBLISHERS LTD of
Eardley House, 4 Uxbridge Street, London W8 7SY.
Trade paperback edition first published
in Great Britain and the USA 2021 by
Severn House, an imprint of Canongate Books Ltd,
14 High Street, Edinburgh EH1 1TE.

British Library Cataloguing in Publication Data
A CIP catalogue record for this title is available from the British Library.

ISBN-13: 978-0-7278-9077-1 (cased)
ISBN-13: 978-1-78029-712-5 (trade paper)
ISBN-13: 978-1-4483-0433-2 (e-book)

Typeset by Palimpsest Book Production Ltd.,
Falkirk, Stirlingshire, Scotland.

To the memory of
Beth Dunnett,
with love

ONE

The grey December afternoon found Langham at his desk in the Ryland and Langham Detective Agency, eating a cold pork pie and reading the manuscript of his latest novel. In the outer office, beyond the communicating door, Pamela was tapping away on the upright Remington.

Between crossing out purple passages in the manuscript, he contemplated living in the country after spending the past ten years in London. He and Maria had booked a second viewing of the property they hoped to buy in Suffolk, though he knew it was just a formality. Maria had fallen in love with Yew Tree Cottage at first sight.

The rattle of the typewriter ceased, followed by a tentative tapping at the door. Pamela poked her head through. 'Another cuppa, Donald?'

He gulped down the last of his pie. 'You've read my mind.'

She took his empty mug and withdrew to put the kettle on.

Life in the country after London . . . He was tired of the city, the constant noise, the increasing traffic and insufferable smog. The village of Ingoldby-over-Water boasted a decent pub and a cricket team, and was only an hour and a half's drive from the city. In his enthusiasm, he'd even promised Maria that he'd consider getting a dog.

His reverie was interrupted by Pamela's return. She placed his mug on the desk and hesitated, biting her lip as she regarded him.

'I wonder if I might have a word, Donald?'

'Fire away.'

She hesitated again, frowning. She was a tall, slim girl in her early twenties, whose piled blonde hair, coral-pink cashmere cardigan and pearls gave her an appearance of sophistication belied by her Cockney accent – which she could switch on and off to order. Her phone manner suggested a Mayfair debutante.

'I was wondering,' she said at last, and winced as if anticipating a rebuff, 'if you and Ralph might consider promoting me?'

Langham picked up his mug and stared at her. 'Promoting?'

'Well, you see . . . I know I deal with clients, and write up the reports, but I have quite a bit of free time. I just thought it might be better spent helping you.'

'Helping in what way?'

She lodged herself side-saddle on the edge of the desk, twining a strand of hair around her forefinger. 'You see, it was while I was typing up one of Ralph's reports – the one about the vicar's stolen parrot – and I thought, "I could do this." Investigate the case, I mean – not steal his parrot. I could talk to the vicar, his neighbours. It didn't exactly take Sherlock Holmes to work out what had happened to the bird, did it?'

Langham smiled. 'No, I suppose not.'

'So, you see, if I handled the smaller cases, did some of the interviewing and what-not, that'd leave you and Ralph free to concentrate on the more important jobs, wouldn't it?'

'I suppose it would, yes; you have a point there.'

'I wouldn't be asking for any more money. I'm happy with what I'm getting at the moment. It's just that . . . well, sometimes I get a bit bored, and I'd like to be out there, helping you.'

She slipped from the desk and smiled at him. 'It was just a thought,' she added tentatively.

'I'll run it past Ralph when he gets back, OK?'

She beamed. 'Thanks a bunch.' She returned to the outer office, closing the door behind her.

Langham sat back and sipped his tea.

Pamela certainly had initiative. She sometimes sat in on their discussions, occasionally making valuable contributions. But the fact was that there was only just enough work, in the quiet period leading up to Christmas, for him and Ralph. Maybe after the New Year, when things began to pick up again, they could think about putting some of the interviews and minor cases her way.

The phone shrilled in the outer office and Pamela answered in her poshest voice. The intercom on his desk flashed and he flipped a switch. Pamela said, 'Donald, it's Maria. I'll put her through.'

Langham picked up the phone, wondering why Maria was ringing from work.

'Darling?'

'Donald. Would it be OK if I popped round to see you?'

'Now?' He was surprised. His immediate thought was that the

estate agent had contacted her to say that someone else had put an offer in for Yew Tree Cottage. 'Is it—?'

Maria anticipated the question. 'The cottage? No. I'll tell you when I see you. Love you, Donald.'

She cut the connection and Langham was left staring at the Bakelite receiver, wondering at her worried tone. He resumed reading his manuscript.

Fifteen minutes later the outer door opened and he climbed to his feet, expecting Maria. Instead he heard Ralph's chirpy tones as he asked Pamela to put the kettle on, then his partner breezed into the office, tossing his trilby at the hatstand in the corner and, as usual, missing.

'How goes it with Major Bruce's stolen diamonds?' Langham asked.

'Piece of cake,' Ralph said, retrieving his hat from the parquet and hanging it on the stand.

'Solved it?'

'Almost. It was the valet – stands to reason. Only bod with the opportunity. I'll stake out his gaff at Barking tonight. I reckon either he'll leave with the sparklers and meet with a fence, or he'll have someone come to his place for a gander. Bob's your uncle. Anything doing here?'

'Quiet as a tomb,' Langham said. 'Oh' – he thumbed towards the outer office – 'Pamela's asked for promotion.'

Ralph's weasel face exhibited pantomime surprise, and Langham recounted their secretary's case for active duty.

He fell silent as Pamela entered the room with Ralph's mug of hot, sweet, milky tea. When she departed, Ralph said, 'I suppose she could do a bit of legwork – maybe after Christmas. Routine stuff, nothing too complex. I mean, she's a young slip of a thing.' He slurped his tea. 'I'll tell her we'll think about it in the New Year.'

Maria arrived five minutes later and Langham could tell, from her brief peck on his cheek, that she was more than a little worried.

'Ralph,' she said, pulling off her thick sheepskin gloves, 'you look freezing cold.'

He was warming his hands before the two-bar electric fire. 'You bet. Perishing out there.'

'Your trouble,' she said, 'is that you don't dress for the winter.'

Langham smiled to himself. Ralph wore a thin polyester suit, summer and winter, and continually whined about the cold.

'I'm a poor gumshoe,' he replied, 'and I can't afford an over-coat. I should be a literary agent, like you.'

She smiled at Langham. 'Maybe we should buy Ralph a thick winter coat for Christmas, *oui?*'

'Rather have a warming bottle of Scotch,' Ralph muttered. 'Anyway, I'll make myself scarce. No doubt you two want to natter in private.'

Maria said, 'No, please stay, Ralph. I'm here on business.'

Ralph flashed Langham a look, then pulled two straight-backed chairs up to the desk.

Maria sat down, opened her handbag – which Langham always thought defied the laws of physics as it appeared tiny yet contained all manner of irrelevant paraphernalia – and pulled out a small white envelope.

'I received this by second post today, addressed to me at Charles's office.'

She passed it to Langham. He opened the envelope and withdrew a white card edged in black.

Maria said, 'Go on, read it.'

He read the brief message out loud. 'Maria Dupré, you are invited to attend a death at six p.m. on the third of December. Maxwell Falwell Fenton, Winterfield, Lower Malton, Essex.'

He passed the card to Ralph, then examined the envelope. The address of the Charles Elder Literary Agency was typed, and the Marylebone postmark was dated the day before.

'Maxwell Falwell Fenton,' Langham said. 'The artist? Do you know him?'

Maria bit her lower lip. 'I did, seventeen or eighteen years ago. He was a regular at my father's soirées at the French embassy before the war. Fenton was a big name then.'

'I'll say,' Ralph put in. 'I've heard of him, so he must've been.'

'This was before he served as a war artist in Europe,' Maria said. 'Even before that he was always a little unbalanced, but I'd heard rumours that the war pushed him over the edge. When he returned to England, he became reclusive and stopped painting. I hadn't heard anything about him for many years, and to be honest I assumed he was dead.'

Langham indicated the card that Ralph was still holding. 'Apparently not,' he said.

Ralph tapped the card. 'The third, Don. That's today.'

Langham took it and read the brief typed message again. He saw something he'd missed earlier. On the top right-hand corner, outside the black-lined border, was a tiny handwritten numeral: 6.

He showed this to Ralph, then to Maria, who said, 'Maybe he numbered the people he was inviting? But what should we do about this?' she went on. 'Call the police?'

Ralph frowned. 'They'd send us away with a flea in our ear. It's not exactly a crime to send out cards like this.'

'But we cannot just . . .' she began.

Langham regarded his wife. 'What do you suggest?'

She shrugged, avoiding his gaze. 'I don't know . . . I was wondering – perhaps we should go down there, see what all this might be about?'

He read the card again. '*You are invited to attend a death . . .*' He shook his head. 'Bizarre, to say the least. In your opinion, Maria, is this Fenton chap someone who'd be likely to kill himself?'

She shrugged. 'I really cannot say. He was always unpredictable, highly strung. I thought him a little mad. So I suppose . . .' She made a pretty moue with her lips and looked worried. 'What do *you* think we should do?'

He bit his lip, considering. 'I don't like the sound of it,' he said. 'If he is unbalanced, then who knows what he might be planning?'

Maria hesitated, looking down at her hands. 'I . . . I think he *is* planning to kill himself.'

'So you think we should go down and try to prevent him?' He shook his head. 'I don't know. I don't like it one bit. I think we'd be better off just informing the police.'

She looked up, her expression suddenly defiant. 'Then, if you will not accompany me, Donald, I shall take the car and drive down there myself.'

Langham looked from Maria to Ralph, who took the hint and snatched up his mug. 'Think I'll make myself another cuppa,' he said.

When the communicating door had closed, Langham leaned forward and said, 'Maria . . . there's something you're not telling me.'

She swallowed and looked down at the gloves she was fiddling with on her lap, her mouth half open as if about to say something.

He asked, dreading the answer, 'I know you said, back there, that you didn't know him well. But you were more than just casual acquaintances, weren't you?'

She winced. 'You must remember, Donald, that I was young. Just eighteen. Fenton was a famous artist . . . and charismatic.'

He nodded, swallowed and asked, 'What happened?'

It was a second before she replied. 'I met him at one of my father's parties, as I said. I was flattered by his attention. I'd just left school in Gloucestershire, and I think I was dazzled by the social life I found in London. And then a feted artist started paying me compliments.'

He hesitated, then said, 'Did you reciprocate?'

'I . . .' She paused, twisting her gloves. 'I was – what is the phrase? – starstruck, I think. I met him on three or four occasions at the embassy, and then he asked me to accompany him to an expensive restaurant. I was not sure that my father would approve – Fenton was in his forties at the time – so I didn't tell him and slipped away one evening.'

'And?'

'Fenton was charming. Of course, I'd heard rumours about him, about how he treated women. But all I could say was that, on that occasion, he treated me like a princess.'

'On *that* occasion?'

'At the end of the evening, he praised my beauty – "speaking from the perspective of an artist, of course," he said. Then he asked me if I would care to sit for him. He had a studio in London, as well as one down at Winterfield.'

'He lived in the sticks back then?'

'Winterfield is his ancestral home,' Maria said. 'It's been in the family for something like three hundred years.'

'You agreed, of course – to sit for him?'

'I was young and impressionable. And flattered. There I was, fresh from school, and this handsome, world-renowned artist said I was beautiful and asked me to sit for him. Of course I agreed.'

'What happened?'

'I sat for him. He painted me.'

'In London?'

'To begin with, yes. I sat for two or three sessions at his Chelsea studio, but he professed himself dissatisfied with something – I can't recall . . . the light or the setting or whatever. So he invited me down to Winterfield. He said that if he could paint me over the course of a weekend, he was sure the portrait would be a masterpiece. There was only one problem.'

'Your father?'

'There was no way my father would have agreed – so I lied. I arranged for a schoolfriend to invite me to her house, then packed a bag and took the train to Chelmsford.'

'You didn't wonder if Fenton had ulterior motives?'

Maria thought about that. 'Donald, it was so long ago. I really was a child, and naive. I knew nothing. Perhaps, to be honest, a little part of me was hoping that what he saw in me was not only a subject fit for a painting, but something more. You do understand, don't you, Donald? I was young and ridiculously romantic.'

He swallowed. 'Of course I understand,' he said. 'So . . . he painted you?'

'He painted me all that first day, a Saturday. And then he had his cook prepare a wonderful meal. I never usually drank, especially wine, but that night . . .'

'My God,' he said, fearing where this might be leading.

'I was a little tipsy at the end of the evening, but not so much that I didn't forget to lock the door of my room. I was naive, but not foolish. Anyway, on the Sunday he continued with the painting, and said that one more session, the following weekend, would see it completed.'

'And you went down again?'

'Not the following weekend – I had planned something with my father. But the weekend after that, yes.'

'How did it go?'

She shrugged, and he saw that she was clutching her gloves again. 'He finished the painting, and it made me look incredible. I was astounded. I wondered if this was how I really appeared, or whether it was just as *he* saw me.'

'Go on.'

It was a while before she could bring herself to continue. 'It was Sunday evening, and he'd plied me with drink. He said he'd like to do another painting, only this time, he said, it would be a nude.'

'Christ,' Langham said. 'And?'

'I was horrified. It was so sudden, so out of the blue. I liked him. I suppose I was attracted to him in a silly, schoolgirlish way, but the thought of doing *that* . . . So I refused.'

'And he accepted that?'

'No. No, he didn't. He was enraged. He turned very ugly, Donald. He was very drunk by this time, and he cursed me.' She screwed her eyes shut, then forced herself to go on. 'And the things he said . . .' She shook her head. 'He called me terrible things – things I cannot repeat. And then he said that I was a little fool if I thought that all he wanted was to paint me. I was terribly hurt and confused. I was in out of my depth. And then . . . then he forced himself on me.'

'The bastard—'

'Or, rather, he tried to.'

Langham found that his mouth was dry. 'What happened?'

'I fought him off. He was very drunk, and although he was a big man, I was young and more athletic. He scared me to death when he grabbed me, and I fought like a cat, scratched him, tried to gouge out his eyes. I was enraged, Donald.'

'Good for you!'

'And then I lurched towards the fireplace, grabbed the only thing to hand and swung it at him. The poker struck the side of his head and he went down like a clichéd sack of cement in a bad thriller. I thought I'd killed him. I felt for his pulse, found that he was still alive, then gathered my belongings and left. I managed to catch the last train up to London and stayed at my friend's house.'

'And that was the last time you set eyes on Maxwell Fenton?'

She shook her head. 'No, Donald. Imagine my horror when he showed up at one of my father's soirées a month later. I tried to avoid him, but he cornered me.'

'What did he say?'

'He fingered the scar on his temple, smiled like the devil and said that he hoped it wouldn't fade as he wanted to have it as a reminder of my tempestuousness. And then he had the temerity to ask me to sit for him again.'

'And you said?'

'I told him to go to hell.'

'Attagirl!'

'And that *was* the very last time I saw him,' she said.

They sat in silence for a while, before Maria looked up at him and smiled. 'So you see, Donald, I want to go down and see if Maxwell Fenton really does intend to kill himself – and, to be honest, I suppose a small part of me hopes he does.'

'Well, if you think you're going there on your own, my girl . . .'
She smiled. 'So you'll come with me?'

Langham sighed. 'Of course, but I'm taking my revolver. Just to be on the safe side.'

He glanced at his watch. It was almost four o'clock. 'If we set off now, we'll be at Lower Malton well before six.'

Maria looked relieved. 'Oh, thank you, Donald. You don't know how much this means to me.'

'You owe me one, my dear.'

They moved to the outer office, and Langham told Ralph they were heading up to Essex.

'It's a fair way,' Ralph said. 'You OK for petrol?'

'Managed to fill up last night at my local station,' Langham said.

Ralph nodded. 'I know a chap down Chiswick way who'll see us right in an emergency,' he said, no doubt referring to one of the many black marketeers he'd got to know just after the war. 'No ruddy Arab's going to stop me driving.'

'Don't curse the Arabs,' Langham said. 'It's your shower, the Tory fools governing the country, who made a mess of Suez. Right,' he said to Maria, 'let's be making tracks.'

She donned her overcoat, headscarf and gloves, and they descended the stairs to the busy, rain-lashed street.

TWO

They drove north-east through the dreary suburban sprawl of the city, chatting about the cottage and Maria's plans to buy new furnishings and curtains. She appeared animated, but it was a superficial enthusiasm belying the fact that her thoughts were elsewhere.

Already the winter twilight was closing in, abetted by rain clouds. The downpour persisted, making the procession of houses, shops and factories seem all the more bleak. Shop fronts were lighted against the gathering darkness, and pedestrians bent into the wind as they hurried homeward. Langham noticed queues of cars at every petrol station they passed.

It was a relief when they left London in their wake and motored through open country. These days he felt as if a weight had been lifted from his shoulders when London with its heaving population was finally behind him. He wondered if it was the imminent prospect of moving from the city that had brought about his sudden antipathy to the capital.

Maria said something, and Langham glanced at her. 'I'm sorry, what was that? Miles away.'

'I said, when all this is over, Donald, I think we should have another little break at the Grange.' A month before they'd spent a weekend at the comfortable old hotel near the village of Abbotsford in west Suffolk.

'"When all this is over",' he said, glancing at her. 'Yes, let's do that.'

They drove on in silence for a while.

'So you really think Fenton intends to kill himself?' he said a little later.

Maria stared into the darkness, grimacing. 'Perhaps the rumours are correct, Donald, and he has gone mad.'

'It certainly sounds deranged to send out invitations to a death.'

'In a way, it is entirely in keeping with his egocentric character. He was always the showman who liked to be the centre of attention. He had talent, yes, undeniably, but it seemed that this was not enough for him. He wanted people to admire him for his eccentricities as well as for his art.' She shrugged. 'He once said to me that his artistic talent came naturally, and that he despised those who lauded it. Do you know what I think?' she added, turning to him.

'Go on.'

'I think he loathed himself. He despised the facility of his talent, and therefore mistrusted those taken in by it. He wanted to be loved for who he was, but people could not love him because he was so terribly flawed and narcissistic.'

'You'd make a good psychiatrist.' He laughed. 'I'll have to watch myself.'

'You have nothing to worry about, Donald. You are at heart a simple, uncomplicated soul, and perhaps that is why I love you so.'

They drove on for another fifteen minutes until they came to a crossroads. Maria pointed to a fingerpost and said, 'Oldhurst, two miles. Lower Malton is just a mile or so further on.'

'Can you recall the way to the house?'

She nodded grimly. 'How can I forget? That Sunday night, fleeing over the fields and down the road to the train station at Oldhurst . . . The house stands a mile beyond the village, in woodland. *Winterfield.*' She shivered. 'Even the name gives me the chills.'

They came to Oldhurst and took a winding lane away from the town and into the darkened countryside.

Lower Malton proved to be a collection of perhaps fifty cottages, a couple of shops, a public house, and a Saxon church on either side of a twisting main street. Langham drove through the village in less than a minute and slowed down as they approached a crossroads.

'Where now? Left, right or straight ahead?'

Maria leaned forward, peering. 'Right, and then an immediate left. The house is about a mile further on.'

Langham turned right, then left along a lane with high hedges and overhung with trees; their headlights bored through the darkness, illuminating a lane that twisted and turned and resembled more a burrow than a road.

Maria pointed. 'There, to the left.'

Langham made out a pair of stone gateposts topped with what looked like griffins rampant. The great wrought-iron gates were open, though hanging off their hinges and leaning back against masses of rhododendron.

He slowed down and looked at his watch. 'Five forty-five. Just on time. At least it's stopped raining.'

'I wonder how many other people he's invited. I hope . . .'

'Go on,' he said, turning into the driveway.

'I hope I'm not the only one.'

'I very much doubt you will be. The invitation was numbered, remember. There'll be others; rest assured.'

They proceeded slowly up the gravelled drive, with looming vegetation closing in on either side. They rounded the bend and the headlights picked out, a hundred yards ahead, the low, many-turreted shape of what looked like an Elizabethan manor house. A roseate glow issued from a single mullioned window to the right of a great timber door.

'And we're not the first to arrive,' he said, pulling up beside a crimson Morgan coupé.

He reached into the glove compartment, withdrew his revolver and slipped it under his jacket.

Maria watched him, smiling tensely. 'I hope you won't need to use it,' she murmured.

'I'm sure I won't,' he said. 'But it's a precaution.'

Langham opened the door and climbed out. He took Maria's hand and they approached the porticoed entrance.

As they were climbing the steps, someone called out, 'I think you'll find it's locked, and that no one will answer your summons.'

They turned to see a small, slim, peroxide blonde stride across the gravel from the side of the house, presumably the owner of the Morgan. She was in her early forties, a pale beauty dressed in a high-collared raincoat and a cloche hat that perched on the side of her head.

'I rang the bell,' she said, 'but there was no reply. So I tried the door and found it locked.' She gestured over her shoulder. 'Then I took a turn around the house, but there's no sign of life.'

She gave them a winning smile and held out a hand. 'Holly Beckwith,' she said. 'You probably know the name from the West End – if you're theatregoers, that is.'

Maria took her hand. '*An Inspector Calls*,' she said. 'Donald and I saw it at the Globe last year. You were superb.'

The actress pressed a hand against her chest. 'So kind.'

Langham made the introductions. The grip of the woman's bird-boned hand was almost ethereal.

He indicated the house. 'I take it you too were invited?'

'So tiresome. I hear nothing from the man for over twenty years, and then this. He always did like to be the centre of attention; it became just *too* much. I was stupid enough to have had an affair with him, darling. It ended in tears – his tears, might I add, when I finished with him.'

Langham moved to the door and drew the bell-pull, then hammered on the door. He moved from the plinth of steps, approached the mullioned window and peered inside. A roaring fire in a vast hearth illuminated a comfortable lounge furnished with three sofas and several armchairs. A trolley of drinks stood beside the fireplace.

'Appears to be set up for a little soirée,' he reported on returning to the women.

The actress eyed Maria. 'And how do you know Fenton? Another one of his conquests, I take it?'

'I sat for him,' Maria replied hurriedly.

'That was one of his many ploys,' Beckwith purred. 'It's a wonder he didn't inveigle you into his little harem.'

'If you haven't seen him for more than twenty years,' Langham said, 'and thought little of the man at the time, do you mind my asking why you came here this evening?'

The actress gave a dazzling smile. 'I came because I wanted to ensure, with my own eyes, that the despicable man was really dead.'

Langham exchanged a glance with Maria. 'You think—?' he began.

'That he intends to kill himself?' Beckwith said. 'Yes, I do, darling. It's entirely in keeping with his character, given that he's dying.'

'He's dying?' Maria said.

'Heard it on the grapevine,' Beckwith replied. 'Cancer or leukaemia or something beastly like that. It isn't like the Fenton I knew to go out with a whimper. I suspect he wants people to watch him go with a bang.'

Langham was about to suggest that they wait in the car, out of the cold wind, when the sound of an engine forestalled him. They turned and watched a pre-war Daimler roll sedately up the drive and draw to a halt beside his Rover.

A small, tubby man leapt out from behind the wheel, ran around the front of the car, and opened the passenger door. His performance had about it the obsequious alacrity of a flunky attending royalty. This impression was reinforced when a small, imperious woman in her mid to late fifties, dressed in an evening gown, stepped from the vehicle. The expression on her plump, querulous face suggested that she thought the gravel might be quicksand.

The little man reached into the car for a fox stole and arranged it around the woman's shoulders with exaggerated solicitude.

She had a bloated, thickly powdered face and a beehive of blue-rinsed hair, and she surveyed the little gathering imperiously through a lorgnette. 'And who might we have here?' she piped.

Langham made the introductions. 'And you are?'

'Goudge,' said the woman. 'Hermione Goudge.'

Behind her, the little man bobbed from side to side, smiling nervously at the company. Langham expected him to return to the car and drive away, and was surprised when Hermione Goudge turned to him almost dismissively and said, 'And this is my husband, George.'

Langham shook his hand in the spirit of camaraderie, already feeling sorry for the fellow. George appeared not so much short as truncated, as if his legs had been amputated at the knees and his ludicrously tiny feet attached to their stumps.

'Any idea what all this is about, old man?' George asked in a reedy falsetto.

''Fraid not,' Langham said. 'My wife received an invitation, and we thought it prudent to turn up. I take it you received—?'

Hermione Goudge turned to him. 'Of course we did. Why do you think we're here?' Her voice had the sharp, hectoring tone of someone who assumed she was always in the right.

'Why the devil are we standing around out here, catching our deaths?' she demanded. 'Hasn't someone—'

Holly Beckwith snapped, 'Of course we have. No one appears to be home.'

'Ridiculous!' Hermione Goudge snorted.

'Would you mind if I took a look at your invitation cards?' Langham asked, looking from the Goudges to Beckwith.

'Why on earth do you want to do that?' Hermione asked.

'Just curious,' Langham said.

'George,' Hermione demanded, holding out a hand.

Her husband fumbled through his pockets and eventually produced two cards which he handed to his wife. She passed them to Langham. The cards were identical to Maria's with the exception of the numerals '2' and '3' handwritten in the top right-hand corners. Beckwith handed him her invitation, which was numbered '4'.

He passed them back without comment.

As if in an attempt to strike up conversation, the actress asked Hermione Goudge, 'And how do *you* know Fenton? I take it,' she added archly, 'that you weren't one of his paramours?'

Hermione regarded her down the length of her nose. 'The impudence!' she snorted. 'I had the unpleasant task of reviewing several of Fenton's exhibitions and writing critically of his mawkish daubs.'

'Of course,' Maria said. 'You're the art critic – didn't you write the biography of Velázquez?'

'Among many other books and monographs, my dear.'
Hermione sniffed.

Langham asked, 'And how did Fenton take your criticism?'

She fixed him with a caustic stare. 'How do you think anyone
of Fenton's shallow, egotistical bent might take criticism? He
was enraged – which, I admit, was rather gratifying to behold.
He was apoplectic that anyone might think his third-rate smat-
terings were anything other than works of genius. I demolished
him in print, and I had the pleasure of doing so verbally when
he bearded me at his solo exhibition at the National just before
the war.'

'When was the last time you met him?' Langham asked.

'That would be 'thirty-nine,' she said, 'and thankfully our paths
have not crossed since. Maxwell Fenton has subsided back into
the obscurity he deserves.'

He turned to George. 'Do you know the artist?'

The little man hesitated. 'We . . . we were friends, many years
ago, before we fell out.'

Langham exchanged a glance with Maria. There was a pattern
developing here, he thought: Fenton had reason to dislike
everyone who had so far accepted his invitation.

Holly Beckwith said to Hermione, 'Did you know that Fenton
was dying?'

The critic sniffed. 'I have heard the rumour, yes. The only
worthwhile thing he might have done in years.'

Another car engine sounded, and a black Ford Popular appeared
around the bend of the drive and drew to a halt beside the Goudges'
Daimler.

Two men climbed out and approached the gathering, now shel-
tering under the portico from the rain that had resumed. The elder
of the two Langham judged to be in his sixties – a nervous, portly,
plum-faced man in a tight suit who hung back and observed the
gathering with darting, piggy eyes.

The younger man in his mid-twenties was small, thin and
epicene, and introduced himself in a languorous drawl as Crispin
Proudfoot, 'the poet'.

Langham wondered if the unlikely moniker was an affectation.
Proudfoot was dressed in a lightweight beige jacket and trousers
more suited to the south of France than to England in winter. His
deathly pale face and white eyelashes suggested albinism.

'Crispin?' Hermione Goudge said. 'What on earth are you doing here? I had no idea you knew Fenton.'

'Hermione, George,' Proudfoot said, beaming at the couple. 'How pleasant to see you both. Yes, I knew him for a time a few years ago.' He introduced the older man. 'This is Doctor Bryce. I was tootling along the lane,' he went on, 'when I saw the doctor and offered him a lift.'

'I live in the village,' the doctor explained in mordant tones.

Holly Beckwith said, 'I take it you were invited here, Mr Proudfoot?'

The poet blushed as if unaccustomed to being addressed by beautiful women. 'Yes. That is, I received this.' He fumbled the card from the breast pocket of his jacket.

'May I?' Langham asked.

He examined the proffered card. The numeral in the top right-hand corner read '5'.

Langham turned to the doctor. 'And yours, if I may?'

Dr Bryce regarded him suspiciously. 'Why the interest?'

'Curiosity, let's say,' Langham smiled. 'Maxwell Fenton's invitation is rather . . . odd, I think you'll agree.'

Hermione Goudge said, 'Odd it might be – but what gives you the right to question us like this? Answer me that, my man!'

'My husband,' Maria said, staring at the woman, 'happens to be a private detective.'

'Off-duty, I assure you,' Langham said, 'although my professional curiosity is piqued, I must admit.' He turned to Dr Bryce and held out his hand. 'If I might see your invitation card?'

The doctor looked uneasy as he fished his card from a threadbare wallet and passed it to Langham. Its numeral was '1'.

Langham regarded the two men. 'I wonder if I might ask how you know Maxwell Fenton?'

'He took me under his wing, rather,' Proudfoot said. 'He admired my verse and introduced me to a few influential figures.'

'When did you last see him?'

'Oh, perhaps five or six years ago.'

Going on a hunch, Langham asked the young man, 'I take it that your parting was . . . acrimonious?'

Proudfoot blinked. 'Why, no. Nothing of the kind. We parted on the most amicable of terms; it's merely that for the past few years I've been living in Paris.'

Langham turned to Dr Bryce. 'And you?'

The doctor looked away. 'What about me?' he muttered.

'When did you last see Fenton, and what is your relationship with him?'

The doctor brought his shifty gaze to bear on Langham. 'I saw Maxwell just a couple of weeks ago, as it happens. I'm his personal physician.'

'You are?' Holly Beckwith said. 'Then you should know if it's true: is Maxwell dying, Doctor Bryce?'

The nervous physician was saved from replying by the sudden report of bolts being shot on the great oak door of the manor house.

'Ah,' Hermione Goudge declared, 'a quorum has been achieved, and we are at last allowed entry – and not before time, I say!'

The vast door swung open and Hermione sallied forth, her husband dancing attendance at her side.

Langham took Maria's hand, hung back for a second or two, then followed the others inside.

THREE

A s they filed into a mahogany-panelled hallway, a po-faced butler asked to see the invitation card of each guest in turn. Hermione Goudge proffered her card and peered at the butler through her lorgnette. 'And where is Fenton, my man?'

'My instructions, ma'am, are to show you to the sitting room.'

He examined Maria's invitation, then held out his hand for Langham's.

'I'm with my wife,' he said.

'I am under express instructions,' said the butler, 'to allow entry only to those with invitation cards.'

Langham held the man's gaze. 'In that case,' he said, taking Maria's arm, 'I'm afraid the evening can proceed without us.'

His words had the desired effect. The butler murmured that he would endeavour to ascertain if an exception might be made in this case, and disappeared along the corridor.

He returned a minute later. 'I have been instructed to make you

welcome,' he said without allowing his neutral expression to slip.
'If you would care to follow me.'

Maria gave Langham's hand a quick, victorious squeeze.

'This is all very well,' said Hermione Goudge as they crossed
the hall, 'but we were expecting Fenton himself.'

'I understand that he will see you presently, ma'am.'

After the chill of the evening, the warmth of the sitting room
was a welcome relief. George Goudge assisted his wife to an
armchair beside the blazing fire and settled her into it as if she
were an invalid.

Crispin Proudfoot marched up to the flames and warmed his
hands. Holly Beckwith made a beeline to the drinks trolley and
fixed herself a Martini, calling over her shoulder, 'Anyone else? I
presume,' she went on, addressing the butler, 'we can help ourselves?'

'My instructions were that I should do everything within my
power to make you feel at home,' the butler said, then slipped
from the room.

Dr Bryce joined the actress and poured himself a stiff Scotch,
then carried it across to the window and stared out. His hand
trembled as he lifted the glass to his liverish lips and took a long
drink.

'Anyone else?' Beckwith asked.

'A vodka and orange for my wife,' George Goudge said as he
approached the drinks trolley.

Langham looked at Maria, who shook her head and murmured,
'Just a tonic water for me, Donald.'

He poured two tonic waters and joined Maria beside the hearth.

From her armchair by the fire, which she occupied as if it were
a throne, Hermione Goudge cleared her throat. 'Someone amongst
us, if you don't mind my saying, must know what all this might
be about.' Her thickly powdered face turned to scan everyone in
turn. 'You, Doctor,' she almost shouted. 'Surely you, as Fenton's
physician, must know what the deuce the man is planning.'

The doctor started at the sound of his name. He swung his
portly bulk to face the woman, his lugubrious expression resembling that of a dyspeptic bloodhound.

'I assure you that I know as much – or as little – as anyone,'
he said, and moved to the trolley where he refilled his glass.
He returned to his station by the mullioned window, his back to
the gathering.

'Perhaps,' Holly Beckwith ventured playfully, 'Maxwell is planning to exhibit his very last work of art—'

'What do you mean by that, girl?' Hermione Goudge snapped.

'He was always an exhibitionist,' the actress said, 'and it would be just like him to shock us all by publicly staging his death.'

'Our invitations stated "a death",' George piped up. 'That doesn't necessarily mean it will be his own.'

The little man had voiced what Langham himself had refrained from mentioning. He cleared his throat and said, 'It struck me that several of you gathered here this evening have in some way incurred Maxwell Fenton's displeasure. I know that's true in four instances out of six.'

'As I said,' Proudfoot stammered, 'we were on the best of terms at our last meeting.'

'Doctor?' Langham said.

Bryce sighed and swung round to face them. 'Ours is the perfect doctor–patient relationship,' he said, his face like thunder.

Langham watched the man. He gripped his glass in his right fist, his fingers white with the pressure he exerted.

'You didn't answer the girl's earlier question, Doctor,' Hermione Goudge said. 'Perhaps you might care to do so now? Is Fenton terminally ill?'

Bryce's slab face gave nothing away. He stared at the art critic. 'What passes between my patient and me is strictly confidential. I am sure you understand that, Mrs Goudge?'

Hermione muttered something under her breath and held out her glass for her husband to refill. He scurried to the drinks trolley and dutifully mixed a second vodka and orange. There was something nauseating, Langham thought, in his slavish devotion to the woman.

The door to the hallway opened and the butler appeared. 'If you would care to proceed to the library, ladies and gentlemen; this way, please.'

Maria found Langham's hand and gripped it. As before, Langham allowed the others to precede him. 'This is it, girl,' he whispered as they left the room. 'This is when we find out what it's all about.'

Maria leaned towards him. 'I have a terrible feeling, Donald.'

He squeezed her hand in reassurance.

*   *   *

The guests crossed the hall and filed down a corridor towards a door at the far end. The butler opened it, and Hermione Goudge was the first to cross the threshold.

She halted in her tracks and muttered something, although Langham failed to catch her exact words. The others crowded behind her, eagerly peering over the small woman's head and murmuring in surprise.

By the time Langham and Maria reached the doorway, the guests had entered the room. At the far end of the book-lined chamber, illuminated in the flickering orange light of an open fire, stood a large, elaborately carved dining chair with a high back and arms terminating in lions' heads – and sitting in the chair was the lank, skeletal form of an old man.

Langham turned to Maria. 'Fenton?'

She was staring at the seated figure with a horrified expression. '*Oui*, but . . . but he is almost . . . unrecognizable.'

As Langham followed the others into the room, he wondered whether the cause of the earlier murmurs of surprise had been Maxwell Fenton's physical condition or the fact that his seat was cordoned off from the rest of the room by a maroon rope, as if the man considered himself an exhibit in an art gallery.

Six chairs were ranged in a semicircle on this side of the rope, facing the seated figure. The butler fetched a seventh chair and placed it for Langham at the end of the row. To the backs of the original chairs, he noticed, were taped slips of paper numbered one to six.

The guests were shown to their respective chairs by the butler, who then departed and closed the door silently behind him.

Maxwell Fenton gripped the lions' heads with hands like claws, his gaunt face expressionless. His corduroy trousers and artist's smock hung loosely on the fleshless bones.

Maria took the penultimate seat, and Langham sat down beside her. He peered along the row at the guests.

Dr Bryce was staring at the floor, his large face pocked with sweat, his beefy hands screwed into fists on his lap. Beside him, George Goudge was gazing down at his fingernails as if embarrassed. His wife was staring at Fenton with an expression of pure loathing, while Holly Beckwith regarded the old artist with wide-eyed wonderment as if she couldn't quite believe what she was looking at. Crispin Proudfoot blinked nervously at the old man.

Maria, Langham noticed, could not bring herself to look at Fenton and was staring beyond him at the shelves of calf-bound books.

A strange hush settled over the gathering, broken only by the occasional crackle from the fire.

At last, Maxwell Fenton spoke. In a frail voice, that nevertheless carried well in the quiet room, he said, 'So here we all are . . . Men and women I once held in high regard.'

He fell silent, his head turning minimally as he took in each guest in turn.

It was hard to determine his age; the silvery skin stretched around his skull appeared ancient, and yet there was a certain vitality in his bright blue eyes which, along with a full head of grey hair, belied the notion that this was a man who stood on the threshold of death.

Only then did Langham noticed the long silver scar that marked his left temple.

It was Hermione Goudge who broke the silence. 'If you would be so kind as to cease your little game and state the reason you dragged us here tonight, Fenton.'

The artist smiled, the expression terrible on his skull-like face. 'All in good time, Hermione. You always were impatient.' His gaze turned to regard the first guest seated at the opposite end of the row from Langham.

'Doctor Bryce, we go back so many years. You have no doubt come to know me well – as I have you. I never considered you a true friend, but I did, once, trust you – before I came to know you better. You are, sir, a fool with a weak will and a penchant for the bottle, whose sins against me cannot go unpunished.'

Maria reached out surreptitiously and gripped Langham's hand. He glanced along the row at the doctor, whose puce-coloured face had turned a shade darker.

'And Mr Goudge . . .' Fenton said. 'Ladies and gentlemen, I have known George for almost forty years. Hard to believe that, just after the Great War, we were good friends for more than a decade. And then came the great betrayal.' He shook his head. 'But there is no need to go into details here. You know what you did, George; you know how much you hurt me.'

The tubby little man stared at Fenton with pop-eyes, his face for a second resembling that of a bloated koi carp.

'What a wonderful irony that it was I who introduced you to

what was to become your life's work,' Fenton went on. 'I refer, of course, to Hermione. You deserve surcease, sir, and I guarantee that it will come to you, sooner rather than later.'

George Goudge gave a strangled gasp, but Fenton was already eyeing Hermione. 'Speaking of betrayal, my dear . . . There can be none greater than that which the esteemed critic, Hermione Goudge, saw fit to visit upon me and so wreck my once great career.'

'I said only what was self-evidently true, Fenton! That you were a second-rate dilettante and a first-rate self-publicist!'

Fenton waved this away. 'But just desserts come to those who most deserve them, Hermione. You have earned the end that awaits you. And now,' he swept on, leaving Hermione red-faced and spluttering, 'we come to the delectable Miss Holly Beckwith, or as I called you, back in the first flush of our romance, "Holly Hock" because of your resemblance to that tall and rather vulgar bloom. We shared a delightful six months, my dear, until your wanton act of vandalism showed me what a selfish, cruel creature you really were. No matter,' he said, waving an airy hand, 'the years pass, and you, too, will suffer the fate you fear most of all.'

Holly Beckwith pressed a fist to her lips and stared at Fenton with a stricken gaze. Langham slipped a hand into his jacket pocket and gripped his revolver.

Fenton moved on to Crispin Proudfoot. 'Ah, Crispin, Crispin.' The artist sighed. 'I saw great promise in you, my boy. I really did. I assisted you in every way I could; I coached you, nurtured your emerging talent, spoke of you to all the right people. And you flew, you prospered, thanks to me – and then . . .' He paused, staring at the young man with barely suppressed rage. 'I know every detail of your theft – and be in no doubt that you, too, will pay for your misdeed.'

The poet hung his head and stared down at his trembling hands.

Fenton gazed at Maria. Her grip on Langham's hand tightened.

'Maria, sweet Maria,' Fenton said, 'one of the most beautiful women I have ever known, and certainly the most beautiful I have ever dared to love. And how did *you* repay me?' He smiled and reached up with a dithering finger to touch the silver cicatrice at his temple. 'You scarred me for life, my dear – but the physical reminder of your perfidy was nothing beside the scar you left upon my soul. But you shall, as they say, reap what you sowed.'

He fell silent. The fire crackled. Holly Beckwith sobbed quietly. Dr Bryce's breathing was stertorous. Hermione Goudge was muttering to herself. Langham could hear the thud of his heart, and at that moment it seemed the loudest thing in the room. Maria's grip on his hand was vice-like.

'My friends, my old friends . . . please remember my words, my avowal of revenge when I am dead and gone.' He stared along the row, one by one, at the guests. 'But first, perhaps, you would like the opportunity to explain yourselves, to excuse your conduct. Doctor Bryce, you first?'

Langham stared along the row at the doctor, who merely hung his head and stared at his lap in silence.

Fenton transferred his gaze to George Goudge.

'George?' he said.

'I, I . . . that is . . .' The little man was red-faced and almost incoherent. 'I did nothing wrong. I followed my heart. You would have done the same in my position!'

'That, my friend, is a moot point; we shall never know. Hermione?'

The art critic stared at Fenton as if he were an insect. 'Your egomania appals me, Fenton, and I refuse to take any further part in your little game.'

The artist ignored her and stared at Holly Beckwith. 'Holly, my Holly Hock?'

She shook her head, choking back the sobs. 'You took my innocence and defiled it, Fenton! And . . . and when I found out what a two-faced manipulator you were, I did what I had to do!' She relapsed into sobs, and Fenton moved his gaze to his next victim.

'Proudfoot?' he drawled, as if bored.

The young man stammered. 'I . . . I never meant that you should know. I always intended to pay you back, as God is my witness.'

'Pay me back?' Fenton laughed. 'Oh, you shall, Proudfoot. You shall!'

Langham's grip tightened around the butt of the revolver as Fenton's gaze settled on Maria.

'And last, but not least, Maria. Perhaps you, being the literary type you are, might be a little more articulate in your own defence.'

Langham stared at her, and never had he seen such an expression of pure, undiluted hatred on her face than at that second. 'You are a despicable human being, Fenton, and you deserve to rot in hell!' The artist laughed at this. 'Oh, I think I might, my dear – I verily think I might!'

His frail, claw-like right hand moved from the lion's head and slid beneath the material of his artist's smock. He withdrew something hitherto concealed there. Langham rose to his feet, fully expecting him to fire the revealed handgun at the assembled guests, one by one.

Instead, Maxwell Fenton raised the revolver, placed its barrel to his skull, and pulled the trigger.

FOUR

Holly Beckwith screamed. Hermione Goudge moaned and slipped from her chair in a dead faint, her husband crying out in alarm. Crispin Proudfoot vomited – but not before reaching the fireplace and the Chinese urn standing beside it, into which he noisily dispatched the contents of his stomach.

Langham turned to Maria. 'Are you up to finding the butler and telling him to phone the police?'

'Yes, of course.' She stood and hurried from the room.

George Goudge was kneeling beside his wife and ineffectively patting her hand. He glanced at the corpse, lolling in the chair. 'I don't suppose there's anything we can do for him?'

Dr Bryce, standing over the body, gave the little man a withering look. 'What the hell do *you* think, for God's sake? He's just shot himself through the blasted head!'

While Proudfoot and Beckwith moved to a chaise longue before the hearth, Langham joined the doctor.

The entry wound at the temple was tiny, but the bullet had blown a disproportionately large hole in the left side of the skull. A section of bone, like a broken teacup, was lying on the floor against the bookcase, and a spray of blood and brain matter was spattered across the calf-bound volumes. The artist's head hung over the side of the chair, bleeding on to the Persian rug.

The doctor was shaking uncontrollably. 'There was nothing we could have done,' Bryce said. 'You saw what happened. I'm his doctor, and even I never saw this coming.'

Langham crossed the room to a drinks cabinet and poured three stiff measures of whisky. He passed one to the doctor, who accepted it with a nod, and one to George Goudge, who was patting his unconscious wife's cheek and murmuring futile entreaties.

Langham drained his own glass, then asked Beckwith and Proudfoot if they'd care for a whisky. The poet declined with a grimace, but the actress nodded and smiled her gratitude. He poured two further measures – one more for himself – and joined the pair.

'I wasn't expecting . . .' the actress began, gesturing towards the corpse. 'I feel . . .' She shook her head, falling silent.

Proudfoot said, 'Guilty?' His voice shook. 'That's how I feel, to be perfectly honest. To think, for all those years he was storing up his hatred, planning *this*. That's what he wanted, you know: he wanted us to feel responsible, guilty. It was his way of avenging himself.'

Beckwith stared at the poet with huge ice-blue eyes. 'But I was well within my rights! He took advantage of me, and—'

Langham interrupted, 'In my opinion, Fenton was deranged. His work fell out of favour, and then he had a terrible war. If you ask me, he was looking for excuses to hate people. You just happened to be his unlucky victims.'

The actress shook her head. 'It could have been worse, I suppose. For a second, I thought he was about to shoot *us*!'

The poet leaned forward, his hands clasped between his knees. 'Can you begin to imagine the state of his mind? The festering hatred! We're all responsible – we all shall bear the guilt. All of us!'

Langham shook his head. 'Rubbish, man. That's exactly what he *wanted* you to feel. His self-hatred exaggerated your perceived slights out of all proportion. He treated my wife abysmally when she was barely a woman – then didn't like it when she stood up for herself.'

Proudfoot held his head in his hands. Beckwith jumped to her feet and paced back and forth, her knuckles pressed to her rouged lips.

The door opened and Maria appeared. She looked flustered and gestured for Langham to join her.

'Maria?'

'The butler – I saw him leave the house.' She took his hand and pulled him from the room. 'It looked as if he was running away.'

They hurried down the corridor, Maria adding, 'I rang for the police and an ambulance.'

The front door stood ajar. Langham ran out into the driving rain. He was in time to see the tail lights of a small car receding into the darkness, not down the main drive but along a track to the left of the house. He took off in futile pursuit, arrived at the corner of the building and came to a halt, panting, as he watched the car disappear through a plantation of pine trees.

Maria joined him. 'But why did he . . .?' she called against the wind.

Langham shook his head, cursing the weather.

He put his arm around her shoulders and turned back to the house. They were passing a conservatory attached to the west wing when he stopped and stared through the glass.

'Donald?'

He moved to the conservatory door and tried the handle. The door was locked, but the wooden frame was rotting; when he applied his shoulder and pressed, the door gave way. In the silvered light of the full moon, he found a light switch and turned it on. An unshaded bulb revealed what must have been Maxwell Fenton's studio, many years ago.

Maria joined him as he moved to a row of six canvases leaning against the wall.

The painting that had caught his attention showed a younger Hermione Goudge, sitting sideways on a window seat and looking almost pretty.

Even more noticeable was the fact that the painting had been vandalized. Three diagonal slashes scored the canvas from corner to corner.

'And look,' Maria said, pointing.

Beside the painting of Goudge was one of her husband, a head and shoulders portrait of a younger, much slimmer version of the man, likewise slashed. Next came a reclining nude of the actress Holly Beckwith, her beauty defaced by three lateral rips; then one of Crispin Proudfoot, sitting cross-legged on a lawn, also vandalized. Alongside it was a close-up of Dr Bryce's bloated face, savagely rent.

Langham moved to the very last portrait. This one was of Maria at the age of eighteen. She had a tumble of raven-black hair, high cheekbones and red, laughing lips. The girl stared from the canvas with a joyous look in her wide brown eyes.

She was recognizably his wife, yet innocent, still almost a child, far too young to be taken advantage of by an immoral artist.

Maria fingered the ripped canvas. 'I remember the girl I was, and how frightened I was when . . . when he tried to . . .' She paused, swallowed and turned from the painting. 'When he'd completed the portrait,' she said, 'that's when it happened, and I struck him.'

'In here?'

She shook her head. 'In the drawing room.' She pressed a hand against her cheek and stared at Langham. 'If he'd tried it in here . . . My God, what would I have done? There was nothing I might have picked up to hit him with. At least we were in the drawing room, near the fireplace.'

'It was a long time ago,' he said, 'and it's all over now.'

'But what happened tonight . . .' Her voice caught. 'He'd let it fester, all the hatred.'

'As I told Proudfoot just now,' he said, 'I think Fenton was mad.'

Maria reached out, lifted her portrait and turned it to face the wall.

'I've been thinking, Donald, about what happened just now.'

'Go on.'

'It doesn't make sense. What he said, and then what he did.'

'All that about you getting what you all deserved, and then his killing himself? Yes, it struck me as odd, too.'

'It was as if he wanted to frighten us with the threat of punishment and yet in the end punished only himself. Unless he thought our "just desserts" would be the guilt we might feel.'

'Perhaps that was it,' he said, uneasy that she had reached the same conclusion. 'But you must remember that he wasn't rational. I'm not at all sure that what he was thinking at the end would make any kind of sense.'

She nodded, frowning at the defaced canvases.

He squeezed her shoulder. 'Come on, we'd better be getting back to the others.'

Maria indicated the door connecting the conservatory to the

main body of the building, and they passed down a long, dimly lit corridor towards the distant hallway.

She paused before they entered the library. 'Donald, why do you think the butler ran off like that?'

'I'm not at all sure. Maybe he saw what'd happened and took fright – he didn't want to be implicated. Rash, because by skedaddling as he did, he makes himself look suspicious.'

Dr Bryce had had the foresight to place a folding bamboo screen before the seated corpse – which served only to draw the eye to the mess of blood on the books and the fragment of skull in the corner.

Hermione Goudge had revived, thanks to a brandy that her husband was holding to her lips. She pushed it away and called out, 'I want to go home, now!'

'I'm afraid that's impossible,' Langham said. 'The police are on their way.'

'The police?' She stared at him with the pop-eyes of the Pekinese she so closely resembled. 'What on earth are you talking about?'

'The police need to take our individual statements in order to satisfy themselves that no foul play has taken place.'

'"Foul play"?' she said. 'What the blazes are you suggesting?'

He sighed. 'I'm suggesting nothing, other than that the police will keep an open mind as to what happened here until our collective statements indicate the facts.'

'I refuse to be interrogated like a common criminal. George, take me away from this infernal place!'

'You're going nowhere,' Dr Bryce said, standing over her. 'Langham's right. George, for God's sake, get another brandy to shut her up.'

'There, there, dear,' George said, patting her hand before hurrying off to refill the glass.

Holly Beckwith ceased her pacing and stared at Langham. 'But what shall we tell the police?'

'We tell them exactly what happened,' he said. 'We tell them about the invitations, Fenton's little peroration, and his final act.'

Proudfoot looked up from the chaise longue. 'But surely we don't have to mention his accusations, do we?'

'Of course not!' Hermione called out. 'The very thought . . .'

Langham stared her down. 'We tell them everything,' he said. 'None of you,' he went on, looking around the group, 'did anything wrong. The police need to know the facts of the case so they can establish that Fenton was of unsound mind.'

Hermione muttered something to herself and gulped down her brandy.

Fifteen minutes later, the ambulance arrived, followed by a police car carrying a detective sergeant, a forensic surgeon and a uniformed constable. Dr Bryce introduced himself as the dead man's physician and formally identified the corpse as that of Maxwell Falwell Fenton. He was the first to be questioned by a plainclothes officer who introduced himself as Detective Sergeant Riley.

The interviews were completed in just under two hours; each of the seven individuals present gave their names and addresses and their version of events and were told that in the course of police investigations there might well be further interviews.

When his turn came, Langham reported the premature departure of the butler just minutes after the shooting.

Riley thought about it and said, 'The butler probably got the wind up at the sight of the blood.' He leafed through his notes. 'He was in the room, I take it?'

'No, there were just the seven of us present, other than Fenton himself.'

The detective shrugged. 'Maybe the butler poked his head in at the sound of the gunshot, didn't like what he saw and scarpered. That'll be all for now, Mr Langham.'

It was almost ten o'clock by the time the guests were granted permission to leave the house.

Langham and Maria were the last to depart, following Holly Beckwith into the hall. The actress was belting her raincoat when the door from the library opened and two ambulancemen emerged bearing a stretcher.

Langham and Maria stood back to allow them to pass. As they did so, the dead man's arm slipped from beneath the covering sheet and dropped over the side of the stretcher.

The actress gasped and pressed her fingers to her lips, staring at the hand in horror.

Maria moved to comfort her, and Langham led the way out into the driving rain.

FIVE

At noon the following day, Maria jumped from the bus and hurried along the King's Road, opening her umbrella and leaning into the headwind. The sound of spattering raindrops was loud on the brolly's nylon dome and the wind was freezing.

She was cheered by the thought of a cottage in the country, from which she could work instead of having to endure the travails of life in grimy London. She would come in perhaps once a week to collect manuscripts or to meet authors, and the rest of the time she would work before the open fire, with Donald tapping away on his next thriller in his own book-lined study. In between times, they would go for long walks in the country, spend evenings listening to the wireless or reading, or nip around the corner for a drink at the Green Man. Donald had said that he might even join the village cricket team, and had promised to think about buying a dog.

Then, as she hurried along the street towards the restaurant where she was to meet Pamela, these pleasant daydreams were usurped by images from the previous evening.

She had screwed her eyes shut when the man had lifted the revolver to his head and pulled the trigger, but what would live in her memory for a long time were the sounds that ensued: the detonation of the gunshot, followed by Holly Beckwith's scream, Hermione Goudge's moan, and exclamations from the men. She had opened her eyes briefly to see Fenton slumped in the chair, then had turned away. Perhaps in a bid to spare her from what followed, Donald had asked her to locate the butler while he took charge of the situation.

Even worse than the sounds and images, however, were the memories that the artist's suicide had brought to the surface of her mind, and which she thought she had long since erased.

Memories. And guilt.

She came to La Maison Blanche, lowered her brolly and shook the rain from it, and pushed through the door. Pamela was seated at a window table and waved as a waiter took Maria's umbrella and coat.

She had first met Pamela Baker at Charles's garden party in August and had immediately taken to the young woman. She was intelligent and possessed a quirky sense of humour that was endearing. Maria had suggested they should meet for lunch, and they had found so much to talk about that they decided to meet more regularly.

Maria squeezed Pamela's hand across the table and slipped into her seat.

'Thank you,' Pamela said when they had placed their orders of French onion soup.

'Thank you?' Maria said. 'For what?'

'For making me ask Donald.'

'Ah, *oui*,' Maria said, laughing. 'But I hardly *made* you.'

'Well, you certainly convinced me that he wouldn't bite my head off!'

'Bite your head off? But Donald is not a cannibal; he is the sweetest of men.'

'I know he is; even so, I was a bit scared. I couldn't have asked Ralph.'

Maria cocked her head. 'And why not?'

Pamela leaned back, pulling a face, as the waiter delivered their soup.

'Because . . . Ralph can be a bit abrupt now and again.'

'That's just his manner, Pamela. He likes to put on a show of brusqueness, a kind of disregard or lack of concern, until you get to know him.' Maria spread a napkin on her lap and nibbled at a crouton.

'They're an odd couple in every way, aren't they?' Pamela said. 'They look so different – Donald is tall and handsome, Ralph small and . . .' She faltered.

Maria smiled. 'Ugly?'

'Well, he doesn't do himself any favours, does he? With his threadbare suit, straggly tash and thinning ginger hair.'

'They're certainly a paradoxical pair. You're right – they are different in every way. Intellectually, politically, temperamentally. Perhaps that's why they make such a good team. That and what happened during the war.'

Pamela spooned her soup. 'What did happen?'

'They were in Madagascar. Ralph was pinned down by gunfire, and a Vichy French soldier was about to shoot him, but Donald . . . he shot the Frenchman dead and saved Ralph's life.'

Pamela was wide-eyed. 'Golly. I didn't even know we were fighting the French!'

'So they are very close – you could say almost like brothers,' Maria said. 'It must create a bond, when you go through something like that together.'

Pamela ate her soup in silence for a while, then surprised Maria by saying, 'Did he sweep you off your feet, Maria? Was it love at first sight?'

Maria laughed. 'Certainly not, to both questions. For the first few years that I knew him, I thought that Donald was – what is the phrase? – a stuffed shirt.'

Pamela covered her mouth and laughed. 'No! But why?'

'Because he was so English and reserved! He would come into the agency every couple of months, as shy as a schoolboy, stammer a few non sequiturs about the weather, then hurry off into Charles's inner sanctum as if eager to get away from me.'

Pamela shook her head in disbelief. 'But what happened? How did you end up married? I want to know all the details!'

Maria laughed. 'What happened? One day Donald staggered into the agency with a bleeding head wound—'

Pamela stared at her. 'What!'

'It's a long story . . . Donald was attacked by a criminal but managed to get back to the agency and stagger through the door . . . Well, not long after that, I knew I had to take him in hand and make him love me. So I did. And let me tell you, it was hard work breaking down that diffident English armour. I think it took me more than six months before he finally consented to sweep me off my feet!'

Pamela was silent for a while. 'Love is strange, isn't it?'

'Life is strange and love is even stranger.'

'Is that a line of poetry?'

Maria smiled and shook her head. 'It's from a short story Donald wrote for me, not long after we were engaged.'

'He wrote you a story? How romantic!'

Maria smiled. 'It was a lovely gesture, and I've always remembered that line. The hero says it to his lover as he goes off to war. And doesn't come back.'

Pamela smiled.

'What?' Maria asked.

'Your funny glum face when you said, "And doesn't come back"!'

'Well, it was a strange story to give me, wasn't it? I suppose Donald was contrasting the love we had with the love that his characters had lost.' She wrinkled her nose. 'It was sweet of him.' She finished her soup. 'But speaking of love, how is Nigel?'

Pamela rolled her eyes. 'Would you believe he wants me to marry him, pack in working at the agency and have his children?'

'No!'

'That's what he said, and he was awfully put out when I laughed at him and said that that was out of the question.'

'Good for you.'

'And wait till I tell him that I've asked for promotion. He won't like that, will he?'

'Certainly not.' Maria laughed. 'What did Donald say when you asked, by the way?'

Pamela shrugged. 'He said he'd have a word with Ralph, and maybe sort something out in the New Year. I was going to ask him this morning if he'd managed to talk to Ralph, but . . .'

'Go on.'

'Well, he seemed preoccupied. I wondered whether he was plotting his latest book. He can get awfully wrapped up in his thoughts when he's writing.'

Maria looked at the heavens. 'Yes, I have noticed!' She hesitated. 'But no, it is nothing to do with his writing. Something happened last night.'

She had no notion, before she began speaking, that she needed to tell anyone about the incident at Winterfield. But she experienced a certain sense of relief as she recounted the macabre events that had unfolded over the course of the previous evening.

Pamela listened, transfixed. 'But that's terrible! More than terrible. He must have been mad.'

'That's exactly what Donald said. He thought that Fenton had killed himself to make those present feel guilty. You see, the artist thought that each of us had, in our own way, grievously wronged him in the past.'

Pamela was slowly shaking her head. 'Even you?'

'Even me. You see, I knew Fenton when I was a girl. I was

barely eighteen, and Fenton was a renowned artist. He dazzled me and asked me to sit for him.'

'And did you?'

Maria nodded. 'Oh, *oui*. Well, I could hardly refuse. It wasn't every day that a famous painter wanted to paint me. I think his request appealed to my girlish vanity.'

'What happened? You said he thought his guests had wronged him?'

'To cut a long story short, he tried to drag me to bed one evening and I grabbed the first thing to hand – a poker, as it happens – and hit him across the temple. I scarred him for life.'

'Bully for you!'

Maria fell silent, thinking back all those years to the night in question.

Pamela said, 'But I wouldn't let him make you feel guilty, Maria – he shouldn't have done what he did.'

Maria found herself murmuring, 'But I do feel guilty, and not because of what I did that evening.'

Pamela narrowed her eyes as she regarded Maria. 'Then, why?'

Maria sighed and pushed her empty bowl away. 'Because I lied to Donald,' she said. After a pause, she went on. 'Pamela, this is between you and me. I wouldn't want Donald to know – at least not yet.'

'Very well.'

'I told Donald that Fenton had painted me, and that we met only on three or four occasions . . .'

Pamela swallowed. 'But?'

'I lied, Pamela. I couldn't bring myself to tell Donald the truth, perhaps because I was ashamed of what happened. I was young. Still a girl. Young and foolish and naive.'

She fell silent, folding her napkin over and over on her lap. She set the napkin aside and went on, 'I did sit for Fenton, three or four times. I was flattered. He was charming, and complimentary, and treated me like a woman. No one had treated me like a grown-up before, and I suppose it went to my head. I certainly discovered I possessed something – a certain power. And when he finished the painting and I saw it for the first time, I was overwhelmed with how beautiful he'd made me appear, and he came up behind me and placed a hand on my shoulder, and kissed my neck.'

She fell silent, staring down at her hands, and what she felt then was not so much a recapitulation of the heady romantic rush she had experienced all those years ago, but a combined sense of shame that she had given in to those feelings, and rage at how Maxwell Fenton had manipulated the young girl she had been.

She shrugged. 'I fell under his spell, and we had an affair, and for a little over a month I saw him every weekend. I was a little fool, thinking myself a sophisticated woman.'

'What happened?'

'Oh, he tired of me, Pamela. Men like that, who can make women fall at their feet, soon get bored with one conquest and move on to the next. He didn't tell me, of course – he was too arrogant to do that – but I could tell from his aloofness, his disregard of me. And when I asked a mutual friend what might be happening, I learned that he was seeing someone else.'

Maria paused, recalling the day she discovered his treachery, then went on, 'And so the following Saturday I left London and took the train to Winterfield and confronted him. I asked him if there was any truth in the rumours that he was seeing this woman. And do you know what he told me? Can you guess?'

Pamela shook her head and mouthed a silent 'No'.

'He didn't deny it, and said that beside me this other woman meant nothing, that she was just a fling, and then he tried . . . he tried to . . . It was as if he thought that I was his by rights. He tried to drag me off to bed . . .' She stopped, gathered her thoughts, then continued, 'And that's when I snapped. I snatched up the poker and swung it at his head with all my strength. I very nearly knocked him out. I thought I'd killed him at first, but when he struggled to his feet and laughed at me – *laughed.* It was all I could do not to hit him again. I dropped the poker and ran away from Winterfield and never went back. Never went back, that is, until last night.'

She stopped, and Pamela just stared at her, open-mouthed. At last the girl said, 'Golly,' and Maria had to laugh.

Maria reached across the table and squeezed her hand. 'And when Donald asked me about Fenton, I lied to him. I *lied.*' She shook her head. 'I love Donald so much that I couldn't tell him the truth for fear that he'd hate me – hate me for the silly wanton little fool I was. And as soon as I lied, it came to me that if I *did* one day tell him the truth, then he'd hate me for lying to him in the first place!'

She felt her eyes brim with tears and dashed them away with her napkin.

Pamela took her hand. 'Donald loves you,' she said quietly. 'He could never bring himself to hate you, either for what Fenton did to you then or for not telling him the truth now. I know he'd understand.'

Maria smiled bravely. 'But would he? A small voice in the back of my head keeps on saying, "What if I tell him and he doesn't understand, and it changes what he feels for me?" Oh, that would destroy me, Pamela!'

'Donald is a good man. He would understand. I think I would tell him, if I were you.'

'I know you're right; I know I should.' She brightened, smiled across at the young girl, at the concerned expression on her pretty face, and said, 'I feel in need of a strong coffee, Pamela, and do you know what else? I might even order a big slice of chocolate gateau.'

'Let's!' Pamela said.

Life is strange, Maria thought, *and love is even stranger.*

SIX

Langham was alone in the office when the clouds parted to let a shaft of unseasonal sunlight come slanting in through the window. Pamela was meeting Maria for lunch, and Ralph was still investigating Major Bruce's purloined diamonds.

He'd left the communicating door open in order to hear anyone knocking on the door of the outer office, and he was trying to concentrate on his manuscript. The events of the previous night, however, conspired to make that impossible.

Aside from the sheer horror of the artist's death, Langham was troubled by something else. Maxwell Fenton's hate-filled diatribe, culminating in his suicide, did not ring true. Fenton had staged the show in order to threaten his guests – and yet the climax of the *Grand Guignol* was not an act of revenge but his own suicide.

And the threats he had issued? *You have earned the end that*

*awaits you . . . You, too, will suffer the fate you fear most of all
. . . You, too, will pay for your misdeed . . .*

But perhaps, Langham thought, what he had said last night was not that far from the mark: Maxwell Fenton had indeed been insane.

He set the manuscript aside and contemplated lunch. He had a bottle of Double Diamond in his desk drawer, and he was debating the relative merits of a pork pie from the butcher's around the corner and an eel pie from the shop across the street, when a faint tapping sounded on the outer office door.

'Come in!' He sat upright and tried to look professional.

One of the perks of this line of work, he often thought, was its unpredictability. He never knew who might next step into the office. He was taken aback, seconds later, when the door opened and a familiar face peered through.

He climbed to his feet and moved to the communicating door. 'Miss Beckwith, this is a surprise.' He gestured for her to take a seat.

The actress appeared hesitant. 'I hope you don't mind. I exchanged phone numbers with your wife last night, and then on hearing that you were a detective' – she gave a dazzling smile and sat down across the desk from him – 'I rang Maria this morning and she gave me your office address.'

'This is about last night, I take it?'

She bit her lip, nodding. 'That's right.'

'First of all, would you care for a tea or coffee?'

'That's awfully kind, but I can't stay long. I've taken time off from rehearsals.' She glanced at a tiny silver watch on her slim wrist. 'I have to be back in half an hour.'

'How can I help you?'

She stared past him, through the window, as if gathering her thoughts.

Her beauty, he thought while he waited, was quite unlike Maria's: while his wife was dark and sultry, Holly Beckwith was slight and pale. Her quick, hesitant movements as she lit a cigarette and blew out the smoke suggested a barely controlled hysteria.

'I wanted to explain – about last night, I mean.'

'Explain?'

'What he said about me . . .'

'What he said?' Even to himself, he sounded like a psychiatrist cajoling a patient into self-disclosure.

'He said some terrible things about all of us, but what he said about me – that I was selfish and cruel . . .' She shook her head, on the verge of tears. 'They were lies, Mr Langham, all lies.'

'I believe you,' he said. 'You really don't have to justify yourself, you know.'

'But that's just it, Mr Langham. I feel that I do.' She inhaled on her cigarette, blowing the smoke high into the air, and went on. 'I first met him when I was rehearsing a play at the Phoenix. He'd been commissioned to design the set.'

'And when was this?'

''Thirty-five. I was in my early twenties, and to tell the truth I was inexperienced when it came to romance. Oh, I dreamed of meeting someone I could fall in love with, but all the men I did meet seemed to be utter cads.'

He smiled. 'Until you met Fenton?'

She returned his smile. 'He seemed different. He was kind, attentive. He bought me things, spent money on me. I was on my uppers at the time, and he bought me expensive stockings and dresses . . . Well, it wasn't long before I was head over heels.'

'Fenton would have been in his forties at the time?'

'Oh, he was an older man.' She laughed. 'He was in his mid-forties, well over twice my age, and famous. And I was a scatter-brained little fool. I understood nothing, not even myself, my own needs and desires. Oh, I thought I did, but I didn't really know what I wanted, deep down. And then . . .'

Langham recalled that Fenton had accused the actress of a wanton act of vandalism. 'Yes?'

She regarded the glowing tip of her cigarette, then located an ashtray on the desk and deposited a length of ash. 'Six months into our relationship, one of the stage-hands at the Phoenix told me that Fenton was married and had a child. I was incredulous at first, but then an actress friend admitted that it was true and hadn't told me in order to spare me the pain. Call me a fool. I thought I was in love, and then to find out he'd been deceiving me . . .'

'What did you do?'

'I'm not proud of my actions, Mr Langham. The next time I was down at Winterfield at one of his big parties, I sneaked off to his studio in the conservatory. He was preparing for a big exhibition in London.'

She shook her head, her eyes wide as she considered what she had done all those years ago. 'I took my cigarette lighter, piled half a dozen canvases in the centre of the floor, poured primer over the lot and set fire to them. Someone saw the blaze, saw me running away, and while the other guests extinguished the fire and saved a few canvases, Fenton caught me and . . .'

Her words ran out and she stared at Langham, slowly shaking her head. 'He was livid, and I was suddenly frightened at what I'd done, and angry with Fenton for all his lies, his deceit. And we fought, verbally and physically. He hit me and I retaliated and screamed my hatred at him. To cut a long story short, someone intervened, or I swore he would have killed me. I took a taxi from Winterfield and never saw Fenton again, until last night.'

She looked at him. 'And to think,' she said quietly, 'that he'd let it fester over the years, his hatred of me. And then it all got too much and he . . .' She closed her eyes. 'Perhaps he did do it to make us feel guilty, and if that is so, he succeeded.'

Langham sighed. 'What happened last night . . .' he began. 'I know it's a cliché – and that what he did was appalling – but if I were you, I'd do my best not to dwell on it, and certainly don't blame yourself. I really do think Fenton was clinically insane.'

'And his threats, to myself and to the others?'

'Confirmation, if any were needed, that he wasn't in his right mind.'

The actress hesitated, and Langham gained the impression that she was considering the wisdom of telling him something she had hitherto withheld.

He said, 'Was that the only reason you came to see me today, Miss Beckwith, to tell me about Fenton's treatment of you?'

'I . . .' She paused, staring at him. 'Yes, it was, Mr Langham. I needed to tell someone, get it all off my chest. Thank you for listening.'

'That's quite all right.'

She stood abruptly. 'I really must dash,' she said.

She moved to the door and hesitated, a hand on the handle. Then she turned. 'There is . . .' she began.

'Yes?'

'No, I'm being silly. It's nothing, really. Goodbye, Mr Langham, and thank you again.'

He stood. 'One moment . . .'

She slipped from the office before he could question her further.

Langham sat down and stared at the cigarette ash piled in the tray.

*   *   *

At one thirty, as he was about to nip around the corner for a couple of pork pies, he heard the familiar sound of Ralph's quick footsteps on the stairs. The outer door opened and his partner breezed in, tossing his hat at the stand and missing.

'You look chipper,' Langham said.

'Case solved, jewels in the major's bank vault, and twenty nicker in my back pocket. Oh, and an extra tenner as a thank you from the old soldier.'

'Just the ticket.'

'Tell you what, let's shut up shop and have a couple round the Bull in celebration.'

'You're a man after my own heart, Ralph. I'll grab a pie on the way.'

Ralph retrieved his hat from the corner. 'And how about telling me all about last night?'

'Where to begin? The invitation to a death turned out to be just on the button. I'll give you the whole sordid story over a pint.'

They were leaving the office when the phone rang.

Ralph swore. 'Ignore it, Don.'

Langham hesitated. 'Might be Maria.'

He returned to the desk and snatched up the receiver. 'Hello?'

'Don, Jeff here.'

'Mallory, as I live and breathe. It's been a while.'

'I need to see you pronto,' Jeff Mallory said. 'I've heard all about last night at Maxwell Fenton's place, and I understand you were present?'

'That's right.'

'This is important. Can you get down here lickety-split? I'm in Lower Malton, staying at the White Lion.'

'*Now*, you mean?'

'Now,' Detective Inspector Mallory said.

'Well, I was just about to go for a pint with Ralph—'

'I've been called in to investigate the death of one Doctor Roger Bryce,' Mallory interrupted. 'He hanged himself in the early hours, only the local boys thought it looked a bit fishy and called in the Yard. And I agree with them. He was murdered.'

So much for a quiet afternoon pint.

'We're on our way,' Langham said.

SEVEN

They drove into Lower Malton at three o'clock, just as the White Lion was opening its doors for the afternoon trade. The rain had held off and a watery sunlight illuminated a row of small cottages and a honey-coloured church on the main street.

Ralph had been silent while Langham recounted the events of the previous evening. 'One thing I don't get, Don,' he said as they pulled up outside the pub.

'Let's hear it.'

'If this Fenton geezer was doolally, and he had a gun, and hated these people he invited, why didn't he just have done and shoot them, instead of topping himself?'

'Who knows what goes on in the head of a madman?'

'But these threats he made?'

'That's the part I don't understand. I thought maybe he wanted the guests to feel guilty – but it seems a very unsatisfying way of getting one's revenge, doesn't it? There's something damned odd about the whole situation.' He indicated the public house. 'Shall we?'

They found Detective Inspector Mallory in the tap room. The big, fair-haired South African was propping up the bar with a full pint of Bass bitter before him. They shook hands. 'Good to see you both,' Mallory said. 'You'll be thirsty after the drive. What'll it be?'

He ordered two more bitters and they moved to a table before the open fire.

'About Bryce,' Langham began, taking an inch from his ale.

Mallory held up a hand. 'First, I want to hear all about what happened last night. I've read Detective Sergeant Riley's report, and a transcript of the interviews, but I'd like to hear what you made of the affair.'

Langham began with Maria's arrival at the office bearing the invitation from Maxwell Fenton, and proceeded to tell Mallory about the next few hours in great detail.

The detective listened with his lips pursed, his long legs stretched out towards the open fire. He nodded and frowned from time to time but refrained from interrupting.

When Langham finished, Mallory picked up on the obvious disparity between Maxwell Fenton's threats and his subsequent suicide. 'In my opinion, for what it's worth, it's too easy an option to ascribe insanity. I'd rather work on the theory that Fenton was sane and try to make sense of his motives from there. Right, as much as I could stay here all day . . .' He finished his pint and climbed to his feet. 'I hope you two have strong stomachs.'

'Grisly?'

'Ever seen a hanged man?' Mallory asked.

Langham shook his head. 'This'll be my first.'

Ralph said, 'I've come across a dozen or so over the years.'

'Ever seen what hanging by the neck can do to a sixteen-stone man?' the detective asked grimly. 'Not a pretty sight.'

As they followed the detective from the tap room, Langham wished he'd refrained from wolfing down two pork pies on the journey from London.

He turned up his overcoat collar against the biting wind as they walked along the main street and past the church. They turned down a narrow, high-hedged lane and continued for twenty yards until they arrived at an old farmhouse set back on a well-kept lawn.

Mallory led them down a cinder drive and around the house, and pointed to an outbuilding across a cobbled yard. A navy-blue Morris Commercial van stood outside the building, and members of the forensics team moved back and forth between the two.

The outbuilding had evidently been used as a garage, as its flagstoned floor was patched with oil, and several petrol cans and a toolkit stood against the wall. It was not these, however, that caught Langham's attention as they entered the building.

The portly Dr Bryce was hanging by the neck from a rope tied to a high oak beam. His fleshy face was almost black, his mouth agape in a rictus of agony, his eyes protuberant. A small wooden stepladder stood close to his dangling brogues. As if to add indignity to injury, the corpse had suffered a leakage common in such cases, and the stench was appalling.

Langham kept his distance and his breathing shallow. A police photographer moved around the body, his flash periodically illuminating the scene.

'He was found by his housekeeper who comes in at nine every morning. The surgeon says he was hanged in the early hours, between midnight and five.' Mallory looked at Langham. 'What time did you say you left Winterfield?'

'It can't have been much after ten. Say five past.' Langham squinted up at the corpse's shirt front. 'Those stains?'

'Whiskey,' Mallory said. 'He'd been drinking heavily before this happened.'

Ralph moved closer to the corpse, grimacing up at the tortured face.

Langham said, 'And you think he was murdered?'

As he said the words, a terrible thought occurred to him. Maria was one of those whom Maxwell Fenton had threatened last night.

Mallory said, 'It's the surgeon's opinion that he was too drunk to have hanged himself. He had help. Shall we go into the house?'

On the way out, Mallory waylaid one of the forensic officers. 'You can cut him down now, and I'd like a report on my desk first thing tomorrow.'

They crossed the cobbles to the back door of the farmhouse and stepped into what Langham thought of as a typical farmhouse kitchen boasting an Aga cooker, a flagstoned floor and low beams.

Mallory indicated an almost empty bottle of Irish whiskey and a shot glass standing on the scrubbed pine table.

'Looks cut and dried, doesn't it? Doctor Bryce comes home after witnessing a particularly nasty incident, hits the bottle and in a bout of melancholy decides to end it all. It'd fit with his profile. Bryce had a history of mental instability, and he had a drink problem. There's something else, though I don't know whether it has a direct bearing on his death. For ten years he worked as a police surgeon at Colchester – until he was removed from his post.'

'Removed?' Ralph said. 'What'd he done?'

Mallory moved to the table and stared down at the empty glass, his hands on his hips. 'Falsified some evidence against a suspect the police knew to be guilty. Bryce just helped the case along. But it came to light, internally. The incident was hushed up, though he was asked to leave.'

'What makes you think he was murdered,' Langham asked, 'other than his being incapable of hanging himself?'

Surprising Langham, Mallory crouched and squinted along the length of the tabletop. 'You won't be able to see it from where you are, but look at it from this angle.'

Langham and Ralph did so, and Mallory pointed to a very faint circle on the timber, directly across the tabletop from the empty glass. 'Forensics think there were two people drinking here last night.'

Mallory crossed to a wall cupboard and opened the door. 'They've taken away the glass for analysis, but look.' He indicated a sheet of lining paper, which was marked by a damp circle beside a line of half a dozen inverted glasses.

'My guess is the killer was known to Bryce. They share a whiskey and the doctor gets sozzled. The killer replaces his glass, helps Bryce to his feet and steers him out to the garage.'

'If so,' Langham said, 'it was planned and set up in advance. The stepladder, the rope . . .'

Mallory nodded. 'Oh, it was premeditated, all right. And well in advance, I'd say.'

Ralph peered at the detective. 'How'd you reckon that?'

'This way.'

Mallory led them from the kitchen, down a low corridor, to a room overlooking the front lawn. This was evidently the doctor's study, with bookcases bearing medical journals and textbooks, and a desk situated before the window.

Mallory pointed to an envelope on the desk. 'It's all right – it's been examined for fingerprints. Clean, of course.'

Langham opened the envelope and withdrew a card bearing the image of a single white lily. 'With sincere sympathy,' he read. He opened the card; it was blank. He passed it to Ralph.

'Someone intended to put the frighteners on him,' Mallory said.

'The envelope is typewritten,' Ralph said, 'and postmarked Marylebone, two days ago.'

Mallory took the card and slipped it into an evidence bag. 'Someone had it in for Bryce, and wanted him to know it. Then, in the early hours, he did the job.'

Langham leaned against the wall. 'Maxwell Fenton threatened his guests in various ways.' He looked at the two men. 'Surely it can't be coincidence?'

'How about this?' Mallory said. 'He has an accomplice. Someone he paid, or coerced, to carry out Bryce's murder after his own suicide.'

Langham pointed at Mallory. 'The butler. He skedaddled pretty sharpish after the shooting.'

Ralph grunted a humourless laugh. 'It were the butler that did it, guv.'

'We need to trace the chap,' Mallory said. 'Could you supply a detailed description of him?'

'Of course,' Langham said. He hesitated. 'If we're right, and someone is carrying out Fenton's threats, then the remaining five guests are in danger.'

'Maria,' Ralph said, only just cottoning on.

Langham nodded, feeling queasy.

'We might be barking up the wrong tree, of course,' Mallory said. 'But to be on the safe side, we'll contact the guests and inform them—'

'Can you offer police protection?' Langham interrupted.

'I'll get on to my Super and see what can be done.'

Langham looked around the study, searching for a phone. 'I need to contact Maria right away.'

Mallory said, 'There's a phone in the hallway near the front door.'

Langham hurried from the study and down the hall. He found the telephone, snatched up the receiver and leaned against the wall. His fingers were shaking as he dialled the local operator, then gave the London number of the literary agency.

The receptionist, Molly, answered with a breezy, 'Hello, the Charles Elder Literary Agency. Molly speaking; how can I help?'

'Molly, Donald here. Is Maria there?'

'She is. I'll put you through.'

Langham blew with relief.

Maria said, 'Donald, this is a surprise.'

He'd already planned what he was going to say. 'Maria, I thought it might be nice if we had a break.'

'A break. What do you—?'

'Listen to me. Leave the office now, book into a small hotel, then ring Pamela to tell her where you are. Understood?'

She gave a puzzled laugh. 'Donald, what is all this about?'

'Just do as I say. And don't go home on the way to the hotel, all right? Go straight to the hotel, then phone Pamela and tell her where you are. I'll meet you there later.'

A silence, then she said, 'I am in danger, aren't I? What Fenton said last night . . .'

'I'll explain everything later – I'm down at Lower Malton at the moment.' He hesitated. 'Maria, you'll be fine. But please do as I say – understood?'

'*Oui*. Yes, of course.'

'I love you,' he said.

'Love you, too, Donald,' she said, then hung up.

His heart hammering, he made his way back to the study.

'Manage to get through?' Ralph asked.

'Told her to book into a hotel.'

There was a tap on the door, and a uniformed constable, his helmet lodged under his arm like a rugby ball, ducked into the room. 'Ah, there you are, sir. There's a woman in the kitchen, a Miss Kerwin, a neighbour. Says she saw someone here last night, late on.'

They followed the constable back to the kitchen, where they found a frail old woman in a tweed two-piece seated at the table, nervously fingering a gold crucifix necklace.

Miss Kerwin looked up as they entered, her eyes concerned. 'Is it true? I've only just heard the rumours. Is Doctor Bryce . . .?' She could not finish the question, and looked from one to the other of the men as if to have her fear dispelled.

Mallory introduced Langham and Ralph as colleagues, then sat across from the woman. Langham leaned against the wall.

'I'm afraid Doctor Bryce is dead,' Mallory said. 'I understand you saw someone at the house last night?'

The old woman fanned herself; the constable brought her a glass of water.

She took a gulp, then fixed Mallory with tear-filled eyes. 'I did, Inspector. It was at twelve thirty, and I was calling for Mr Baldwin.'

'Mr Baldwin?' Mallory said.

'My tabby,' Miss Kerwin said. 'I don't like him staying out at night. The foxes, you see.'

'Quite,' Mallory said. 'Now, this person?'

'I saw her leave in a car. I live just across from the doctor, so naturally I see everything that goes on. Of course, it's not uncommon – Doctor Bryce, for all he was a gentlemen, was a bit of a rogue, you know.'

'A rogue?'

'Oh, many's the time he had his ladies call and stay the night, though this one left at twelve thirty.'

'And you saw the woman? Can you describe her?'

Miss Kerwin frowned. 'I'm afraid I can't, Inspector. It was dark, and I must admit that I wasn't paying very much attention. I was more concerned about Mr Baldwin. I saw the woman walk along the side of the house to her car and then drive away.'

'Are you absolutely sure it was a woman?' Mallory asked.

'Oh, absolutely. She had long dark hair, and the way she walked – it was very definitely a woman.'

'Was she tall, small? Well built or slight?'

'She was small. Petite, I think the word is.'

'And the car? Could you possibly describe it, the make?'

The old woman shook her head. 'I'm sorry, Inspector. As I said, it was dark, and I'm not very good with cars.'

'I don't suppose you've seen the same vehicle before at Doctor Bryce's?'

'I'm afraid I couldn't say, Inspector.'

Mallory thanked Miss Kerwin and asked the constable to show her out.

When they were alone, Ralph whistled. 'Well, blow me down. A woman!'

'So much for the butler,' Langham said, 'though they might be in it together.'

Mallory shook his head. 'But would a petite woman have the strength to assist a sixteen-stone man across to the garage and up a stepladder, presumably against his will?'

'Touché,' Ralph said.

'How about this?' Langham said. 'There *were* two of them – the woman might have been joined by the butler at some point – and they did it together.'

'The sooner we trace the butler, the better,' Mallory said. He rose and moved to the door. 'Right, I've just about finished here. I'm going back to the White Lion to compare notes with my sergeant.'

They left the house, and Mallory had a last word with the forensics team before walking back into the village.

Outside the pub, Mallory turned to Langham. 'By the way, Caroline sends her best wishes.'

'Still going strong?'

'From strength to strength,' the South African said. 'I wasn't going to mention this, but last week I screwed up the courage and popped the question.'

'You did? You old dog! What did she say?'

Mallory grinned. 'Well, when she stopped crying, she accepted.

We're having a small register office do just before Christmas. You're all invited, of course.'

Langham shook the South African's hand and Ralph made a caustic comment about a lifetime of servitude.

'Don't listen to that cynic, Jeff. Wait until I tell Maria,' Langham said. 'Which reminds me, I'd better phone Pamela.'

Mallory said goodbye and entered the pub, and Langham crossed the lane to a phone box and hauled open the door. He got through to the office and Pamela answered instantly.

'Pamela, did Maria—?'

'A minute ago,' she said, 'and it's all arranged. Only, there's been a change of plan.'

'There has?'

'Rather than go to the expense of booking a hotel room, Donald, I suggested she cancel the room – you can both stay at my place in Bermondsey. Maria's meeting me here in an hour. There's a spare room, and you'd be more than welcome.' She hesitated. 'Can I ask what's—?'

'Later,' he said. 'It's a long story. I'll tell you both when I get back.' He thanked her and rang off.

'Everything tickety-boo?' Ralph asked.

Langham told him what Pamela had said.

'Sounds like a good idea to me. The girl has her head screwed on tight. What now?'

Langham thought about it. 'Seeing as we're here, what say we go and take a poke around Fenton's old pile?'

'Lead the way,' Ralph said.

They climbed into the Rover and drove through the village.

EIGHT

L angham drew to a halt in the drive and stared out at Winterfield's ruined facade.

The old house appeared even bleaker now, seen in the weak winter sunlight. Most of the windows in the east and west wings were shattered, save for those of the sitting room where the guests had gathered the night before. A thick growth of ivy covered most of the brickwork, and several of the tall chimney stacks were missing bricks; some had collapsed entirely, the masonry piled precariously in the eaves.

Ralph jumped from the car, approached the front door and tried the handle. 'Locked.'

'Thought it would be,' Langham said. 'But there's more than one way to skin a cat.'

He led the way along the front of the house and around the gable end to the conservatory. Sunlight picked out panes of mildewed glass and several more reduced to jagged shards. He pushed through the rotting door and indicated the portraits leaning against the far wall.

'Maria and I found these last night,' he explained, 'after we'd chased the fleeing butler. Look.' He pointed to the slashed canvases and knelt to examine them more closely.

He fingered the ripped edges. 'These have been cut recently. See the edge of the tear, there? It's white. Do you have a penknife handy?'

Ralph dug around in his jacket pocket and passed Langham a knife. He opened it, moved to the portrait of Hermione Goudge, and sliced the margin of the canvas. He considered the result. 'The same white edge.'

'So the paintings were slashed recently,' Ralph said, fingering his straggling ginger moustache. 'Yet according to what he said last night, he'd nursed his grudges for a while.'

Langham stood and led the way to the door to the west wing.

As they moved down damp, cobweb-festooned corridors, Ralph whistled. 'It's like the set from a ghost film, Don. Christ, what a criminal waste.'

'Piles like this cost a packet to keep up. It's a wonder Fenton didn't resort to torching the place for the insurance.'

They moved through the ground-floor rooms one by one. It was impossible to tell what function they had originally served, as room after room was vacant, the floorboards rotting and, in one or two cases, missing altogether. Rats and mice had taken up residence, and growths of mould and fungus coated walls and ceilings.

Only three rooms on the ground floor had been maintained. One was the sitting room where the guests had gathered the previous night; another was the library where the shooting had occurred, and the third was a small room next door to the library.

'And what do we have here?' Ralph declared as he opened the third door.

This room had evidently served as a bedroom – and the bedroom of an invalid. An adjustable hospital bed stood against the far wall, and an oxygen cylinder was propped next to it, attached to a breathing mask.

Ralph approached the bed and knelt down, picking up an empty cardboard packet. 'Drugs. Chlormethine.'

'Apparently, Fenton was suffering from some kind of cancer.'

Ralph nodded, looking around the room. 'Bedpans, empty syringes, medicine bottles. He was nursed here. We need to check nursing agencies, talk to whoever looked after him.'

Langham crossed to a Queen Anne bureau in the corner of the room and pushed the roll-up lid. Something scurried from a nest of papers and leapt to the carpet, startling him – a huge grey house mouse, disgruntled at having its habitation invaded.

Gingerly, he sorted through those papers not shredded into nesting material, and at the back of the bureau discovered a sheaf of bank statements.

He leafed through them one by one.

'Take a look,' he said, passing them to Ralph. 'Notice anything interesting?'

'The cash deposits paid in on the second of every month, always for the same amount.'

'Twenty-five quid going back' – Langham thumbed through the statements – 'going back almost five years.'

'So Fenton was paid twenty-five quid in cash as regular as clockwork.' Ralph scanned the statements. 'That was aside from his pension. That's all he had coming in.'

'Which might account for the state of this place.'

Langham rooted amongst the papers and found the stubs of three cheque books going back almost a decade. He sat on the bed and went through the dockets meticulously.

'Find anything?' Ralph asked.

'No, nothing. Wait a sec.'

In the most recent book, a cheque had been written without the stub being filled in. Langham tilted the book to the light and made out the impression of handwriting on the uppermost cheque. He read aloud: 'Thirty guineas, paid to the Kersh and Cohen Theatrical Agency, two weeks ago.'

'What the blazes did he want from a theatrical agency?'
'Search me,' Langham said. 'Hired a troupe to entertain him in his old age?'
'I'll look them up tomorrow,' Ralph said, 'along with butlering agencies. Hang on. What if this butler chappie was nothing of the sort, but an actor hired to play the part?'
Langham frowned. 'Why was the butler necessarily an actor? If he was in on all this, and an accessory to murder, then he's unlikely to be someone Fenton hired to play a part, is he?'
'Right,' Ralph said. 'But I'd still like to know why Fenton shelled out thirty guineas to this theatrical outfit.'
Langham sorted through the rest of the bureau but found nothing of interest. They left the bedroom and searched the rest of the ground floor before moving upstairs. Here, again, the rooms were for the most part unused and in many cases derelict. Langham opened the door to one bedroom to be met by a cold wind blowing in through the smashed casement. Ivy had invaded the room and coated the entirety of the far wall, and swallows had made their distinctive cupolaed nests in the cornices.
The neighbouring bedroom had evidently been used recently, judging by the made-up double bed and a pile of clothes on a chest beneath the window. Langham sorted through them: trousers and shirts that would fit a smallish man. They went through drawers, cupboards and the chest, but found nothing of further interest.
They moved on, finding more empty, unused rooms in varying states of dereliction, until Langham opened the very last door on the corridor.
'Another one,' he said, and led the way into the room.
The only item of significance here, other than the made-up bed, was a small table and mirror positioned against the wall. Langham found an array of cosmetics in the drawer and what looked like a tube of greasepaint.
'What do you make of these?'
Ralph frowned, fingering the tube. 'Maybe he hired an actor who used this room?'
'Possibly. The recently occupied bedrooms tie in with the theory that Fenton hired two people to carry out his dirty work after his death. They came here to receive instructions.'
Ralph sat down on the bed. 'What I don't get, Don, is why they'd agree to do that? Was he paying them hundreds?' He gestured.

'Going by the state of this place, he didn't have that much cash to flash around. OK, so did he have some kind of hold over these people, enough to force them to kill, after his death? But that wouldn't work – if they were coerced into killing, surely when the geezer topped himself, they'd simply say, "Sod this for a lark".'

'My guess is that they weren't forced into doing this,' Langham said. 'They're doing it of their own volition, because they want to. So who the hell are they, and what's their motive?'

Ralph laughed. 'Work that out, Don, and we're laughing.'

'Seen enough? I want to get back and make sure Maria's safe and well.'

They left the house, drove through the village and turned on to the London road.

NINE

Maria left the office and caught a bus to Earl's Court. She sat on the top deck, at the very front, and stared out at the rain as the bus made its laborious stop-start way through the grey streets of the capital.

She wished, now, that she'd pressed Donald to tell her the reason he wanted her to book into a hotel. He was at Lower Malton, for some reason, and she wondered if he'd found something at Winterfield that made him fear for her safety.

She recalled Maxwell Fenton's threats. But Fenton was dead, and the dead could not harm the living, could they? Not harm them physically, that is: she remembered what Donald had said about the artist's wanting to instil guilt into his guests. So why, then, had he insisted that she book into a hotel?

Far better, she thought, to take up Pamela's invitation to stay at her place. She would have company the next morning, as Pamela had said that she didn't intend to go into the agency.

She stepped from the bus at Earl's Court and crossed the road, hurrying through the rain past the Lyons' tearoom. She climbed the steps to the Ryland and Langham Detective Agency, smiling to herself at the gold lettering on the glass door-panel. Donald had been inordinately proud of the legend when he'd showed it off to her a couple of months ago, and told her that Ralph had had it done on the cheap by a friend. It showed, she thought; the first 't' in Detective was peeling. She had refrained from telling Donald that it made the word look more like 'Defective'.

Pamela was slipping the cover over her Remington upright when Maria entered the outer office.

'All set,' the girl said. 'You didn't mind cancelling the hotel booking? Only, it'll be nice to have people around the place.'

'Not at all; I'd rather stay with you. As you say, why go to the expense of paying for a room?'

Pamela hesitated in the process of pulling on her coat. 'Did Donald tell you what it's all about?'

As Pamela locked the office door, Maria said, 'He said he'd tell me later. But he thought it a good idea that we stay with you.'

They waited five minutes at the bus stop across the road from the agency, then caught the number eighty-eight across the river to Bermondsey. The bus carried them through a city thronged with pedestrians but noticeably free of traffic. The petrol rationing was having its effect.

At one point, Pamela asked, 'Have you thought any more about telling Donald?' She raised her pencilled eyebrows.

'I've been thinking about nothing else all afternoon. I know I should tell him, and I will. But I need to find the right moment to do so.'

She turned and stared through the rain-splattered window.

They alighted at Bermondsey High Street, and Pamela led the way past the illuminated shop fronts and turned left along a street of tiny red-brick terrace houses. Another left turn brought them into an identical street, this one adorned with sycamore trees planted at regular intervals along the pavement.

Pamela pushed open the gate of a mid-terrace house and unlocked the front door.

What immediately struck Maria was how tiny the place was compared with her own spacious Kensington apartment, and then how tasteful the decorations in the front room were: green-and-white striped wallpaper, a beige carpet, and a jade-green three-piece suite.

When she admired the room, Pamela said, 'All thanks to the agency, Maria. I couldn't have afforded to redecorate on the wages I was getting at the gallery.'

Maria looked around the room, noticing the Baird radiogram in the corner. 'Do you rent?'

'It was my mum and dad's,' Pamela explained as she moved into the adjacent kitchen and put the kettle on. 'They left me the house when they passed away last year.'

She leaned against the doorframe, tea caddy in hand, and smiled at Maria. 'It's OK. They'd both been ill for some time. It was a release in the end. Milk and sugar?'

'Milk, no sugar.'

They sat side by side on the two-seater sofa and sipped their tea from oversized mugs.

Maria said, 'Donald and I won't be in the way, when you and Nigel . . .?'

'I only see him every Saturday,' Pamela said, 'and sometimes on a Friday night. He's out the rest of the time with his mates. It's either the pub, football or the dogs – I hardly get a look in. Tonight it's the greyhounds at White City.'

Maria recalled what Pamela had told her over lunch about Nigel's wish to marry her. The girl had made it obvious that there was nothing further from her mind.

She thought back to when she was Pamela's age, and her life then: a poorly paid job in publishing, few friends, and chronic suspicion when it came to men.

Pamela said, 'Still thinking about what to tell Donald?'

Maria smiled. 'Oh, it's not that,' she said. 'I was considering Fenton. Donald thinks what he did last night might have been intended to inspire guilt in the guests – but Fenton made me feel guilty even when he was alive, after what happened at Winterfield back in the thirties.'

'You were very young,' Pamela began.

'The awful thing is that what he did . . . It made me feel as if it were *my* fault. I felt guilty for striking him, and yet guilty for giving myself to him as I did. Afterwards I knew he'd manipulated me, preyed on my naivety – but that made me feel even more guilty for the fool I'd been. I was very mixed up for years, and it was a long time before I learned that I wasn't to blame, and that Fenton was responsible for what happened.'

She shook her head, thinking back to the grim, lonely war years working as a secretary in London.

'It made me very suspicious of men, Pamela. I thought they

were all like Fenton – out for themselves. I had a few brief, unsuccessful relationships, but I could never commit myself, and it was
me who always broke it off. I didn't want to be hurt again, like
the first time.'

'I'm sorry, Maria,' Pamela said, taking her hand.

Maria laughed. 'In my early thirties I'd resigned myself to
spinsterhood! Imagine that.'

'And then Donald came along.'

'I suppose I got to know him, to trust him, over the long period
when he couldn't bring himself to ask me to dinner. Charles spoke
so much about him, said what a "fine fellow" he was, that I felt
I knew him even before we got together.'

Pamela squeezed her hand. 'So, you see, Fenton hasn't had the
last word.'

'And yet even now, after all those years, and after his death . . .
I hate him for coming between Donald and me, and for how I feel
now – guilty and afraid of what Donald might say. I'm being
foolish, aren't I?' She smiled and jumped up. 'But enough of all
that. I'm going to make another pot of tea.'

At six o'clock they peeled potatoes and carrots, and Pamela
turned on the cooker and took three Cornish pasties from the larder.
As the vegetables boiled, they drank their tea, and Maria asked
Pamela about her work at the detective agency.

'You do realize, don't you, that if you get promoted, the jobs
they'll give you will be boring and routine? It isn't every day they
investigate anything of interest. Mainly, it's petty thefts and errant
husbands.'

'I know – I type up the notes, remember? But anything would
be better than sitting behind a desk all day. I'd like to get out of
the office from time to time.' She leaned back against the cooker,
warming herself. 'But Donald likes the job, doesn't he?'

Maria frowned. 'I'm not at all sure that he does,' she said. 'He's
always complaining that it takes him from his writing. I think he
started work at the agency as a favour to Ralph, though he thought
it might help with his writing.'

'You don't think he'd leave, do you?'

Maria smiled at her. 'Between you and me, when we move to
Suffolk, I intend to ask him if he'd think about cutting down his
working hours.'

'What do you think he'll say?'

'I think he'll be agreeable. More time to write, after all.'

'And Ralph?'

'He would, as the saying goes, take it on the chin. He'd have to.'

At six thirty a loud knocking at the door heralded Donald's arrival. Maria let him in, and he stepped into the front room and looked around. 'What a nice place you've got yourself, Pam.' He pulled off his overcoat and tossed his hat on the sofa.

Maria smiled as she watched Donald make polite small talk with Pamela, complimenting her taste in paintings. They were Constable and Turner copies, which Pamela said had belonged to her parents and which she couldn't bring herself to discard.

Donald looked tired, and normally he would have slumped in an armchair, pulled Maria on to his knee and told her all about his day.

He did at last drop into a chair and stretch out his legs towards the two-bar electric fire as Pamela passed him a mug of black tea.

Maria sat on the arm of the chair, took his chin and directed his face towards her. 'And now, please, tell me what is happening, *oui*?'

He grimaced, pointed to the corner of the room where Pamela was setting the Formica-topped table and said, 'Over dinner, *non*?'

Maria ate with little appetite as Donald told them about Dr Bryce's death.

'The killer made it look like suicide, but Jeff's men are certain it was murder.'

Maria swallowed a tasteless wedge of Cornish pasty. 'He threatened us,' she said in almost a whisper. 'Fenton threatened us all. It can't be a coincidence, can it?'

'Jeff's working on the theory that someone's carrying out Fenton's last wishes, for whatever reason. Maybe two people. A woman was seen leaving Bryce's place in the early hours. And Jeff's keen to trace the butler.'

Maria shook her head, her mind racing. 'But he threatened us all. You think we're *all* in danger, which is why—'

Donald reached out and took her hand. 'A precaution,' he said. 'That's all. A precaution, until we get to the bottom of this.'

Later that night, in bed in the tiny second bedroom, they lay awake in the moonlight that shone through the thin cotton curtains. For the past fifteen minutes Maria had thought of nothing else but her lies to Donald about her affair with Maxwell Fenton.

He stroked her cheek. 'Maria, everything's going to be fine.'
She turned to face him and kissed his lips. 'I know it is, *mon cheri*,' she said.

TEN

The following morning Langham drove from Bermondsey to
Pimlico and hurried up the steps to the Charles Elder
Literary Agency. Molly beamed at him from behind the
reception desk.

'His nibs in?' he asked.

She pointed to the office door, and he crossed to it and knocked.

'Enter,' came the baritone summons.

Langham stepped into the sumptuous room. Charles Elder sat
behind his vast mahogany desk, his snowy white hair piled above
his big, triple-chinned face.

'My boy, how wonderful to see you on this bleak and blustery
morn. You bring a ray of sunshine to the day!' He frowned. 'But
this isn't about Maria, is it? She did depart rather hastily yesterday.
She is well, Donald?'

'She's fine,' Langham said, taking a seat. 'But this is the situation . . .' And he proceeded to tell Charles about Maria's invitation
to Winterfield, Maxwell Fenton's suicide and the murder of Dr
Bryce.

'But that's terrible, my boy! Appalling! And are you sure that
Maria is safe in Bermondsey?'

'As safe as houses,' he said. 'But I think it wise if she doesn't
come into the office until we've got to the bottom of this.'

'Of course, of course. As long as it takes . . .' The big man
looked worried, cupping his multiple chins with his be-ringed right
hand.

'I've come to collect a couple of manuscripts she was working
on—'

'But there's absolutely no need, Donald! Maria shouldn't be
working, what with everything else she has to worry about.'

'She insisted,' Langham said. 'I think it'll help to take her mind
off the situation.'

'But this is terrible, terrible,' Charles wailed. 'I do think it calls for a little drink.' And so saying, he pulled a bottle of whiskey from his desk and poured himself a peg. 'You will join me, my boy?'

'Bit early for me, Charles. I need to keep a clear head.'

'Here's to your investigations,' Charles said, hoisting his glass and accounting for the measure in a single gulp.

He locked the bottle away and stared across the desk at Langham. 'I have been thinking, my boy. And this latest development only serves to confirm my convictions.'

'About?'

'About the wisdom of your continuing to work as a detective. I fear for you, I really do. And now Maria has been dragged into the dangerous mire of underworld shenanigans.'

Langham smiled at his agent's hyperbole. 'The fact is that this has nothing to do with my work, Charles. Fenton would have invited her whether I worked as a PI or as a choirmaster.'

'Even so, you cannot deny that, in your line of work, you do face danger on a daily basis.'

Langham frowned. 'Make that monthly,' he corrected.

Charles waved. 'My point still stands. You would be better off resigning and concentrating on your novels.'

'But would I? I think that my experiences as a private detective feed well into my books.'

'But I worry for you, my boy! I worry!'

Langham reached out and patted his agent's plump hand. 'I assure you, Charles, that you have absolutely no need. I can look after myself.' He climbed to his feet. 'Right, I'd better be making tracks. Is Albert well?'

Charles beamed. 'Never better,' he said. 'Did I mention that we're taking a little break before Christmas?'

'Maria did say something. Tangiers, isn't it?'

'A week of midwinter sun will do wonders for my spirits. But we'll be back in time for Christmas. And don't forget, you're invited up to Suffolk for the festivities.'

'We're looking forward to that,' Langham said, and moved to the door. 'Oh, one more thing,' he said. 'If anyone comes sniffing around here, asking for Maria or enquiring about her address, would you please contact me immediately?'

Charles's expression of woe intensified. 'I certainly will, my boy. I certainly will.'

Langham thanked him and left the office.

He found the bound manuscripts Maria had mentioned, said goodbye to Molly and drove to Earl's Court.

At the office, he warmed himself by the radiator and stared through the window. The sky was as dull as pewter and a fine rain fell ceaselessly. Three big Leyland double-decker buses ground slowly along the high street, one after the other, and old Alf was taking his mongrel mutt for its morning walk.

Langham was wondering what was delaying Ralph, who was usually in the office before him, when the phone rang and his partner's Cockney tones sounded down the line. 'Don, would you ruddy Adam and Eve it – the tank's dry. That geezer down Chiswick I told you about – well, he ain't got a drop to spare.'

'We could always siphon some from my tank.'

'Thanks, but don't bother. I'll come in on the Tube. Be a pal and meet me at Charing Cross in an hour, would you?'

'I'll be there,' Langham said.

'Oh – one more thing. I did some digging yesterday when I got back, and found the address of the Kersh and Cohen Theatrical Agency.'

'Good man.'

'Then I rang round two or three agencies who hire out butlers and suchlike, and struck gold. They were contacted a couple of weeks back by one Mr Smith from Winterfield, Essex, who hired a butler by the name of Joseph Gittings. I have his address in Battersea. We could nip along to his gaff this morning, then talk to the bods at the theatrical place later.'

'Good work,' Langham said, and rang off.

An hour would give him time to have a cuppa at the Lyons' tearoom next door and a glance at the morning paper. He was about to leave the office when the phone rang again.

'Ryland and Langham—' he began.

'Don, Jeff here,' Mallory said.

'Developments?'

'Not as such, but I need your help.'

'Go on.'

'I went round to see the Goudges at their Chelsea apartment last night. Odd couple.'

'You're telling me.'

'I explained the situation, told them about Bryce's murder and said that, taking into consideration Maxwell Fenton's threats and the doctor's subsequent death, it would be wise if they were to lay low for a while. I suggested they leave the city and book into a hotel somewhere until I contacted them with the all-clear. God knows, judging by the pile they live in, they could afford a hotel.'

'What did they say?'

Mallory grunted a laugh. 'The woman did all the talking, while her husband flapped around her like a nursemaid with St Vitus's dance. I've never met a woman who could load every word she speaks with such acerbity.'

Langham smiled as he recalled the art critic from the evening at Winterfield.

'Anyway,' Mallory went on, 'the upshot is that they refuse point-blank to believe that Bryce was murdered, and certainly not by anyone connected to Fenton.'

'Despite his threats?'

'Despite his threats,' Mallory said. 'Hermione Goudge pooh-poohed the whole idea and said that the notion that they were at risk was preposterous. I think her husband was alarmed, but too afraid of his wife to open his mouth and object.'

'What do you want me to do?'

'Go and see them and stress the danger. Lay it on thick. Shock the silly woman into seeing sense. Here's their address.'

Langham made a note of it and smiled to himself. 'I think I know exactly how to do that,' he said.

'Oh, one other thing. We contacted this Crispin Proudfoot chap and told him to make himself scarce, but we drew a blank when we tried to contact the actress, Holly Beckwith.'

'Strange. Didn't she give her address to Riley the other night?'

'She did – a boarding house in Peckham. But when we checked yesterday, we were told she'd moved out that morning and hadn't left a forwarding address.'

'She did say she was rehearsing something in London,' Langham offered.

Mallory sighed. 'Thanks, but do you know how many plays – professional and amateur – are running in the city at any one time? It'll take us days to plough through the programmes.'

'Just a sec, Jeff. Beckwith said something yesterday about exchanging addresses with Maria. You could check with her; of course, the address she gave might be the Peckham place.'

He gave Mallory Pamela's telephone number, then said, 'What's the situation concerning police protection for the guests?'

'Don't worry, I'm just about to pop along and see my Super about it,' Mallory said, and rang off.

Langham glanced at his watch. Almost nine thirty. So much for a quiet cup of tea while poring over the morning paper.

He locked the office and hurried down the linoleum-covered stairs, pulled his hat down against the rain and ran across the pavement to the Rover.

One good thing about the petrol shortage was that there were fewer vehicles on the road; on the minus side, profiteering garage owners were hiking their prices. He still had half a tank remaining, which, if he was careful, might last a couple of days. He drove from Earl's Court to Charing Cross, a journey which, thanks to the light traffic, he completed in fifteen minutes.

He parked across the road from the Underground station and watched the dour, bedraggled-looking commuters emerge from the exit in their droves. Another thing he wouldn't miss about London, aside from the traffic and the smog, was the cattle-like hordes of grim-faced citizens who thronged the public transport system. With the move to the country imminent, he wondered how he'd tolerated the capital for so long.

Ralph emerged from the Underground looking like a drowned rat in his tatty grey raincoat and trilby pulled down low over his narrow forehead. He crossed the road and slipped into the passenger seat with a curse.

'So I phoned Irish Pat, didn't I, and all he said on the petrol front was "No can do, bejesus." Just like that – and me an old customer!'

Langham commiserated and pulled from the kerb. 'Oh, change of plan. Jeff called – you might like this.'

He went on to tell Ralph about the sceptical Goudges and his idea to put the frighteners on the couple.

'Sounds just my cuppa,' Ralph said, rubbing his hands. 'I like the thought of putting the wind up a pair of toffs.'

Langham found himself trailing a double-decker all the way along the King's Road, its black exhaust fumes adding to the smog, then turned off towards the Thames. Presently they pulled up outside the Tivoli Mansions. The rain was still teeming down.

Ralph slipped the revolver from the glove compartment and followed Langham along the pavement.

'Just a mo,' Langham said, pointing across the road to a young man who had just emerged from the driver's seat of a black Ford Popular. Crispin Proudfoot saw Langham, waved frantically and hurried across to join them. The poet looked beside himself with fear.

'Langham!' he cried. 'Am I glad to see you!'

Langham found it impossible to tell whether it was rain or tears streaming down the young man's wan face, but he suspected the latter.

'The police came to see me yesterday,' Proudfoot said, taking Langham's arm in a desperate grip. 'They said Doctor Bryce was dead – murdered! – and that I should make myself scarce.' His face crumpled. 'And then, this morning, I received this . . .'

He pulled a sodden card out from beneath his gabardine mackintosh and waved it under Langham's nose. 'I was going to talk to Hermione, to see if she might reassure me.'

Langham looked along the road and saw a café. He turned to Ralph. 'I'll meet you in the foyer of the Tivoli. Give me five minutes while I . . .' He gestured to the poet, who was dripping in the street and looking pathetic.

'Righty-ho.' Ralph nodded and hurried into the red-brick and white stucco pile. Langham took Proudfoot's arm and propelled him along the street to the café.

They removed their coats and hats and sat down at a window table. 'You don't know how relieved I was to see your friendly face,' the poet said. 'The way you took charge of the frightful situation the other evening, before the police arrived . . .'

Langham ordered two coffees from the waitress while Proudfoot pulled a silk kerchief from the pocket of his beige jacket and mopped the tears, and the rain, from his face.

'Do you mind if I take a look at that card?' Langham asked.

The poet passed it across the table. Langham said, 'What did you do with the envelope?'

'It was sopping wet, so I discarded it,' Proudfoot said. 'I was taking the card to Hermione to see what she might make of it.'

The card was identical to the one Dr Bryce had received, illustrated with a single white lily and bearing the words, *With sincere sympathy*.

'When did this arrive?'

'First post this morning,' Proudfoot said, lifting his coffee cup.

His hand shook, and it was all he could do to steer the cup to his lips without spilling its contents. 'But if Doctor Bryce was murdered—'

'Keep it down,' Langham said, aware that a couple of customers were looking askance at the poet's hysteria.

'I'm sorry. This is all a bit much to take in, Mr Langham.'

'I know, I know,' he said soothingly. 'It isn't every day one finds oneself caught up in a situation like this.'

'But you, as a private detective . . .'

Langham smiled. 'In my real life, I'm a writer. Thrillers. I work as a detective part-time. Underneath this calm exterior, I'm as worried as you are. Perhaps more so. My wife is threatened, too.'

'Yes, of course. I'm sorry. I take it you've arranged for her to stay somewhere safe?'

'We're staying with a friend for the time being,' he said. 'Until all this blows over.'

Proudfoot smiled in uneasy camaraderie. 'What I don't understand, Mr Langham, is who can be doing this. Maxwell Fenton is dead. We saw him shoot himself. But his threats . . .' He took another trembling sip of coffee. 'You don't believe in revenge from beyond the grave, do you?'

'Of course not.'

'Then what do you think—?'

Langham interrupted. 'It's pretty obvious. Fenton had an accomplice, and it's he – or she – who's carrying out his dirty work.'

'But that's fantastical!' the poet cried.

'Nevertheless, it's the obvious conclusion.' Langham hesitated. 'I take it you took the advice of the police and moved from your usual address?'

'I found an attic room in Muswell Hill and moved in last night.'

Langham stared at the poet, alarmed. 'But you said you received the card this morning.'

'That's right – I had to pop back to my place in Knightsbridge for a few things and found this waiting for me.'

'You'd better give me your new address so I can keep in touch. Does it have a telephone?'

The poet nodded, then scribbled the address and phone number in a notebook, tore out the page and passed it across with shaking fingers.

Langham recalled the evening at Winterfield and Maxwell Fenton's acrimonious listing of his guests' supposed misdemeanours. The artist had said something about Proudfoot's theft.

'Look here, I need to build up a picture of Maxwell Fenton – get to know the kind of person he was in order to understand his motivations. He mentioned, the other evening, that you'd stolen something from him.'

Proudfoot turned bright red and stammered, 'I–I, that is . . .'

'This will go no further than you and me,' Langham assured the young man. 'I need to know why he felt so aggrieved, what motivated the man.'

Proudfoot took a deep breath. 'Fine, very well. I'm not at all proud of what I did, Mr Langham, but in my defence I must say that I was penniless at the time, and desperate. This was five years ago, just before my move to Paris. I'd fallen on hard times; I was reviewing in order to subsidize the pittance I earned from my poetry and short stories, and I needed money so that I could get away from London.'

'What happened?'

'Max often invited me down to Winterfield. He held weekends where artists, literary types, actors and the like would gather. They were . . . some of the parties were rather wild, though I never went in for anything like that myself.'

'And?' Langham prompted, suppressing the urge to smile.

The poet shrugged and looked forlorn. In the heat of the café, steam rose from his fair hair. 'I was a little drunk at the time. I was in Max's study. This was in the early hours. The party was winding down. Max and I were the last ones left drinking. We'd been discussing something – I can't recall what – and Max said he was turning in and staggered off.'

Proudfoot swallowed, his prominent Adam's apple bobbing, and looked everywhere but at Langham. He continued in an undertone, 'I knew where he kept his money – in a drawer in his desk. I honestly don't know what made me do it. As I said, I was drunk – and desperate. I opened the drawer and took what was in there.'

'How much?'

Proudfoot shrugged, swallowed and said almost inaudibly, 'Two hundred pounds.'

Langham whistled. 'Quite a tidy sum.'

'So I took it, God help me, and left the house at dawn before anyone was up, then boarded the train to Dover, en route to France.' He sighed, regarding his thin, long-nailed fingers on the tabletop before him. 'Obviously, Max worked out that it was I who stole the money, and had held it against me ever since.' He looked up, staring at Langham. 'But I swear that I always intended to pay it back, just as soon as I had the funds.'

Langham took a sip of his coffee, considering the young man's words. 'As you say, Fenton found out and held it against you ever since. However . . .' He hesitated.

'Yes?'

Langham shrugged. 'While the theft of two hundred pounds is no small matter, Fenton's desire to see you dead because of it is something of an overreaction, don't you think?'

'But you don't know Fenton,' Proudfoot almost wailed. 'He had a hair-trigger temper and took offence at the slightest provocation. I've seen him flying into a rage if he found one of his paintings hanging at what he considered to be the wrong height, and he'd accuse gallery owners of attempting to thwart his career. He was paranoid.'

'Insane?'

The poet hesitated. 'I've heard that charge levelled against him,' he said, 'though I'm in no way qualified to give an opinion.'

'Do you know if Fenton was married?'

Proudfoot shook his head. 'I'm sure he never married, though I've heard he had multiple affairs.'

'I understand he had a child, back in the thirties?'

Proudfoot widened his eyes as if in surprise. 'If so, it's the first I've heard of it. He never spoke of anything like that – his personal life, his affairs. He kept his cards close to his chest in that department.'

'Did you like him, Crispin?' Langham asked, watching the poet closely as the young man blinked and turned his empty cup in his long fingers, around and around.

'I respected him, and I was grateful for everything he did for me, his championing my poetry, the people he introduced me to.' He reddened, staring across at Langham, and went on, 'I can see what you're thinking. I respected him, and yet that's how I repaid him, by taking two hundred pounds from his desk.'

Langham shrugged, watching the poet. 'Do you know if Fenton had friends, acquaintances, who were so close to him that they might carry out his wishes posthumously?'

The young man shook his head. 'He had few really close friends, Mr Langham. His paranoia tended to drive people from him, after a time.'

'And yet there's a very real possibility that someone, or more than one person, has seen fit to carry out his threats.'

Proudfoot screwed his eyes shut. 'Don't! Please . . . don't . . . say . . . *that*!' he almost sobbed. 'Christ knows, I'm well aware of what's happening. What do you think it's like, suffering like this?'

Langham felt like slapping the poet across the face but restrained himself. 'You'll be fine if you take the advice of the police and lie low. Don't tell a soul where you are, and try not to go out, certainly not to your usual haunts, wherever they may be.'

Proudfoot swallowed, nodded and smiled his thanks. 'I wonder . . . You've been so good, Mr Langham. Could I have your number, so that if I need to contact you in an emergency . . .'

Langham wrote the agency's telephone number on a page of his notebook, tore it out and handed it to the poet.

Proudfoot read it, then looked up. 'You don't know how grateful I am, Mr Langham. I had intended to talk to Hermione, but your wise words have helped me no end.'

'My partner and I are heading there now, as it happens. Trying to talk sense into the stubborn woman.'

'Talk sense?' the poet repeated, wide-eyed. 'Do you mean . . .?'

Langham sighed. 'She refuses to believe that she's in danger and wants to stay put.'

'Hermione can be recalcitrant when she wants to be,' Proudfoot said. 'Please try to make her see sense, would you?'

Langham smiled. 'I'll do my very best,' he said. 'Now, I'd better pay up and get back to it. My advice to you is to drive straight back to Muswell Hill and lie low, all right?'

The poet smiled and said he would do just that. Langham paid for the coffees and hurried across the street to the Tivoli Mansions.

ELEVEN

Ralph was kicking his heels in the reception area when Langham pushed through the revolving door.

'That sorry specimen,' Ralph said scathingly, 'was one of the guests from the other night, right?'

Langham laughed. 'Crispin Proudfoot, a poet.'

'A poet, eh? That'd figure. A right drip. You held his hand and dried his tears?'

'In a manner of speaking. He had the vapours about being on the hit list. I told him to lie low. Now, you all set?'

Ralph patted the pocket of his raincoat where the revolver nestled. 'Let's do it.'

Langham crossed to the concierge's glass cubicle. The old, moustachioed man wore a crumpled grey uniform with chunky epaulettes. 'Goudge, apartment twelve. If you could inform them that Donald Langham would like a word.'

The concierge turned to an intercom, flipped a switch and spoke briefly into a microphone. Langham made out the querulous reply, and the concierge said to Langham, 'If you'd care to take the lift, sir. Third floor.'

They crossed the foyer, waited for the lift to descend and open, then stepped inside.

They ascended in silence and stepped out on the third floor.

Langham led the way along a plush, carpeted corridor until he came to a polished timber door marked with the number twelve. He pointed out the spyhole set into the centre of the door. Ralph knocked, then stepped to one side so as not to be seen through the spyhole.

Langham pressed himself to the wall, out of sight of whoever should answer the summons. Ralph slipped the revolver from his pocket and held it behind his back.

Bolts were shot and a lock turned. The door opened and George's falsetto voice said, 'Mr Langham? What—?'

Without waiting to be invited inside, Ralph brandished the handgun and barged into the apartment.

'Oh!' George cried. 'Oh, my!'

'Quit the wittering and get into the lounge!' Ralph snapped.

Pressed against the wall, Langham smiled as he heard Hermione Goudge call out, 'George? George, what in heaven's name . . .? Oh!'

He waited twenty seconds, then strolled into the apartment and followed the sound of George's whimpering down the corridor until he came to a luxuriously appointed sitting room equipped with a grand piano and decorated with an array of undoubtedly expensive works of art.

George and Hermione Goudge sat side by side on a chaise longue, drip-white and staring at Ralph, who stood over them with his handgun directed at the woman.

When Hermione caught sight of Langham as he appeared, smiling, and stood next to the gunman, she stared at him pop-eyed and stammered, 'Langham! What the devil . . .? What in God's name is all this about, you vile creature?'

Langham smiled. 'Just a little demonstration, Hermione, to point out the fact of your errant stupidity.'

'Why, I've never been so insulted!'

'Prepare to be even more insulted,' Langham said, pulling up the piano stool and straddling it. 'Ralph, put the shooter away. Hermione and George live to fight another day.'

Chuckling to himself, and giving the trembling George a theatrical wink, Ralph slipped the revolver under his raincoat and leaned against the wall as if settling himself to enjoy what was about to take place.

'You're fools,' Langham said, 'both of you. Crass and utter fools. Yesterday Detective Inspector Mallory told you of the danger you were in, and what do you do?' He looked from Hermione to George. 'You do nothing. You think you know better than the police, who, you might be surprised to learn, have a certain expertise in these matters. But no, the Goudges think they know better.'

George, at least, had it in him to look shamefaced. Hermione stared defiantly at Langham. 'Mallory called yesterday with some half-baked story about Bryce's murder—' she began.

'Half-baked?' Langham was incredulous. 'Bryce was hanged by the neck by an unknown assailant.'

But Hermione was not to be talked down. 'That was Mallory's theory,' she said. 'But it doesn't quite fit with what we know, does it, George?'

She gave her husband a withering look, as if daring him to demur, and he murmured, 'No, dear.'

Langham looked from George to Hermione. 'And what *do* you know?'

'We happened to offer the doctor a lift on leaving Winterfield,' she said. 'It was a foul night, and I wouldn't have seen a dog out in such weather. And Lower Malton was on our way.'

'And?'

'And he was sullen and morose for the duration of the journey, though he did say one thing.'

Against the wall, Ralph glanced up from inspecting his nails. 'What was that?'

'He said that he felt like going home and drinking himself to death. Those were his exact words. I think George muttered something about it being a terrible business and suggested the doctor have a nightcap and go straight to bed, and Bryce said – and these were his exact words – "I feel more like drinking myself to death, to be perfectly frank." There! And hours later he was dead, killed by his own hand.' Hermione stared triumphantly from Langham to Ralph.

Patiently, Langham pointed out, 'Hermione, Bryce didn't drink himself to death. He was hanged. He'd had a drink, granted – but in the opinion of the police surgeon, he would have been too drunk to hang himself. Also, there was evidence that he wasn't alone when he was drinking. Someone was with him – the same person who assisted him out to the garage and hanged him.'

Hermione waved this away. 'Supposition! I heard with my own ears what Bryce said.'

Langham sighed. 'You also heard, I take it, Maxwell Fenton's threats to you all before he killed himself?'

'Threats? More like the ravings of a lunatic, if you want my opinion. And what are you suggesting? That Fenton came back from the dead to murder the doctor, and is now threatening the rest of us?'

Langham exchanged a pitying glance with Ralph, who rolled his eyes.

'What I'm suggesting, backed up by the police, is that Fenton had an accomplice who is enacting the artist's final wishes.'

Hermione goggled at him. 'Preposterous! I've never heard of anything so ridiculous in my life! I think you've been watching too many trashy movies, my man.'

'But you don't deny that all those gathered at Winterfield the other night had, as far as Fenton was concerned, wronged him in some way?'

'That's what the man assumed, yes, but he was clearly delusional.'

Langham thought about it. 'Do you have any idea what Bryce might have done to incur Fenton's wrath?'

George Goudge lifted a hand like a pupil requesting the teacher's permission to speak. 'Ah . . .'

'Go on.'

'I heard a rumour – this was back in the war – that Doctor Bryce had treated one of Maxwell's lovers, and word was that it went horribly wrong and she died, and Bryce was responsible.' He shook his head. 'But I don't know the details, or even if it's true.'

It sounded unlikely to Langham: why, if this were so, would Fenton have kept Bryce on as his personal physician?

He climbed to his feet and strode to the window which, with art deco flamboyance, curved around the corner of the building. He stood with his back to the room and stared out. Buses grumbled along the street, their diesel fumes adding to the grey fug of the winter's day. Pedestrians hurried back and forth, totally oblivious to everything but their own private concerns. He wondered what Maria might be doing now.

He turned and stared at the toad-like pair seated side by side on the chaise longue. He decided to change tack.

He leaned against the wall and said, 'I want to know a little more about Maxwell Fenton.'

'Why on earth—?' Hermione began.

'I'm trying to understand the man,' Langham said. 'The better I understand him, the greater the chance I have of working out why he planned what he did – and whom he might have hired to carry through those plans.'

Hermione began to protest, but Ralph snapped, 'Shut up and listen, for Christ's sake!'

Hermione pursed her lips and avoided Ralph's disdainful gaze.

'When did you first meet Maxwell Fenton, Hermione?'

'Why, that would be at some point in the late twenties.'

'"Some point"? That's not good enough. I want to know exactly.'

Hermione pulled a sour face and thought about it. 'Very well . . . It would be 'twenty-nine.'

'George?' Langham asked.

The little man tapped his lips, staring at the chandelier. 'We met at art college after the war, in 1919. Fenton was tutoring there.'

'Were you close to him then?' he asked George.

'We became friends later, in the twenties. We agreed on certain things. We were both politically conservative, and shared a disdain for modernism in the arts then sweeping Europe. After college, I decided I couldn't cut it as an artist and began art dealing in a small way. I sold some of Fenton's early pieces.'

Langham interrupted. 'And was Fenton as egotistical then as he was in his later years?'

George hesitated. 'Maxwell was always self-assured. And opinionated. He was quick to take issue with people and was easily offended.'

'Was he paranoid?'

'Some people opined that he was, yes. As for myself . . .'

'Yes?'

'I don't think he was paranoid at the time, but became so later, in the late thirties.'

'When his work fell out of favour?'

'Around then, yes.'

Langham moved from the window and sat on the piano stool. 'Fenton mentioned, the other night, something about your betrayal. What happened, George?'

The little man went red and stared down at his sausage-like fingers.

'I asked you a question!' Langham snapped.

George jumped as if shot and shifted uncomfortably.

Hermione spoke up. 'Don't say a thing if you don't want to, George. He has absolutely no authority to ask such impertinent questions.' She stared at Langham. 'What business is it of yours, young man?'

Langham sighed, then said reasonably, 'I'm trying to investigate a murder, Hermione. I'm also, though you might find this hard to believe, trying to help you – to save your skins, even. It might be useful if I knew why Maxwell Fenton held such a grudge against your husband.'

She continued to stare at him, and Langham was reminded more than ever of a truculent Pekinese. She said, 'I assure you that it has not the remotest bearing on this case, Mr Langham.'

'If that's how you want to play it,' he murmured to himself.

He stood up again and moved around the room, examining the paintings adorning the walls. He recognized a few names: Nicholson, Spencer, Freud – contemporary painters whose work was much sought-after.

He came to a portrait of a woman he recognized. It was Hermione herself, perhaps in her early twenties, and Langham was surprised to find himself thinking that, back then, she had been almost attractive in a compact, dark, mysteriously brooding way.

He was even more surprised when he made out the artist's signature: *Max Fenton, '29.*

The woman smiled out of the painting, her mouth wide, almost laughing, and there was an unmistakably mischievous light in her eyes. He thought he'd seen the same dancing light portrayed in another canvas he'd seen recently . . .

He turned and leaned against the wall, between Hermione's portrait and a Nicholson still life.

Going on a hunch, he asked, 'How long after you met Fenton, in 'twenty-nine, did you fall in love with him?'

The reaction of those in the room was interesting: George closed his eyes in a gesture almost of despair or resignation; Hermione opened her mouth as if to deny the question but was silent – which Langham found interesting in itself. Across the room, Ralph stared at him, open-mouthed.

'Well?' Langham prompted.

'I . . .' Hermione stared down at the array of diamond rings that encrusted her fingers.

It was gratifying, Langham thought, to see the woman speechless for once.

'It was a brief fling, nothing more,' she murmured at last. 'I was young and foolish. I knew as little then about men as I did about art – my knowledge of both came much later.'

'What happened?'

'What do you mean?' she snapped.

'You left him, am I right?'

She hesitated, then said, 'After we had been together for perhaps three months, I became aware of his unfaithfulness.'

'He was seeing other women?'

'Several other women, Langham. He was an incorrigible philanderer with not a moral bone in his body. I confronted him, then broke off our affair. Not long after that, I met George.' She reached out and, in a show of affection Langham found oddly touching, took her husband's hand and squeezed it.

'How did Fenton take it?' he asked. 'Both your breaking off the affair and your subsequent engagement to George?'

'Like all philanderers, who think nothing of being unfaithful to their partners, he didn't like the taste of his own medicine. He was cut to the quick when I said I had no desire to see him ever again. He begged me to reconsider, but I told him, in no uncertain terms, to go to hell.'

'And he resented you ever since – as much for what he saw as your betrayal as for your later condemnation of his art?'

She held his gaze. 'Perhaps that is so, Langham, but I can assure you that my criticism of his work had nothing to do with our affair. He was a poor painter, period, and it was my duty to declare him such.'

'And yet,' he said, turning to her portrait, 'you display his painting of you?'

She glanced down at her fingers. 'It is one of his few competent pieces,' she said hurriedly, 'and anyway it's worth a fair amount. And I must admit that it reminds me of my . . . my youth.'

Langham looked across at George Goudge. 'So back in the thirties, you meet Hermione, fall in love, and marry. And your friendship with Maxwell Fenton, I surmise, hits the rocks.'

George shrugged. 'We'd been drifting steadily apart anyway,' he muttered.

'And your taking up with his old flame,' Langham went on, 'was the final straw for Maxwell. He accused you of betrayal, and had resented you for it ever since.'

George burst out, 'Maybe so – who can see into the mind of a madman?'

Langham smiled and gestured as if to concede the point: *Who indeed?*

'I've heard that Fenton was married,' he said.

Hermione said, 'I heard rumours that he'd tied the knot, yes. In the early thirties, I think it was.'

'To? Do you happen to know her name?'

Hermione frowned. 'I think she was called Prudence, or was it Patience? As for her surname . . . No, it's gone – if I ever knew it at all.'

'And was it with this woman that he had a child?'

'I've no idea with whom it might have been,' she said, 'though I did hear he'd become a father.'

'Do you know if the child was a boy or a girl?'

'I really can't recall – but I did hear on the grapevine that the poor thing died in infancy.'

Langham drew a long breath. 'And a few years later, as a war artist in Europe, he witnessed things that finally became too much, and unhinged him.'

'So the story goes,' Hermione said.

'You don't believe it?'

She sighed. 'I really haven't the faintest idea how to untangle what might be the facts of the case from the self-propaganda with which Fenton liked to glamorize himself. He was ever the egotist, and had a penchant for playing the role of the tragic artist.'

'And it all ended at Winterfield, with a bullet in the head,' Langham said. 'And yet . . . and yet his resentment lives on.'

He rose to his feet abruptly, startling the pair. 'I've done my best to warn both of you of the danger you face. If you're stubborn enough to ignore Fenton's threats, then so be it.'

He nodded to Ralph and was about to suggest that they leave when he heard a rattle from the hallway, followed by the slap of letters landing on the parquet.

Ralph pushed himself from the wall and disappeared into the hall. He returned, smiling to himself and clutching an envelope.

'Well, well, well,' he said, 'what do we have here?' He looked across at Langham and raised the envelope. 'Shall I?'

Langham smiled. 'Go ahead.'

Ralph passed Hermione Goudge the envelope, and Langham said, 'On the day he died, Doctor Bryce received an anonymous card – identical, I suspect, to the one you're now opening.'

Hermione looked from him to the envelope, then opened it. She pulled out a card, grimaced and passed it to George.

Langham saw that it was indeed identical in every respect to Bryce's, decorated with a single white lily and bearing the legend 'With sincere sympathy'. It was, unsurprisingly, unsigned.

Langham nodded to Ralph and they made their way from the room.

Before he reached the hallway, Langham paused and turned to

the stupefied couple, still staring down at the card. 'Take my advice and leave London as soon as possible, OK?'

Hermione looked up. 'We'll make arrangements to leave this afternoon, Mr Langham,' she said quietly.

Langham nodded and followed Ralph from the apartment.

In the lift to the ground floor, Ralph said, 'Nice bit of detective work there, Don. I didn't see it coming – that Fenton and the old bag had an affair.'

'I would never have guessed it, if it hadn't been for the painting.'

'Think they really will see sense and skedaddle?'

'They'd be bloody fools not to, Ralph. What now?'

'How about we tootle along and drop in on this butler chappie?'

Langham led the way to the car.

TWELVE

They motored across London Bridge and along the Old Kent Road.

'You ever met an off-duty butler before?' Ralph asked.

'Can't say I have.'

'Strange coves.'

'In what way?'

Ralph frowned and lit up a Capstan, filling the car with its acrid fumes. 'They're just like you and me, really. Underneath. No better and no worse. Only, see, they think they're a cut above everyone else.'

'How's that?'

'Well, I reckon it's 'cos they work all the time with toffs. I mean, stands to reason, doesn't it? You hob-nob with aristocracy from sparrow-fart to midnight, and what happens? It rubs off on you, is what.'

Langham smiled to himself. 'What rubs off on you?'

Ralph blew a plume of smoke at the windscreen. 'Superiority is what. The idea that you're better than everyone else. I mean, just think about the bitch we just left. Right piece of uppity goods, she is. The way she looks down her snout at everyone, her hubby included. Well, butlers are just like that. Mark my word, you'll see when we meet this Gittings character. He'll think he's God's gift, and no mistake.'

'We'll see,' Langham said.

'And if it's OK with you, Don, I'll do the talking.'

'Fine by me.'

'I know how to handle these types. Don't let 'em get above themselves, and if he tries it on, take him down a peg or two.'

Langham turned left along a street of small, red-brick houses in the shadow of a vast gasometer. 'What number is it?'

Ralph peered out. 'Forty-five. There,' he said, pointing.

Langham slowed down and pulled into the kerb.

'Least it's stopped raining,' Ralph said. He peered up and down the street and sniffed. 'We looked at a house a couple of streets away, after the war. Annie wanted to be closer to her mum in Deptford, but I reckoned nothing to the area. Give me Lewisham any day. I mean, just look at it! Grim.'

He finished his cigarette and flicked the butt end through the window. Langham was about to suggest they make a move when the door of number forty-five opened and a tall, dark-haired man in his forties, smartly dressed in a Crombie coat and bowler hat, stepped from the house and walked along the street away from the car. He carried a rolled-up newspaper under his right arm and looked for all the world like a city banker.

'That the chap?' Ralph asked.

'That's him,' Langham said.

'We could nab him and ask him to accompany us back to his place?'

'Wait,' Langham said, pointing.

Joseph Gittings stopped at the kerb, looked both ways and crossed the road towards a public house. As they watched, he pushed through the door to the snug.

'Better still,' Langham said, 'how about we join him for a jar?'

'Could murder for one,' Ralph said, jumping from the car.

They gave Gittings a couple of minutes to buy his drink and find a table, then crossed the road and entered the Globe Tavern. The butler had settled himself at a corner table and was opening his *Daily Mirror* and taking an inch from the top of his Guinness.

'I'll get them in,' Langham said, 'while you mosey over and say hello, friendly like.'

Ralph nodded. 'Mine's a Fuller's.'

Langham ordered two bitters. Ralph sat next to Joseph Gittings and showed the butler his accreditation. Gittings scowled suspiciously at Ralph, then looked across the room and saw Langham. His expression registered recognition, quickly followed by alarm.

Langham picked up the pint pots and crossed to the corner table, nodding cheerily. 'We meet again, Mr Gittings, under somewhat more auspicious circumstances this time.'

The butler shrugged and, as po-faced as ever, looked from Ralph to Langham. 'Said all I have to say to the rozzers,' he muttered.

'So they caught up with you?' Ralph said.

'They came and went last night, and they don't have anything on me.'

'And why should they?' Langham said. 'You've done nothing wrong, have you?'

'Not a thing,' Gittings said. 'So why're you nosing around?'

Ralph said, 'We just want to know more about the geezer who employed you, don't we? This Maxwell Fenton chap.'

Gittings took a mouthful of Guinness. 'What makes you think I know much about him? He hired me for the night, gave me instructions, then slipped me a fiver and left me to it.'

'And then,' Langham said, 'he blew his brains out all over the library wall at the end of the night.'

Ralph lit up another Capstan. 'Bit unusual, that, eh? Not what your employers normally get up to, is it? And then you high-tail it before the boys in blue turn up.' He shook his head. 'How do you think that looks, chummy?'

Gittings lifted his pint. His hand shook. 'So what if I heard the shot, looked in and saw . . .?' He shrugged. 'I ask you, what could I do? He was dead, stone-cold dead.'

'So you panicked and ran?' Langham said.

'I suppose I did. Best out of there, I thought. Didn't think the rozzers would trace me. Nor you, for that matter.'

'When was the first time you met Maxwell Fenton?'

The butler took another drink. 'That afternoon two days ago, as arranged. He told me that he was expecting guests, six of them, and they'd all have invitations. I was to show them into the sitting room, then liaise with him about when I should escort them all to the library.'

'And when I showed up, without an invitation?' Langham asked.

'I thought I'd better clear it with Mr Fenton. He didn't like it, but when I said you'd take the missus home if you weren't allowed in, he instructed me to let you in and set out an extra chair.'

'And he said nothing about what the little get together was all about?' Ralph asked.

'Not a thing.'

'Did he say anything about the guests, who they were, his dealings with 'em?'

'No, nothing like that.'

Ralph knocked ash from his cigarette into the tray with a flick of a nicotine-stained finger. 'And when you got to Winterfield that afternoon, there was no one else about?'

'Not a soul – only Mr Fenton.'

'You sure about that?'

'Absolutely.'

'What about a car in the drive?' Ralph asked.

'Nothing, no car. Nothing at all. Made me wonder how Mr Fenton got around. I reckoned he used taxis.'

'And once inside,' Ralph went on, 'you didn't get the impression that there was anyone else in the house – keeping themselves to themselves, like?'

'No, as I said, there wasn't a soul about – only Mr Fenton.'

'He didn't mention anyone else? Friends, relatives, acquaintances?'

'No, no one. He gave me his instructions and left me to arrange the drinks trolley.'

'What time was this?' Ralph asked.

'When Mr Fenton contacted the agency, he left instructions that I was to arrive no later than five. I arrived at Winterfield at one minute to and rang the bell at five on the dot.'

'Commendably punctual,' Langham murmured.

'And how did Fenton seem at this point?' Ralph asked.

'Seem?'

'I mean,' Ralph said, drawing on his Capstan and watching the butler through narrowed eyes, 'did he look like a geezer who was planning to blow his skull to smithereens?'

Gittings took a long drink, considering the question. 'That's the strange thing,' he said reflectively. 'You see, looking back, that's what struck me as odd. He didn't seem in the least preoccupied or melancholy. Not at all like someone who was planning to kill himself. He seemed, well, quite chipper, to tell the truth.'

'Chipper?' Ralph said, dubious. 'Like, happy-go-lucky?'

Gittings frowned. 'I wouldn't say happy-go-lucky so much as breezy, confident. He was smiling and quite chatty, asking me about the trip down and about how long I'd served as a butler.'

'And that is, as a matter of interest?' Langham asked.

'Almost twenty-five years, fifteen of them for Lord Hailbury. When he passed away, I decided to go part-time, and I joined the agency.'

'So back to that night,' Ralph said. 'He gave you instructions about greeting the guests, but what about afterwards?'

'He said the evening would end at approximately ten o'clock, and that I was to be on hand to see the guests out.'

Langham exchanged a look with Ralph. 'What were his exact words?' Langham asked, leaning forward.

Gittings regarded his half-finished pint. 'Just that: he expected the evening to end at ten, and that I should be ready when the guests left.' He hesitated. 'That's why, when he did what he did, it was so shocking.'

Langham sat back, regarding his pint.

Again, he thought, there was something not quite right here. Fenton's words had not matched his deeds – just as his threats to the guests on that fateful evening had not matched the act of taking his own life.

There was something very wrong about the whole thing, but for the life of him Langham could not guess what that might be.

An old man bustled into the bar with a tray, selling cockles, pork scratchings, and pickled eggs. Ralph bought three eggs and wolfed them down in short order.

'So you looked in on hearing the gunshot,' he said around a mouthful of masticated egg, 'saw what he'd done and off you scarpered?'

'That's about the top and bottom of it, yes,' Gittings admitted.

Langham said, 'And you drove straight back to London?'

'When I reached Ilford, I decided I needed a drink to steady my nerves. I stopped at a pub and had a quick few pints.'

Langham said, 'And you didn't, on the way, take a detour to the village of Lower Malton and the house of one of the guests, Doctor Bryce?' He paused. 'You didn't happen to meet up with a dark-haired woman at Bryce's place—?'

'I don't know anything about any woman,' Gittings said. 'But the inspector asked me about Bryce. He wanted to know what I was doing between midnight and five in the morning.'

'Let me guess,' Ralph said. 'You told the rozzers you were tucked up all comfy in your pit, right?'

'Not at all,' said Gittings, relishing what he said next. 'I told them that between midnight and five I was locked in a cell at Battersea police station.'

Langham leaned forward. 'Come again?'

'You see,' Gittings said, 'I had one or two too many at Ilford, and after leaving the Swan and almost making it home, I was pulled over just around the corner and found to be drunk in charge. I spent the night in a cell at Battersea.'

'Well, blow me down,' Ralph said, laughing, 'if that ain't about the best alibi I've ever come across!'

'Never thought I'd be glad to find myself in the slammer for the night,' Gittings admitted. 'Funny how things work out, isn't it?'

Langham finished his pint and pointed to the butler's glass. 'Care for another?'

'I don't mind if I do, sir.'

Langham took half a crown from his pocket. 'I'll put this behind the bar for a couple more,' he said, 'and then we'll be on our way. Thank you for your time, Mr Gittings, and be careful how many you have. You don't want to spend another night in the cell, do you?'

The butler smiled. 'I'll mind your advice, sir, and limit myself to just one more.'

Back in the car, Langham said, 'Well, so much for your theory that all butlers are uppity aristocrats-in-waiting. He seemed quite a decent chap, all things considered.'

'The exception that proves the rule,' Ralph muttered.

'So, what do you make of what he said?'

'Only thing that struck me as odd, Don – Fenton's manner. Chatty and breezy, not like a man planning to snuff himself.'

'That's what I thought. Right, what now?'

'I want to nip round the corner and check with the rozzers to see if Gittings was banged up like he claims.'

'You doubt him?' Langham said, pulling into the road.

'Just crossing all the t's and dotting the i's, Don.'

Langham drove to the end of the street, turned left, then right, and motored along the main street until he came to the police station.

Ralph hopped out. 'Back in a jiffy.'

A few minutes later he tapped down the steps of the station and resumed the passenger seat.

'Well?' Langham asked.

'He's legit,' Ralph said. 'Found drunk in charge of a road vehicle and thrown into the cell at five to midnight, released at dawn.'

Langham set off and headed north. 'Next stop,' he said, 'the Kersh and Cohen Theatrical Agency.'

THIRTEEN

They parked on Holborn High Street and walked down an alleyway towards a Chinese laundry, a grille at ground level belching out clouds of steam and the overpowering reek of bleach.

'The agency's above the Chinese place,' Ralph said. 'I had a stroke of luck on the blower. I asked the receptionist if any of their acts had been hired by a Maxwell Fenton. Then I added "Maxwell Fenton of Winterfield, Essex" and, hey presto, the woman said that someone called Mr Smith of Winterfield, Lower Malton, had booked an actor a couple of weeks ago.'

'Odd. Why would Fenton use an assumed name?' Langham asked.

'Search me. Good job I mentioned Winterfield, though, or we might never've had the lead.'

'That's what's worrying about this job so much of the time – how we rely on chance and blind luck.'

'And brains and legwork, Don. Don't forget that.'

'I supply the former and you the latter, right?' Langham said, straight-faced.

'Aye, and your old mum was the Queen of Sheba.'

They halted before the Chinese laundry. Beyond an open door, a flight of cracked linoleum steps rose to the theatrical agency. Ralph led the way up to the first-floor office.

A harried-looking man in shirtsleeves was barricaded behind a desk overflowing with papers and folders. He was in his sixties and balding, with thick black glasses and a Biro pen lodged above his right ear. Buried in the avalanche were two constantly ringing telephones and an ancient upright typewriter.

'The Astounding Baldini at the Metro, Bracknell, on the fifth? Of course. Five guineas a night.' He waved Langham and Ralph to a padded bench that ran along the wall opposite the desk, then slammed the phone down and answered the second.

'Hello? Right, right. You doubt me? I swear! Fine act. Listen to me, he was treading the boards with Irving. No word of a lie.' He scribbled something in a ledger and picked up the first phone when it began ringing. 'Kersh and Cohen. The Carringtons? They're the finest man-and-wife mind-readers north of the river. Six guineas a turn, available from the tenth.'

At this rate, Langham thought, they could be waiting till dusk.

The walls of the office were plastered with black-and-white photographs depicting, presumably, the many acts that Kersh and Cohen represented: debonair matinee idols and sultry leading ladies, stand-up comedians and clowns, plate-spinners and magicians. Several pictures showed the man behind the desk smoking a fat cigar, his arms yoked possessively around the shoulders of blonde starlets.

He slammed the phone down and a sudden, ringing silence descended.

'God help me,' he shouted as if still on the blower. 'What a business! The world is full of chisellers and crooks, my friends. And me, poor Mannie Kersh, I'm in the middle, squeezed between grasping impresarios and griping talent. And you are?'

'Ryland and Langham,' Ralph said, 'I phoned yesterday—'

Mr Kersh raised a hand. 'Don't tell me! Comedians, right? And you' – he pointed to Langham – 'you're the straight man.'

'I spoke to a Miss Mankowitz—' Ralph tried again.

Kersh rolled his eyes. 'Between you and me, I'd be better off employing a monkey. Would you believe she called in sick again? Influenza this time.'

'That's terrible, but . . .' Langham began.

'I'll say. I can't be answering the phone all day.' He looked from Langham to Ralph. 'Go on.'

Ralph blinked. 'I beg your pardon?'

Kersh clicked his fingers impatiently as if keeping time to a bossa nova. 'Let's have it, but I warn you – I've seen 'em all before. And double acts? Hard sell these days. Individual stand-ups, fine. But double acts—'

The phone shrilled and he snatched it up. 'Kersh and Cohen. That's right. He's a star, and reliable. You won't be disappointed. Three guineas a night and board and lodging. I'll send him along.'

As soon as Kersh dropped the receiver, Ralph said, 'We're not comedians, Mr Kersh.'

The agent blinked. 'Mind-readers, right? But as you'll no doubt know' – he laughed at his little joke – 'I'm fully booked with mentalists.'

'We're private detectives,' Langham said, 'and we're here to enquire about one of your customers, a Mr Smith of Winterfield.'

Mr Kersh spread his hands. 'But why didn't you say, boys? Private detectives! I've had everything in here, my friends – but gumshoes, never! A first!' He leaned forward. 'How can I help?'

'Mr Smith booked one of your acts,' Ralph said. 'According to Miss Mankowitz, this was a fortnight ago. We'd like to know the identity of the person he booked.'

'He's not in trouble?'

'No, but we're investigating the suicide of Mr Smith, so we'd obviously like to speak to anyone who had dealings with him.'

The phone rang and Mr Kersh snatched it up and listened. 'I'm sorry. I'm very sorry. No, that's impossible. Klaxo the Clown is dead. You didn't hear? Heart attack, the last act at the Brighton Hippodrome. Tragic. We're all in mourning here. Sadly missed. A rare talent . . . A terrible, terrible business. Goodbye.'

He blinked at Ralph. 'The name again?'

'Smith.'

Mr Kersh propelled his swivel chair over to a filing cabinet and pulled open a drawer. His fat fingers marched down a wad of dog-eared files. He pulled one out and examined a typewritten list, his lips moving as he read.

'Here we are. Smith, Winterfield. Booked one of my best, Edgar Benedict.'

'An actor?' Langham asked.

Mr Kersh's bushy eyebrows leapt high above his round glasses. 'An actor, he asks! A star! Worked alongside the finest – Olivier and Gielgud and all the big names. Though, granted, this was before the war. He's knocking on now – in his seventies.'

'Fallen on hard times?' Langham suggested.

'Perhaps lean times would be a better description,' Kersh said.

'Do you know why Mr Smith hired him?' Ralph asked.

Kersh read the notes and shook his head. 'I'm afraid not, my friends. But he paid well – thirty guineas. My guess is a soliloquy, or maybe a reading at some country house soirée.'

'We'd like Mr Benedict's address,' Langham said.

Kersh pushed himself over to a second filing cabinet and pulled out a heavy drawer. He found a file and opened it on the desk, then copied out the address in small, neat handwriting and passed the slip of paper to Langham.

'Twelve Laburnum Grove, Forest Hill,' he read.

'And Mr Benedict didn't say anything about the booking, when it might've been for?' Ralph asked.

'Not a dicky bird, but then I haven't seen Edgar for a while. He's not as well as he was. His glory days, I'm afraid, are behind him. But what glory days! He even acted in Hollywood, you know?'

The phone shrilled again and he snatched it up. Langham quickly thanked him and gestured to the door.

Mr Kersh waved as they slipped from the office. 'The Amazing Mr Waldo is available and his rates are *very* reasonable, my friend.'

They left the office and made their way back to the car. 'How about we go and see this Mr Benedict, Ralph, then call it a day, and I'll drop you at home?'

As they drove from Holborn and headed south, Ralph asked, 'How's Maria taking it?'

Langham tapped the steering wheel, considering. 'She's bearing up, all things considered. At least she's safe at Pamela's.'

The traffic was abnormally light for a Friday afternoon. Langham kept his distance behind an overloaded coal lorry and considered taking Maria out for a meal. A nice red wine at a quiet Italian place would be the perfect way to wind down after a busy day.

'How well did she know this Fenton chappie?' Ralph asked, slipping down in the passenger seat and lighting up a Capstan.

'Well, I think she was smitten. She was only eighteen at the time, and Fenton was a big name in the art world.'

Ralph glanced at him. 'They weren't . . .?'

'Lovers?' Langham laughed. 'No, of course not. As I said, she was young. A kid. Fenton painted her.'

Ralph blew out a plume of smoke. 'You never said why Fenton had her on his hit list, Don.'

Langham recounted Maxwell Fenton's behaviour at Winterfield all those years ago, and Maria's response with the fire iron.

'And he harboured a grudge ever since?' Ralph said. 'Enough to want her killed?' He shrugged. 'Sounds a bit of an overreaction to me.'

'Well, he wasn't in his right mind towards the end.'

Ralph grunted. 'The bastard's better off dead, if you ask me,' he said. He was silent for a while as they motored south-east through the suburbs. 'I've been mulling it over.'

'Go on.'

'This Edgar Benedict chap. Fenton hired him, right? But Mr Kersh couldn't say for what. Presumably some acting work.'

'That's the favourite.'

'But – this is a long shot – what if it was this Benedict fellow he got to do his dirty work?'

Langham shook his head. 'So he rings up Mr Kersh and hires the actor Edgar Benedict to kill half a dozen innocent people? It's a theatrical agency, Ralph, not a hiring house for hitmen.'

'I know, I know. But what if he had something on the actor?'

'What do you mean?'

'What if he was blackmailing him?'

'What on earth makes you think . . .?'

Ralph pointed a nicotine-stained finger at him. 'Remember those bank statements we found at Winterfield? The twenty-five nicker going into Fenton's account every month? So what if the dosh was from the actor, to keep Fenton silent about something?'

'It's a theory,' Langham allowed, 'but a very tentative one.'

'And how about,' Ralph went on, 'Fenton then put the pressure on the actor? Stopped demanding cash and wanted something more from him. Perhaps what he had on the actor was enough for Fenton to force him into killing these people?'

Langham glanced at his partner. 'You really think that?'

Ralph gazed through the windscreen for a while, then shook his head. 'Not necessarily. What would make Benedict kill these people when the bloke who's blackmailing him is dead?'

'Exactly,' Langham said. 'We might find out more when we talk to Edgar Benedict.'

Laburnum Grove was an affluent, leafy suburban street lined with red-brick semi-detached villas dating from the nineteenth century. They found number twelve and parked outside. An orange light burned at a downstairs window, cosy in the gathering twilight.

They left the car and stood under the small portico before the front door as rain began to fall. Evidently the house had been divided into flats; four bell-pushes were labelled with the occupants' names.

Langham pushed Benedict's and waited.

Ralph sniffed. 'I expected something a bit posher from an ex-Hollywood thesp.'

'Kersh did say he'd fallen on lean times.'

'Probably explains why he accepted acting work from Fenton,' Ralph said, adding, 'or maybe he decided to become a hitman in his old age?'

'Can it.' Langham laughed, pressing the bell again.

A lace curtain in the bow window twitched aside, then fell back into place. Through the door's stained-glass window, Langham made out a vague shape advancing down the hallway.

The door opened and a blue-rinsed matron regarded them through half-moon glasses. Ralph was ready with his accreditation, which he hung before the woman's startled gaze.

'Private detectives?' she exclaimed.

'We'd like a word with Mr Edgar Benedict,' Ralph said.

'I am afraid Mr Benedict is away at the moment.'

'Do you know when he might be back, Mrs . . .?'

'Miss,' she corrected. 'Miss Wardley. As to Mr Benedict's return, I'm afraid I couldn't possibly say. He is an actor, you see, and he's liable to go away at short notice and for indefinite periods.'

'You know him well?' Ralph asked.

'Mr Benedict has been renting a room from me since the end of the war,' she said. Then plucked up the courage to ask, 'I wonder if you would mind telling me what this might be about? Mr Benedict isn't in any kind of trouble, is he?'

'He's in no trouble at all,' Langham reassured her. 'We'd merely like to speak to Mr Benedict in relation to someone whose movements we're investigating.'

The landlady looked relieved. 'As I said, Mr Benedict is not currently at home—'

'I take it you have the key to his room?' Ralph said, peering past her into the hall. 'We'd like to take a look.'

'Well . . .' Miss Wardley lifted an uncertain hand to her wattled throat.

'We wouldn't be long,' Langham said, smiling at her, 'and you can accompany us.'

'In that case, very well,' she relented, and led them into the house and up two flights of stairs.

'Mr Benedict has rooms in the attic,' Miss Wardley explained as they climbed. 'He has a little sitting room up there, as well as a bedroom. It's all very self-contained.'

'How long has he been away?' Langham asked.

'That would be almost a week,' she replied. 'He left last Saturday.'

They came to a landing and paused outside a door. 'And he hasn't been back since then?'

'He hasn't,' she said.

'Did Mr Benedict mention where he was going? Does the name Winterfield in Essex ring a bell?'

'I'm afraid he didn't mention his destination, and I don't recall him mentioning Essex. For all that I have known Mr Benedict for over ten years,' she said, 'he is very reserved and hardly ever vouchsafes anything of a personal nature. You might say he's the perfect gentleman.'

'He's secretive, eh?' Ralph suggested.

The landlady pursed her lips. 'I would prefer to use the term "discreet".'

She moved to the door and unlocked it, showing them into a spacious area under the sloping roof. The sitting room was furnished with a chintz-covered sofa and armchairs drawn up to a small gas fire, next to which stood a bulky radiogram. Black-and-white photographs adorned the walls, visual mementoes of a lifetime treading the boards.

Langham moved around the room, admiring the photographs. They showed the same young man in a variety of stage roles – and one or two obviously taken while on film sets – as well as signed pictures of well-known stars. One photograph showed Benedict on the beach in his early twenties with his arms around another beaming, bare-chested young man.

Langham turned to the landlady, who was smiling with fondness at the photographs. 'I take it that Mr Benedict wasn't married?'

She blinked. 'Whatever makes you think that? In actual fact, he *was* married. Four times.'

Ralph laughed. 'A bit of a lad, eh?'

Miss Wardley blushed. 'I'll have you know that Mr Benedict had the tragic misfortune of losing two of his wives to premature deaths.'

'But he's single now, I take it?' Langham asked.

'His last wife passed away in 'forty-five, just before he moved in here. As far as I know, he has had no liaisons since then. But, as I mentioned, he does not speak much of his personal affairs.'

'Children?' Ralph asked.

Miss Wardley shook her head. 'One of his greatest regrets,' she said, 'is that he never fathered a son or daughter. His first wife died in childbirth, and his second just months after they married. In many ways, gentlemen, Mr Benedict leads a quietly tragic life.'

Langham turned to the photographs and smiled sadly to himself, repeating *a quietly tragic life* . . . How terribly descriptive, and just the kind of phrase a spinster like Miss Wardley would use.

'And yet very fulfilled,' he said, gesturing to the gallery, 'going by these?'

'Fulfilled? I'm not at all sure that Mr Benedict would describe his career in that way,' she said. 'Oh, he had many roles in his early years, but he never had leading parts or long runs on the stage. He was, I think the phrase goes, a jobbing actor. And latterly the parts had dried up somewhat. He was hired occasionally for radio plays, but I think he secretly craved to be back on the stage.'

'Don,' Ralph said from across the room, 'come here and take a gander.'

Langham ducked under a sloping beam. Ralph pointed to a black-and-white photograph showing a group of men and women posed in the sunlight before a country house.

He noticed two things almost simultaneously. The first was that the house was unmistakably Winterfield – with its crabbed mullioned windows and twisted, turreted chimneys – and the second was that one of the young women in the picture was Maria.

Ralph glanced at him. 'It is Maria, isn't it? And the house: Winterfield, right?'

Langham nodded. 'Yes, to both.'

He stared at the young girl his wife had been, laughing out at the camera. She was standing next to a tall, slim older man who had a hand placed, almost possessively, on her shoulder. The intimacy exhibited by the pair made him feel more than a little uneasy.

Ralph pointed. 'Fenton, right?'

Langham stared at the tall, good-looking, dark-haired man standing beside Maria. 'It must be. He's dressed for the part in a paint-smeared artist's smock.' He contrasted the full-faced, handsome Maxwell Fenton depicted here with the aged wreck who had taken his own life just two days ago.

'And this chap here' – Ralph indicated a tall man in his mid-fifties, familiar from the other photographs, garbed in tennis whites and standing on the other side of the artist – 'must be Edgar Benedict.'

'So Benedict was a guest at the soirées down at Winterfield in the thirties,' Langham murmured.

Ralph scratched his head. 'I don't geddit, Don. He knew Fenton, right? Look, he has an arm around the artist's shoulders. They were friends. And yet when Fenton hires him via the agency to come down to Winterfield, he uses the name Mr Smith.'

Langham shook his head. 'Why? Why would he do that? Why not just use his own name? And why go through the agency to contact his old friend?'

He unhooked the photograph from the wall and turned to the landlady. He indicated Benedict and Fenton standing side by side. 'I don't suppose Mr Benedict ever mentioned the artist Maxwell Fenton, did he?'

Miss Wardley took the photograph and stared at it, frowning.

'As a matter of fact, yes. Yes, he did. In fact . . .' She moved to the bedroom door. 'I don't suppose Mr Benedict would mind my showing you this.'

She ushered them into the small bedroom under the eaves and pointed to an oil painting hanging over the single bed. It depicted a beautiful auburn-haired woman reclining on a chaise longue, her bare arms extended above her head as she smiled insouciantly at the artist.

'Mr Benedict's second wife, Amelia Carswell, the actress. Mr Benedict told me that Amelia passed away just months after this was painted. A brain haemorrhage, I believe. She was just twenty-eight. And the artist was Maxwell Fenton.'

Langham moved closer to the oil and peered at the bottom right corner and the signature *Max Fenton, '37*.

He stood back and admired the painting, recalling Hermione Goudge's withering assessment of Fenton's canvases as 'daubs'. He didn't profess to be an expert, but the painting of Amelia Carswell seemed more than just technically accomplished: the way he had depicted the woman's playful demeanour, the ray of sunlight slanting through the window, was little short of brilliant.

'Do you know if Mr Benedict and Maxwell Fenton met recently?'

'I really don't know. If they did, then Mr Benedict didn't mention it.'

'And Fenton never visited Benedict here?' Ralph asked.

Miss Wardley shook her head. 'Not to my knowledge.'

They ducked out of the small bedroom and returned to the sitting room. Langham searched the photographs of Edgar Benedict for the most recent, and found one depicting the actor with silvered sideburns and wrinkles around his eyes. He appeared to be in his late fifties.

He indicated the photograph and the group scene taken outside Winterfield. 'Would you mind terribly if we borrowed these? I promise I'll return them just as soon as we've completed the investigation.'

Miss Wardley appeared unsure but relented. 'Very well, yes. But what should I tell Mr Benedict when he returns?'

Langham removed the photographs from their frames and slipped them into his pocket, then gave the landlady a calling card. 'If you would be good enough to give him this, and tell him it's vitally important that he contact us when he returns, I'd appreciate it enormously.'

Miss Wardley took the card and stared at it, nodding her agreement.

She led them back downstairs to the hallway, and they thanked her and left the house, hurrying through the rain to the car.

Ralph sat in meditative silence as Langham drove through the quiet streets towards Lewisham, then said, 'OK, listen to this.'

Langham glanced at his partner. 'You've revised your earlier theory, right?'

Ralph grinned. 'How'd you guess?'

'I can read your mind as if it were a book.'

'Go on, then. What am I thinking?'

'Your earlier hypothesis, about Fenton blackmailing Benedict to do his dirty work. You now think blackmail might've had nothing to do with it. You're thinking that Benedict, as a friend, was all too willing to help Fenton out.'

'Well, something like that,' Ralph said. 'What about it, Don?'

Langham shook his head. 'I don't buy it.'

'Not even as a long shot?'

'Not even then. You'd have to be a ruddy great friend in order to agree to kill half a dozen innocent men and women. And even if he had a personal reason to hate these people – and we've no evidence to make us think that Benedict did – it's highly unlikely that a quiet, reserved thespian would suddenly become a mass murderer at the behest of an old friend.'

'Well, put like that . . . But we don't rule it out, OK?'

'We don't rule it out,' Langham agreed. 'But there's another thing. As I said earlier, if Fenton did want Benedict to do his killing after his death, why did he use the Mr Smith moniker and go through the agency?'

Ralph swore. 'It doesn't stack up.'

'There's something about the whole business that doesn't stack up.'

They reached Lewisham and drove down the long street of modern terraced houses where Ralph lived, pulling up outside number eighty-eight.

'Right,' Ralph said, 'what about tomorrow?'

'We should meet Jeff and pool everything we've found. He needs to know about Benedict. It's imperative we trace the actor. If he isn't actively involved, then he might have information we need to know.'

'I'll see you at the office,' Ralph said. 'I'm meeting a chap tonight about getting a jerrycan of petrol. Wish me luck. How about a cuppa while you're here?'

'I'd better not, thanks all the same. I want to get back to Maria. I think we'll go out for a meal – I feel like getting well and truly sloshed tonight.'

'Have one for me while you're at it,' Ralph said, and climbed from the car.

Langham started up and headed for Bermondsey.

That evening, over a lasagne and Sicilian wine at a tiny bistro on Greek Street, Langham discussed the details of the case with Maria.

He mentioned Edgar Benedict, and her eyes widened. 'And the odd thing,' he went on before she could speak, 'is that Fenton and Benedict knew each other. We found a photograph at his lodgings showing the actor together with Fenton before the war at Winterfield.' He considered mentioning that Maria featured in the same photograph, but stopped himself.

She reached across the table and clutched his hand. 'But I knew this Edgar Benedict, Donald! He was a regular guest at my father's parties, and I met him once at Winterfield.'

'Do you know how close Benedict and Fenton were?'

'Oh, they were best friends, Donald. As thick as thieves. They even agreed politically – they were closet Mosleyites.'

'I like the sound of Fenton less and less,' he said. 'Ralph has a hare-brained theory that Benedict might be doing Fenton's posthumous dirty work.'

Maria laughed. 'Well, I wouldn't put it past him. Benedict was an awful man.'

Langham lowered his glass. 'What?'

'He really was a vile character. Why are you looking so surprised, Donald?'

'It's strange,' he said. 'You talk to people about a third party and you form an impression about them. From what Kersh and Benedict's landlady said about the actor, I rather built up the picture of a quiet, reserved English gentlemen.'

Maria blew in mock disgust. 'Don't you believe it, Donald! Benedict was vain and egotistical, and he treated women appallingly. Some people even say,' she went on, leaning close to him and lowering her voice, 'that Edgar Benedict had a hand in the death of his second wife.'

He stared at her. 'But she suffered a brain haemorrhage,' he said.

Maria shook her head. 'No, she didn't. She died while on holiday in Jersey. She fell to her death from a clifftop. Only some people say that she was pushed. Benedict was having an affair at the time, you see, and the marriage was turning sour.'

'Well I never!' he said. He shook his head. 'But no. However awful he might have been, it's too much to think he'd willingly kill for his old friend, isn't it?'

Maria rocked her head. 'Human beings are very, very strange, Donald. You should know that by now.'

He raised his glass in acknowledgement, drained it, and ordered a second bottle from the passing waiter.

FOURTEEN

The alarm went off at eight, drilling into nebulous dreams that vanished as Langham blinked himself awake. He sat on the side of the bed and held his head in his hands. He had a thudding headache and a raging thirst. He found his dressing gown, moved to the bathroom and splashed his face with ice cold water. He returned to the bedroom feeling a little better and lay down next to Maria.

He groaned.

She reached out and stroked his cheek.

'I should never have ordered that second bottle.'

She propped herself up on one elbow. From the humorous skew of her lips, he knew she was about to mock him. 'Donald, does your mouth feel "as dry as a camel's crotch after a three-week trek through the Sahara"?' It was a line he'd used in his first novel, which Maria had thought hilariously bad.

'Worse,' he said. 'It feels like a camel's crotch after three *months* in the desert.'

'My poor darling,' she said, stroking his cheek. 'What are you doing today?'

'If I survive,' he said, 'I'll catch up with Jeff Mallory and go through the case with him.'

A tap sounded at the door and Pamela called out, 'Don, the phone.'

He pulled a surprised face at Maria. 'I wonder who that might be?'

He moved to the sitting room, and Pamela indicated the telephone next to the sofa. He slumped down and took up the receiver. 'Langham here.'

'Don, it's Jeff.'

'Speak of the devil. I was just saying to Maria that we need to—'

Mallory interrupted. 'Can you get yourself down to the Tivoli Mansions quick sharp?'

Langham swore. 'The Goudges?'

'How did you guess? I'll see you there.' Mallory rang off.

He returned to the bedroom, massaging the back of his neck and recalling the Goudges, sitting side by side on the chaise longue, shocked by the sympathy card that had just arrived.

'Donald?' Maria reached out a hand.

'That was Jeff. I think the Goudges . . .'

She looked shocked. 'What?'

'He didn't say.'

'But you think—?'

'I don't know,' he said. 'Look here, I'd better be off.'

He dressed quickly, then took Maria's hand and kissed her fingers. 'I don't want you going out today, OK? Just to be on the safe side. Have a quiet day indoors, all right?'

'I intended to get some reading done anyway.'

He pecked her cheek and hurried from the bedroom.

Pamela appeared in the doorway to the kitchen with a plate of toast. 'Would you like—?'

'No time,' he said, pulling on his overcoat. 'Must fly. Oh – would you be a dear and ring Ralph? Tell him to meet me at the Tivoli Mansions as soon as he can.'

'Tivoli Mansions,' she said. 'Will do.'

He ran out to the Rover, drove over Tower Bridge at speed and headed west. The traffic was light. It had rained during the night and the streets glistened in the early-morning sunlight. As he made his way down the King's Road, his progress hampered by a dawdling Co-Op milk float, he found himself considering the imperious Hermione Goudge and her put-upon husband. He could not stop himself from wondering how the killer had gone about his business.

Three police cars, Mallory's Humber and a navy-blue forensics van were pulled up outside the mansion. A bobby patrolled the pavement and another stood sentry before the revolving door.

Langham gave his name and said that Detective Inspector Mallory was expecting him.

'In you go. The inspector's in the foyer.'

He pushed through the revolving door and found Jeff sitting on a settee in reception. He was leaning forward with his head in his hands. When he looked up at Langham, his eyes were bloodshot and his blonde thatch dishevelled.

'I had a man stationed outside all night,' the detective said, 'and the bloody concierge didn't see a damned thing.'

Langham nodded, feeling queasy. 'Ralph and I gave them the hard word and left around midday. They'd just received a sympathy card. They said they'd make arrangements to leave that afternoon.'

'I had a man phone them around two o'clock, suggesting they get out ASAP. George said he'd tried to book a room in a hotel they used in Hampshire, but it was full that evening. He said they'd leave first thing in the morning, so to reassure the couple I had a constable stationed outside the place from four o'clock.'

'What happened?'

Mallory sighed and climbed to his feet. 'Been in the force for over twenty years,' he said, leading the way to the lift, 'and I've never seen anything like this. We're not dealing with your run-of-the-mill killer, Don. This one's a psychopath.'

They rode the lift to the third floor, and Mallory led the way along the corridor to apartment twelve.

The door stood open. A forensics officer came out, carrying a plastic specimen bag. 'We've dusted, photographed and gathered all we need, sir. Over to you.'

Mallory led the way down the hallway to the sitting room. 'They were found at eight thirty this morning by the cleaner,' he said. 'Watch your step: that's hers.' He pointed to a pool of vomit on the parquet threshold of the sitting room, and Langham did a quickstep around it.

He looked across the room and saw the bodies. 'My God . . .'

The Goudges had been stripped naked and arranged side by side on the chaise longue, their throats cut from ear to ear. The blood had dried on their chests, like black bibs, contrasting starkly with their abundant white flesh.

'The surgeon estimates they were killed between six o'clock and midnight yesterday,' Mallory said. 'They evidently knew the killer; there's no evidence of forced entry. They either opened a bottle of wine, or the killer brought one, which he or she laced with a sedative. They were unconscious when the killer did that to them.'

Langham saw two empty wine glasses on a coffee table. 'A third glass?'

'As with Doctor Bryce, there's evidence that the killer joined them in a drink, then washed up the glass and replaced it in the kitchen.'

Langham stepped closer to the corpses, but not too close.

'I suppose that's a small mercy,' he said. 'So they weren't aware of what was happening, and didn't feel anything?'

'Apparently not. They were dead to the world.' Mallory caught himself and grimaced.

'But what kind of person would have . . .?'

'Some sick bastard with a hell of a grudge, is who.'

Langham pointed to a small occasional table beside the chaise longue.

The killer had undressed the couple, then taken great care to fold the discarded garments and place them in a neat pile on the table, exhibiting a fastidious attention to domestic detail that pointed up the savagery of the slaughter.

'I know,' Mallory said. 'As I said, we're dealing with a psychopath. And an abnormally tidy psychopath, at that.'

Langham moved to the window and stared out. As if on cue, a dark cloud obscured the bright winter sunlight and the heavens opened, drenching the streets. Pedestrians hurried for cover, happily oblivious of the scene of carnage in the exclusive third-floor apartment.

'But if you had a bobby outside from four, and the surgeon said they were killed between six and midnight . . .' Langham looked at the detective. 'You think your man nipped off for a quick cuppa?'

'He swears blind he never left his post, except once when he came into the foyer out of the rain and had a natter with the concierge – but neither of them saw a thing.'

'You think he's lying?'

'My sergeant swears he's trustworthy. But it would've only taken a second for someone to have slipped past them if he was hobnobbing with the concierge. There's an alternative scenario, of course. The killer didn't come in from outside.'

'Meaning he or she was already in the building?'

'There's nowhere they could have hidden for long without being noticed by someone, the concierge or the residents. But how about this – the killer was already living here, in one of the apartments. They'd been renting it for a while, all the time planning the murders. I have someone checking the other apartments and their occupants.'

'How many are there? Occupants, I mean.'

'According to the concierge, twelve apartments and twenty residents. Well, eighteen now.'

Langham turned from the window and looked around the room.

His gaze settled on Maxwell Fenton's portrait of Hermione Goudge, painted when she was much younger, and almost pretty.

'Bloody hell,' he said.

Mallory turned. 'What?'

Langham gestured to the painting, and the three lateral slashes scored across the canvas.

Mallory said, 'Identical to the canvases back at Winterfield.'

'Which begs the question,' Langham said, 'who defaced the Winterfield paintings? Fenton or the killer? The slashes in those canvases appeared to have been done recently.'

Mallory gestured to the portrait. 'Copycat vandalism?' he suggested. 'Which would make sense as the killer seems to be doing Fenton's sick bidding.'

Langham stared at Hermione's smiling face, and he was struck by the unbearable sadness of the young woman's blithe ignorance of the fate awaiting her many years in the future.

He heard footsteps from along the corridor, and Ralph walked into the room. He stopped in his tracks when he saw the bodies. 'Strewth! The bobby downstairs said it wasn't a pretty sight. He wasn't lying, was he?'

Langham recounted the salient details and Ralph listened in silence, stroking his straggling ginger moustache.

'Same modus op as the Bryce hanging,' he said. 'Quiet drink with someone known, victims don't suspect a thing, then Bob's your uncle and they're dead.'

He looked from Mallory to Langham. 'You brought Jeff up to speed on the gen from yesterday?'

'What was that?' Mallory asked.

Langham told the South African about their interview with Gittings the butler, their meeting with Mr Kersh at the theatrical agency, then their inquiries at the Forest Hill boarding house run by Miss Wardley.

'So Fenton hired his old actor friend Benedict for purposes unknown,' Mallory said. 'But why use the name of Smith when booking Benedict?'

'Why go through the agency at all?' Langham pointed out. 'Ralph wondered if Benedict might be carrying out Fenton's last wishes.'

'We need to find this Benedict character,' Mallory said, 'and pronto.'

Langham remembered the photographs he'd taken from the

guest house and removed the one of Edgar Benedict from his overcoat pocket. 'This is Benedict in his late fifties.'

He passed it to Mallory, who looked at the actor and grunted. 'Doesn't look like your usual murder suspect, does he?'

Langham glanced across the room at the ivory-handled telephone on a table in the corner. 'If you don't mind, I just want a quick word with Maria.'

He crossed to the telephone table and sat down, wondering how he might tell Maria about what had happened without alarming her. He considered, briefly, not phoning at all, but realized that he wanted to hear the reassuring sound of her voice.

He got through to Pamela's Bermondsey number and Maria herself answered.

'Donald?'

'Maria – I just wanted to make sure. What I said earlier, about not going out. Promise me you won't move a muscle till I get back?'

'Of course, Donald. As I said, I'm reading today. Pamela has just popped out for some bread for lunch. Donald, the Goudges?'

He drew a breath. 'I'm sorry, Maria.'

She exclaimed, then said, 'They're dead?'

'Maria . . .'

'How . . .?' she began.

'Later, OK?'

'But—'

'Look, I'd better get off. I love you.'

'Love you, too, Donald. Bye.'

He replaced the receiver and rejoined Mallory and Ralph.

'I was just telling Jeff,' Ralph said, 'I was motoring past the Lyric and what did I see? Ruddy Holly Beckwith's name up in lights, is what. Plain as day for the world and his wife to see.'

Mallory said, 'I had a word with her yesterday, told her to make herself scarce. She agreed to move from her current lodging house to a friend's place, but she didn't say she was appearing in a bloody play. I thought it was still in rehearsal.'

'You're right,' Ralph said. 'But the opening night's the day after tomorrow.'

Langham said, 'We could pop along and try to get her to pull out of the production.'

'Could you? And if she doesn't take heed, I'll drop by and make her see sense.'

Ralph stared across the room at the corpses. 'I just hope we can do a better job than we did with the Goudges.'

A uniformed constable appeared at the end of the hallway. 'Inspector, Detective Sergeant Venables would like a word.'

Mallory led the way from the apartment, and a plainclothes officer hailed him from along the corridor and gestured towards an open door.

'I think we might have something here, sir.'

FIFTEEN

The apartment was smaller than that of the Goudges – not enjoying a prime corner position – and the sitting room looked out into an alleyway at the back of the building. It was minimally equipped with utility furnishings and possessed all the individuality of an anonymous hotel room. Langham made out not a single personal belonging in either the sitting room or the adjacent bedroom.

'The apartment was let to a certain Miss Hilary Shaw two weeks ago, on a six-month lease,' Detective Sergeant Venables said, referring to his notebook. 'I've checked with the letting agency, and all the business transactions were done either over the phone or by post. Miss Shaw gave her previous address as being in Bournemouth, but I've looked it up and it doesn't exist.'

Mallory nodded. 'This looks promising.'

Venables said, 'According to neighbours, Miss Shaw was rarely in residence. In fact, she was seen only once or twice over the course of the past fortnight. Only one person spoke to her – Miss Etheridge, a retired librarian from apartment eight. A constable is bringing her along now, sir.'

'Good work,' Mallory said. 'I take it no one heard or saw anything last night?'

'I've spoken to every resident in the mansion, sir, and no one noticed anything suspicious.'

'Not that they would,' Mallory said. 'If this Miss Shaw was the killer, all she needed to do was lie low until the corridor was quiet, knock on the Goudges' door, and in she goes. She probably made a date to see them in advance.' He looked at Langham. 'The Goudges didn't mention anything about meeting anyone for drinks yesterday, did they?'

'No, not a thing.'

'I wonder if the concierge or the constable saw anyone leave the building last night,' Mallory mused. 'When I've seen Miss Etheridge, Venables, get them up here, would you?'

'Very good, sir.'

A constable appeared at the door escorting a tiny, timid-looking woman in her eighties. With her high lace collar, severe black bodice and buttoned boots, she looked like an elderly maiden aunt from a Victorian melodrama.

Mallory showed her to an armchair by the window, and she seated herself and peered timorously at the four men standing over her. Mallory gestured for everyone to sit down, and Langham settled himself on a footstool in the corner.

'But is it true?' Miss Etheridge began, her pale hands fluttering at her throat. 'Hermione and George? No, no it can't be! It's just too horrible to contemplate.' She looked pleadingly at Mallory. 'Arthur – that's our concierge – told me that someone had *murdered* the Goudges! Please tell me he was mistaken, Inspector.'

'I'm afraid we are investigating a double murder, Miss Etheridge,' Mallory said solemnly. 'If you don't mind, I'd like to ask you a few questions. I shan't keep you long.'

'Oh, my!' She pressed her fingers to her papery cheeks, reminding Langham of Munch's *The Scream*. 'The Goudges were such nice people. She was a renowned art critic, you know, and would do anything for anyone, and her husband was so devoted to her. Who would do such a terrible thing, Inspector?'

'That's exactly what we're attempting to ascertain,' Mallory said, opening a notebook on his lap.

'But what about the other residents? If there is a killer loose, then are we safe in our beds?'

'Let me assure you that no one is in any further danger. The perpetrator has fled, and I'll have my men patrolling the area until this business is cleared up. Now, I understand you've spoken in the past to a certain Miss Hilary Shaw who rented this very apartment.'

'That's correct, Inspector. Is she . . . please don't say that the killer also—'

'We'd like to know a little more about Miss Shaw in order to eliminate her from our enquiries.'

Miss Etheridge looked shocked. 'Miss Shaw is a suspect? And to think we actually exchanged pleasantries!'

'When did you meet her,' Mallory asked, 'and can you recall what was said?'

'Oh, it was perhaps a week ago, and we exchanged the briefest of greetings. I believe I asked her how she was settling in.'

'And what did she say?'

Miss Etheridge screwed up her pink, powdered face in concentration. 'I believe she said she liked her rooms, Inspector, though she didn't like the view.'

'She didn't say anything else? Where she came from, whether she knew the Goudges?'

'No, nothing like that. She did ask me how long I had been in residence here – and I told her twenty years. I moved in here when I retired, you see.'

'Now – and this is important – can you describe Miss Shaw to me?'

She pursed her lips in recollection. 'She was small, I recall, and as slim as a wand.'

Langham exchanged a glance with Ralph. The witness who lived opposite Dr Bryce had described his female visitor that night as being petite.

'Do you recall her face, the colour of her hair?' Mallory went on.

'She had a pale face, as I recall – and I do recall her hair, because it isn't every day that you see anyone with such a striking head of ginger hair. Bright red, it was.'

Mallory made a note of that. 'And her eyes?'

Miss Etheridge shook her head. 'I really can't recall, Inspector. You see, I met her in the corridor, and the lighting there is none too bright.'

'Quite,' Mallory said. 'And how old do you think Miss Shaw was?'

'Oh, very young, I should say. No older than thirty, certainly.'

'Now, is there anything else, anything at all, that you recall about Miss Shaw? Did you see her in the street, for instance? Do you know if she drove a car or travelled by bus or taxi?'

'Now that you mention it,' she said, brightening, 'I do believe I saw her using the bus. Indeed, yes. I saw her climbing aboard the sixty-three just a little while after she moved in. Might that be important, Inspector?'

Langham hid his smile as Mallory said, 'That might be very helpful indeed, Miss Etheridge. Thank you very much for your time.'

'Will that be all, Inspector?'

'For now,' Mallory said, 'but I'll send a police artist round a little later today, if you would be good enough to give him a detailed description of Miss Shaw.'

The old lady almost beamed her delight, the horror of the Goudges' murder apparently forgotten. 'Oh, how exciting, Inspector!'

Mallory gestured to the constable, who took Miss Etheridge's elbow and escorted her, still expressing her delight at the prospect of assisting the artist, towards the door.

Ralph said, 'We're on to something. That Miss Kerwin described Bryce's visitor as a dark-haired, petite woman. Ginger would appear dark at night.'

Mallory was frowning down at his notes. Langham said, 'You're not convinced, Jeff?'

The detective sighed. 'I'm not sure. The kind of murders they were . . .'

'Come on,' Ralph said, lighting up a Capstan, 'women can be just as psychopathic as men, you know. I've seen them do some bloody awful things in my time, I can tell you.'

'I'm not dismissing this Miss Shaw,' Mallory said, 'but I'm not going to concentrate on her to the exclusion of other possibilities. OK, she gave a fictitious previous address. But people can do that, you know, without being killers.'

'We need to link this Miss Shaw to Maxwell Fenton,' Langham pointed out. 'A last fling in his old age, a protégée?'

'A lover or a protégée who'd be willing to *slay* for him?' Mallory grunted.

'He did seem to have a certain allure over women,' Langham said.

'Some bloody allure!' Ralph said.

The constable appeared at the door again, this time with another uniformed constable and the elderly, moustachioed concierge in tow.

Mallory gestured to a couple of seats, and the men sat down.

The inspector directed his first question at the concierge. 'We understand this apartment was rented by a certain Miss Hilary Shaw?'

'That's correct, sir, though she isn't often here. In fact, she hardly uses the place.' He shook his head. 'Some people have more money than sense, if you ask me.'

'How often have you seen her?'

'Since she took the place a fortnight ago?' He shrugged. 'Two or three times.'

'And have you ever spoken to her?'

'Nodded and said "morning" and "evening", as you do.'

'But nothing more?'

'No, not that I recall, no.'

'Could you describe her to me?'

The concierge shrugged. 'Small – small-boned, she was. A redhead, pale-faced, not particularly attractive.'

'Would you go so far as to say ugly?'

'No, not ugly. I'd say more plain than anything. Certainly not a head-turner.'

'And did you see Miss Shaw at any time yesterday?' Mallory asked.

'Yes,' he said. 'Yes, I did. She came down in the lift around nine last night and left the building. I remember that because I recall thinking it was odd because I didn't know she was at home.'

'Around nine, you say? Can you be any more specific?'

The concierge shrugged. 'I'm sorry. Must've been around nine, thereabouts, 'cos the news had just started on the Third Programme.'

The uniformed constable nodded. 'I saw a small woman leave the building just as the church bells'd finished striking the hour. Arthur's right, it was nine.' He looked sheepish. 'I'm sorry, sir. I was told to keep an eye out for people *entering* the building, not leaving.'

Mallory grunted something non-committal and asked, 'Did Miss Shaw seem in any way agitated, nervous?'

'I can't really say, sir. She seemed normal enough. I tipped my helmet, said good evening, and watched her down the street.'

'In which direction?'

The constable frowned. 'East, sir. I believe she hailed a taxi.'

'Can you recall what she was wearing?'

'A blue raincoat. And a beret – a purple beret, as I recall.'

'Excellent. Venables, send someone round to all the local taxi ranks and see if they picked Miss Shaw up from outside the Tivoli just after nine.'

'Will do, sir.'

'I take it there's a back entrance to the building?' Mallory asked the concierge.

'That's right, Inspector. We use it for deliveries and such.'

'Is it kept open?'

'No, it's locked at all times.'

'And who has copies of the key?'

'Just me and Bert.'

'On your person or in the office?'

'Hanging in the office, Inspector, on account that we don't use the back door very often.'

'Do you think anyone could have taken the key long enough to have made an impression from which a copy could have been made?'

The concierge frowned. 'Well, I can't rightly say, Inspector. S'pose anything's possible.'

Mallory looked from the concierge to the constable. 'Is there anything else, anything at all, that you can recall which might shed light on this business?'

The men stared at the floor for a time, frowning, then shook their heads. Mallory thanked them and said that a police artist would be in touch in due course to sketch the likeness of Miss Shaw.

When they were alone again, Ralph said, 'So, we have two theories: Miss Shaw and the possibility that someone nabbed the back-door key from the office and had a copy made.'

Mallory climbed to his feet. 'That just about wraps things up here. I'm going to write up a report for the Super, then have a natter with forensics. I'll be in touch if we come up with anything.'

As they passed number twelve, on the way to the lift, Langham recalled the last sight he'd had of the Goudges alive, side by side and staring at the sympathy card.

He stopped in his tracks and stared at Mallory. 'Why didn't it occur to me earlier?'

'What, Don?'

'The invitation cards the six guests received from Maxwell Fenton . . . They were numbered, one to six. As were the backs of the chairs in the library, and Joseph Gittings, the butler, had been instructed by Fenton to show the guests to their own individually numbered chairs. Bryce was the first, George and Hermione Goudge second and third, Holly Beckwith the fourth, Crispin Proudfoot the fifth, and the sixth, Maria.'

Mallory pointed at him. 'And Bryce was knocked off first, the Goudges second and third. And Beckwith's next . . .'

Ralph said, 'We'd better hotfoot it to the actress, Don.'

'They rehearse in rooms on Archer Street behind the Lyric,' Mallory said. 'At least, that's where I found her yesterday. I have a man on the door and someone inside, and I've arranged to have a couple of men watch her friend's place in Dalston.'

Langham led the way to the lift and they hurried out to their respective cars.

SIXTEEN

Maria set aside the manuscript she was working on and stared into space. The story of romance among the dreaming spires of Oxford, while well written, failed to hold her attention, its depiction of academic privilege at odds with her present situation. She felt more like a character from one of Donald's thrillers, with the killer on the prowl and her life hanging by a thread.

She jumped up and paced the room, considering what Donald had told her over the phone an hour ago. The Goudges were dead, which put paid to her notion that the death of Dr Bryce had been a coincidence, or that the police had got it wrong and it had been no more than a tragic suicide after all.

The lulling, back-and-forth drone of the Hoover from upstairs, as Pamela busied herself with the housework, was oddly reassuring, a familiar reminder of everyday domesticity. It reminded her, also, of her childhood in Paris in the twenties, when her father had made a present of an electric vacuum cleaner to their housekeeper. The memory made her smile.

She moved to the kitchen and made a cup of tea, then returned to the sitting room and tried to read the manuscript.

She finished her tea and paced the room again, biting her bottom lip as her thoughts raced. The drone of the Hoover ceased and she heard Pamela singing to herself on the staircase. She wondered if the girl was polishing the woodwork now, and if she should offer to help.

The previous night, at the Italian restaurant after her third glass of wine, she had almost told Donald what had really happened between Maxwell Fenton and her before the war.

She considered how close she had been to telling him – and winced at the thought of how Donald might have reacted, hating her either for submitting to the artist's charms back then or for lying to him now.

There was no way, she thought, that she could emerge from this situation without damaging their precious relationship. He would either hate her for a slut or for a liar.

And if she continued to keep her secret, she would hate herself all the more.

But wasn't her assessment of how he might react demeaning to Donald himself? Pamela had said that she was sure he would understand if Maria told him the truth.

But could she be *sure* he would understand?

She was too afraid to take the risk.

She sat down on the sofa and held her head in her hands.

Maybe, just maybe, when all this was over and she had time to think about it rationally, she might be able to tell him then.

Her thoughts were interrupted when Pamela entered the living room and moved quickly to the window. She stood against the wall beside the curtains like a heroine in an espionage film, moving the material a bare inch and peering out.

'What on earth are you doing?' Maria asked.

'She's still there.'

Maria's heart seemed to miss a beat. 'Who is?'

Pamela let the curtain drop and turned to her. 'I noticed her when I was Hoovering the bedroom. She walked along the road, on the other side, and back again. Then she stopped and looked across at the house.'

Maria swallowed. 'Are you sure? I mean – are you sure she was looking at this house?'

'I'm sure.'

Maria stood up and casually glanced through the window but saw no one in the rain-washed street.

'I don't see—' she began.

'Come here!' Pamela hissed, beckoning her.

Maria joined Pamela, moved the curtain back and peered out. 'To the left,' Pamela said, 'just beyond the postbox.'

Maria made out a grey shape in the mist fifty yards away. 'She's walking away from us,' she said. 'Maybe she was just posting a letter?'

'I saw her walking up and down the street, and then she stopped and stared across at this house.' She looked at Maria, wide-eyed. 'Didn't Donald say the other night that a woman had been seen at the doctor's house on the night he died?'

Maria shrugged, uneasy. 'The old lady *thought* she'd seen a woman. But people often walk up and down the street—'

'In the pouring rain?' Pamela said. 'Back and forth, and stop and stare?'

'Anyway,' Maria said, taking another peek, 'she's gone.'

Pamela peered out. 'For now,' she said.

Maria moved to the kitchen and asked Pamela if she wanted a cup of tea, more for something to do than because she wanted another cup herself.

'No, not now,' Pamela said.

Maria boiled the kettle and mashed the tea, wondering if her friend had been imagining the woman's odd behaviour. She poured herself a cup and resumed her seat on the sofa. She would read for a while, then distract herself by making an elaborate evening meal.

'She's back!' Pamela cried from the window. 'There she is, passing the house again, looking across . . .'

Maria's heart thudded, her mouth suddenly dry.

Pamela moved away from the window with grim-faced determination. 'I'm going out there to ask what on earth she's doing.'

Maria stood and took Pamela's hand. 'You're doing nothing of the kind! I won't let you. If she – if she is the . . .' She gestured, unable to say the word. 'You'd be foolish to take the risk, Pamela.'

They stared at each other. Maria reached up and cupped Pamela's cheek. 'Please, stay here.'

Pamela hesitated, then nodded.

Maria glanced through the window. She saw a vague shape in the mist on the other side of the street, walking away from the house.

Pamela moved to the kitchen. 'I think I will have that cuppa now.'

Maria sat back down and took up the manuscript.

She heard the kettle bubbling as she read of effete undergraduates sipping Darjeeling from china cups in genteel tearooms. The kitchen door swung shut.

She had read another five pages when she became aware of the silence. She looked up and called the girl's name. There was no reply.

'Pamela?' she said, leaving the sofa and opening the kitchen door.

The room was empty.

Pamela had closed the back door but had left the Yale unlocked.

The knife drawer, beside the larder, was open a couple of inches, which it certainly hadn't been ten minutes ago.

Maria opened the door and stared out into the grey, twilit afternoon. All she saw was the yard, the alley beyond and the line of terraced houses across the way.

She returned to the sitting room and peered through the window.

There was no sign of either Pamela or the mysterious woman. A car passed, sluicing a wave of rainwater on to the pavement. A postman, hunched against the weather, hurried along on his second round of the day.

She began pacing again, her teeth worrying her bottom lip. When Pamela returned, she'd tell the little fool what she thought of her.

She saw the phone on the occasional table in the corner of the room. She wondered if Donald had left the Goudges' apartment and gone to the Earl's Court office. She crossed to the table and snatched up the receiver, dialling the number from memory with trembling fingers.

'Please be there,' she said to herself. 'Please pick up the phone!'

The dial tone rang and rang, filling her with despair.

If the woman attacked Pamela, then came for her . . .

She slammed down the receiver and paced to and fro, hardly daring to peer out into the fog-shrouded street as she came to the window again and again.

Five minutes passed, ten . . .

She moved to the kitchen, took a carving knife from the drawer and returned to the sitting room.

After five minutes she heard the back door open, very carefully, and her heart leapt. The kitchen door stood ajar, and through the gap she made out Pamela creeping across the room and replacing the knife in the drawer.

She didn't know whether to feel relief or rage.

The kettle bubbled, and in due course Pamela emerged, clutching a mug of tea and smiling breezily as if nothing untoward had happened.

Maria stared at her. 'I told you,' she said, 'not to go out there. I was frightened to death when I realized you'd gone.' She produced the knife from behind her back. 'Look, I even armed myself, thinking the woman would attack you and come for me!'

Silently, Pamela moved to the sofa and sat down. She was no longer smiling, and Maria noticed, as the girl set her mug on the sofa's wide arm, that her hand was shaking.

'Pamela?'

'She was there,' she said in a small voice, 'staring across at the house when I came out of the passageway further along . . .' She gestured vaguely. 'She saw me and scarpered. I followed her, Maria. She *was* watching the house. I know it, or else why did she hurry off like that?'

'Did you get close enough to see . . .?'

Pamela shook her head. 'She dived into a car and drove away. She was a long way off.'

'Could you describe her to the police?'

Pamela chewed her lip. 'All I could make out was that she was small and wore a raincoat and a hat like a beret.'

Maria crossed the room, sat beside the girl on the sofa and took her hand.

'No more heroics, *oui*? I'll phone the police.'

The girl nodded, and Maria locked and bolted the front and back doors, then crossed to the telephone in the corner of the room.

SEVENTEEN

The rain had blown over by the time Langham and Ralph reached the theatre.

They made their way to Archer Street and a red-brick

building guarded by a uniformed constable, his waterproof cape glistening with raindrops.

Ralph showed his accreditation and the bobby nodded. 'Inspector Mallory said you might be calling by.'

Langham gestured to the door set into the red-brick wall. 'Is this the only entrance?'

'From this side it is, sir. There's a communicating door through to the theatre itself, and a colleague is manning that.'

'I don't suppose you've noticed any suspicious characters loitering around – a small woman with ginger hair, for instance?'

The policeman shook his head. 'No, sir. No one, other than the actors and such, that is.'

Langham thanked him and pushed through the door. They found themselves in a short, dimly lit corridor. A door stood ajar at the far end, through which Langham made out the raised voices of actors at work.

They slipped into the room and stood unobtrusively against the wall.

A dozen actors sat on straight-backed chairs placed in an oval around the performance area in which Holly Beckwith and a tall Bohemian-looking man strode back and forth, rehearsing a scene.

Langham looked around the room. 'The killer would be a fool to try anything here,' he said. 'There's safety in numbers. I'm more worried about Beckwith's vulnerability coming here and leaving. And her appearing in the play.'

'What d'you reckon? Someone'll take a pop at her from the stalls?'

Langham shrugged, stuffing his pipe and lighting up. 'Who knows? The three deaths so far have been along the same lines, but who's to say the killer would stick to the script? He or she might improvise with a gun, for all we know.'

'You going to read Beckwith the riot act?'

'I'll say. Her life is at stake, that's for certain. She might have landed a starring part in a West End production and won't like having to pull out, but she'd like the alternative even less.' He grunted. 'The final curtain, as it were.'

Holly Beckwith, clutching a folded play-script, confronted the actor. 'That's all very well,' she declared, 'but have you for one minute considered your wife's feelings?'

The director moved around the pair, two fingers pressed to his pursed lips as if examining a work of art. 'Excellent, darling! Now, James, if you could be a little more earnest in your response.'

The actor nodded. Beckwith repeated her line, and James delivered, 'I'm sorry, but the only woman I care about is *you*.'

'And Holly,' the director said, 'when you turn away, raise your hand to your lips as if in shock.'

'Like this,' Holly said, obeying the director's commands.

'Perfection, darling. Wonderful! Now, from the top of the page, everyone.'

Three other actors stood and took their chalked marks on the bare floorboards. If Beckwith had noticed Langham and Ralph's arrival, she gave no indication.

Directly across the room, a tall man lounged against the far wall, timing the scene with a stopwatch. To Langham's right, a small young woman sat on a high stool, going through a script with a red pen. She set it aside, sighed as if monumentally bored, and drew a Pall Mall from its red packet with her lips. She tapped her trouser pocket, looking for matches, then scowled.

Langham left Ralph and moved around the edge of the room. He proffered his box of Swan Vestas, and after a brief glance at him she smiled and accepted a match.

She lit up and frowned at Langham through the smoke. 'Don't tell me,' she said. 'You're an agent?'

He showed his accreditation. 'Private detective.'

She raised her eyebrows. The woman had short blonde hair and a pale, expressive face. 'On duty? Or are you a stage-door Johnny come to drool over our leading lady?' Langham detected just a trace of resentment in her reference to Holly Beckwith.

'On duty,' he said. 'And you?'

She pulled down her rouged lips in a pantomime of gloom. 'Actress. Understudy. Ever the understudy!'

'Let me guess,' he said, smiling. 'Holly's role, yes?'

'Got it in one, Detective. But look at her! How do I match that? She has talent *and* looks.' She gazed at Beckwith in a show of abject despair that Langham found almost comical.

'Oh, I don't know. I'm sure you have talent, and with a wig . . .'

He watched her, but her expression showed no response other than glum dismissal of his well-meaning words.

He tried to see her as a killer in a ginger wig but failed. She was too pretty, for one thing. The concierge had described Hilary Shaw as being plain.

'Have you noticed anyone hanging around here recently, acting suspiciously?' he asked.

'Other than yourself and your sidekick, you mean?' She blew a smoke ring towards the ceiling. 'No, no one.'

'Or *not* acting suspiciously? Just hanging around, watching? A small woman in a ginger wig, a purple beret and a blue raincoat?'

'Again, no. But I'll tell you if I see her. What has she done, other than committed a crime against good taste?'

Langham smiled. 'We just want to dismiss her from our enquiries,' he said non-committally.

She drew on her cigarette as she watched the rehearsal. 'There have been a few chaps knocking around, showing an interest.'

'In Beckwith?'

She nodded. 'Ogling the star.'

'Strangers, or have you seen them before? And when was this?'

'Yesterday, a chap in a gabardine looked in, standing just where your mate is.'

'Could you describe him?'

The woman frowned, then shook her head. 'Sorry, no. I don't take much notice of . . .' She stopped herself and looked away. 'No, I'm sorry. He just watched Holly for a while, then went away.'

Langham wondered if it might have been one of Mallory's men, checking on the actress's whereabouts.

'And the others?'

The actress shrugged. 'Too numerous to mention. Ask Holly yourself.'

Within the oval of chairs, the director clapped his hands and called out, 'Let's leave it there, boys and girls. An hour for lunch. See you all back here at one?'

The woman sighed and jumped down from the stool.

'Hey, don't be so glum,' Langham said. 'I have a feeling you're about to get your big break.'

'In my dreams, buddy,' she said in a mock American accent, then joined the actors as they drifted towards the exit.

Holly Beckwith looked across the room and her expression of flushed thespian bonhomie faltered and became one of sudden uncertainty.

Langham lifted a hand in laconic greeting.

She switched on a bright smile and crossed to him. 'Why, Mr Langham . . . And I see you've brought reinforcements,' she went on as Ralph joined them.

Langham introduced Ralph, who said, 'Charmed, as they say in the movies.'

'We'd like a quiet word, if you wouldn't mind,' Langham said.

Beckwith gestured to the departing gaggle of actors. 'I was about to accompany . . .'

'How about you join us instead?' Ralph suggested. 'I know a cheap Italian place around the corner.'

She looked unsure. Langham said, 'It is important, Miss Beckwith.'

She sighed. 'Very well.'

Ralph led them from the building, down the alley and along the street to a small, steamy bistro. Langham was gratified to see the uniformed constable follow them; he stationed himself discreetly across the street as Langham sat down at a window table.

Behind the counter, a coffee machine hissed and steamed like a miniature traction engine, and waiters called back and forth in sing-song Italian.

Beckwith ordered coffee and a slice of gateau, Langham and Ralph coffee and toasted teacakes.

Langham said, 'I'm sorry. This is going to come as a shock, Miss Beckwith, but George and Hermione Goudge were killed last night.'

In the process of lighting a cigarette, the actress stopped and let her hands fall to the tabletop. 'Killed?'

'Murdered,' Ralph said.

She swallowed. 'A gentleman from Scotland Yard spoke to me yesterday,' she said evenly. 'He told me about Doctor Bryce, and said that I – that everyone who had attended that awful evening . . .' She shook her head. 'He said that we were all in danger.' She looked from Ralph to Langham. 'What happened to . . . to the Goudges?' she murmured.

'They were sedated, then had their throats cut,' Ralph said, clearly intending to shock her.

Her face crumpled and she wept. Ralph found a napkin and offered it to her. She blotted her eyes. 'I can't pretend to have liked Hermione, but . . .' She shook her head, sniffing and drying her eyes.

Ralph said, 'The killer means business. The invitations were numbered, remember, along with the chairs.'

Holly Beckwith looked aghast. 'Bryce, George and Hermione . . . And I was number four!'

'The police are doing all they can,' Ralph said. 'But you can make their job a lot easier.'

'Of course, I'll help in any way I can. What do you need to know, gentlemen?'

The waiter arrived with their coffees, gateau and teacakes.

Langham said, 'It's not so much what we need to know as what we want you to do. I'm sorry, but I'm afraid, for your own well-being, you must step down from your role in the play, as of now.'

If anything, Beckwith appeared more shocked at this than on receiving the news of the slaying of the Goudges.

'Leave the play? But I've worked so hard for the part. I couldn't possibly . . .'

Startling her, Ralph reached across the table and gripped her fine-boned wrist. 'Your life's at stake, for Christ's sake. We're dealing with a madman, miss. A cold-blooded lunatic who appears to relish killing his victims.'

She grimaced at the severity of his grip, and he released her arm. She looked from him to Langham, as if pleading. 'But the police . . . I have police protection. Surely—?'

Ralph leaned forward, lowering his voice so as not to be over-heard. 'The Goudges had police protection, too. The killer worked out how to get at them, even so.'

'If I hired someone to . . .'

Langham watched Ralph as he tried not to lose his temper. 'Do you want to know the grisly details?' his friend snapped, then continued before she could reply. 'Very well, then. Here goes. The Goudges were sedated with drugged wine and then, while they were still alive, they were stripped naked and their throats were slashed, from here'– Ralph graphically demonstrated the cut – 'to here. We're not only dealing with a killer, miss, but a deranged maniac who's killed three people so far and won't stop there, mark my word.'

'If I were you,' Langham said, pressing the advantage, 'I'd go back to the rehearsal rooms with the friendly bobby and tell your director that you're withdrawing from the play immediately. You have an understudy, so—'

'Tina?' The actress laughed. 'She couldn't understudy a plank of wood!'

'That's really beside the point,' Langham said. 'Tell the director that you can't possibly play the part.' He reached across the table and patted her hand. 'And it isn't as if it's permanent. Just as soon as all this is cleared up, and the killer is in custody, you can resume the role.'

'But when might that be?' she wailed.

Langham stuck out his metaphorical neck. 'I'd say in a matter of days.'

Holly Beckwith stared at him, her gateau untouched on the plate before her. She shook her head. 'Who would do such a thing?' She lodged her elbows on the table and held her head in her hands. 'This is a nightmare!'

'Indeed, who would do such a thing?' Langham said. 'We need to work out who was close to Fenton recently. Intimate with him. It's someone, obviously, with his interests at heart, for some twisted reason. I know you've no doubt been asked this before, but can you think of anyone who might fit the bill?'

She spread her hands helplessly. 'It's such a long time since I had anything to do with the vile man.'

'Have you heard rumours or read anything in the press—?'

'About?'

Langham shrugged. 'I don't know . . . Fenton's liaisons, lovers?'

She worried at her bottom lip in furious thought, finally shaking her head. 'Nothing comes to mind. As I said, I last saw him years ago, before the war.'

Langham nodded. 'How about his lovers back then? Can you recall their names? There was a woman called Patience or Prudence . . .'

She shook her head. 'I can't recall anyone by that name.'

'What about other women?' Ralph said.

'Well . . . there were a few girls who were hanging around him at the time I knew him.'

'Can you recall their names?' Ralph asked, ready with his pencil and notebook.

'There was a Felicity . . . Felicity Smythe, and her set.'

She went on to list five women whom she knew had shown an interest in the artist back in the late thirties, and Ralph took down their names.

Langham said, 'In the past few weeks, have you happened to set eyes on a small woman with red hair?'

She repeated the description. 'I really can't say. That is, not that I noticed. Why, is she—?'

'There is a possibility that she might be involved,' he said.

'No, I recall no one of that description.'

'Have you noticed anyone else, man or woman, watching you during the past week or so?' Langham asked. 'Yesterday, for instance, at rehearsals?'

She smiled. 'There was a nice man who popped in yesterday morning,' she said. 'But he was a police officer checking the security of the place.'

Langham considered something that Beckwith had told him when she'd visited the office – and something Hermione Goudge had mentioned.

'When you called at the office,' he said, 'you said that, back in the thirties, Fenton had had a child.'

'That's right.'

'Do you know whether it was a boy or a girl?'

She frowned, then shook her head. 'No, I don't. I'm sorry.'

'I mentioned this to Hermione Goudge yesterday, and she said that she'd heard that the child hadn't survived. Apparently, according to her, it died in infancy. But is this true – was Hermione correct?'

Beckwith spread her hands. 'I honestly can't say.'

Ralph leaned forward. 'What are you getting at, Don?'

Langham shrugged. 'A long shot. What if this child, a girl, *did* survive, despite what Hermione thought?'

Ralph whistled. 'The red-headed girl?'

Holly Beckwith looked mystified. 'But what if she did?'

Langham said, 'It's a connection with Fenton. Someone intimate with him, who might, in the circumstances, be willing to do his bidding.'

Beckwith pulled a distasteful face and shook her head. 'But why would his daughter – if she did survive – why would she kill for her dead father? It doesn't make sense.'

Langham sat back and sipped his coffee. He recalled the trip to Forest Hill the previous day and their interview with Miss Wardley.

'If not a daughter,' he went on, 'then how about a friend, or someone beholden to the artist?' He withdrew the photograph of Edgar Benedict from his coat pocket and slid it across the table to the actress.

'Do you recall this fellow from your time at Winterfield in the thirties?'

Without picking it up, she lay a finger on the portrait. 'Yes, I do recognize him.'

'Edgar Benedict,' Langham said. 'He and Fenton were good friends. Best friends, apparently.'

'Benedict was always down at Winterfield.' She looked up at Langham. 'Not a very nice man, as I recall. But they weren't best friends – well, I say that . . . They *were* best friends at one point, but then they had a big falling out.'

Langham stared at her. 'They did? What about?'

Beckwith shook her head. 'I'm sorry. It was after my time – long after I'd sworn never to set eyes on Fenton again. Early in the war. Someone mentioned that Maxwell and Edgar had had an almighty bust-up.'

'And you don't know what about?' Langham pressed. 'You didn't hear rumours?'

She shook her head. 'No, I'm sorry. I'm not even sure if I was told, and forgot, or if I never knew. I tried to wipe away all my memories of the awful man, forget that I ever knew him.'

Langham stared at the photograph of the actor. If Fenton and Benedict had fallen out during the war, then why had the artist contacted the theatrical agency and booked the actor for purposes unknown?

Holly Beckwith laid her fingers on his cuff, tapping. 'Just a tick! I do recall *something*. This was years ago, just after the war. I don't know who – perhaps a mutual acquaintance – but someone told me that Edgar was so cut up about the row that it had made him quite ill. Apparently, he'd approached Fenton again and again in the hope of a rapprochement. He begged to be forgiven, apparently, for whatever he was supposed to have done.'

'But you don't know what that was?' Langham asked.

The actress shook her head. 'No, I'm sorry. It's all so long ago. It's gone.'

Ralph indicated the untouched wedge of gateau before the actress. 'Aren't you going to eat that?' he asked.

She regarded the cake. 'Do you know something?' She smiled

at him. 'I've quite lost my appetite.' She looked at her wristwatch. 'Snakes alive! I'd better dash – they'll be getting back.'

Langham wrote Pamela's Bermondsey telephone number on the back of his calling card and passed it to the actress. 'In case you remember anything else concerning Fenton,' he said.

She thanked him and slipped the card into her bag.

'You promise to do as I said?' Langham pressed. 'Go back with the constable, tell the director that you're indisposed, then return under escort to your friend's place.'

'I'll have to inform my agent,' she began.

'I'm not bothered what you have to do – but please, just do it, OK?'

She nodded, gathered her hat and handbag, and made to rise.

Langham recalled her visit to his office and her hesitancy on leaving. She had been about to tell him something then but had thought better of it.

He said, 'One more thing. The other day, just as you were leaving my office, there was something you were about to say. Considering everything that's occurred since, would you mind telling me what that was?'

She thought about it, then sat down again. 'That night, at Winterfield, Mr Langham . . .'

'Yes.'

She looked uncertain, then said, 'As we were leaving, and they brought the body out . . .'

'Your reaction to seeing the corpse's hand,' Langham said, recalling her expression of horror.

'Exactly.' She fell silent, staring down at her handbag.

'Well?'

'You're going to think I'm mad!'

'Try me.'

She shook her head. 'I don't know. I might be imagining it, after the shock of what's happened and everything.'

Ralph leaned forward. 'Imagining what?' he asked.

She fixed Langham with her bright blue eyes. 'Well, when they brought the body out, on the stretcher, and I saw the hand, just hanging there. I know this is going to sound stupid, but I thought *that isn't Max Fenton's hand*.'

Langham stared at her. 'What?'

'I told you you'd think me crazy.' She buckled her forehead in a frown. 'But at the time . . . it might have been the stress of the occasion, but I was struck by the fact that it couldn't possibly be Fenton's hand.'

'But you'd seen him earlier, face to face,' Langham said. 'Were you in any doubt then?'

She frowned prettily again. 'No. That is, I was shocked at his appearance, at how his illness had ravaged him. But I put the change down to just that – his illness. But when I saw his hand—'

'What was different about it?'

'You see, Max had big hands – workman's hands. Blunt, with short fingers. But those I saw that night were thin, long.' She shook her head. 'No, I'm imagining it, aren't I? It was only a glimpse, after all. Or perhaps the illness would account for the change. But at the time it struck me as odd.'

She glanced at her watch again. 'I really must dash,' she said. She smiled from Langham to Ralph, rose from the table and hurried out into the street.

Langham stood and moved to the door, wiping a porthole in the condensation and peering out to ensure that the constable had seen her and was following.

The bobby spotted her, signalled to Langham and hurried across the road to meet the actress.

He returned to the table, lost in thought. If Beckwith was right, and the corpse was not that of Maxwell Fenton . . .

Ralph was staring at him. 'Christ, Don. You don't think . . .?'

'I do – if we're thinking along the same lines.'

'That if the corpse wasn't Fenton's,' Ralph said, 'then it was Edgar Benedict's, right?'

Langham frowned. 'But ruddy hell, Ralph. It *must* have been Fenton. His own doctor identified him. I recall Bryce doing so when the police surgeon arrived. And anyway, if it was Edgar Benedict playing the part of Fenton, pretending to be him – why? Why did he go through the rigmarole of assuming the artist's identity, threatening the guests, and then blowing his brains out? It just doesn't make any kind of sense.'

'What now?' Ralph asked.

'Jeff needs informing. I'll phone the Yard and try to reach him.'

He asked Ralph to order him another coffee and hurried from the café.

EIGHTEEN

Langham found a phone box thirty yards along the street.

He got through to Scotland Yard and asked to speak to Detective Inspector Mallory. A desk sergeant put him through.

'Jeff. Developments.'

Briefly, he recounted the interview with Holly Beckwith, her claim that the actor Edgar Benedict had fallen out with Fenton during the war, and that the corpse's hand had not resembled that of the artist.

'So how about this, Jeff – the corpse was that of the actor, Benedict?'

'Christ,' Mallory said. 'OK. Where are you now?'

'Not far from the Café Neapolitan on Rupert Street—'

'I'll be there in five minutes.'

Langham walked slowly back to the café, lost in thought.

Ralph was troughing into the actress's gateau with a busy fork. He looked up like a guilty schoolboy caught in the act. 'Well, she didn't want it . . .'

'You have the appetite of a gannet,' Langham said.

The waiter brought two more coffees.

Ralph said, 'I've been thinking about it, Don. Could it really've been the actor? I mean, everyone there that night had known Maxwell Fenton. Surely they'd twig an imposter?'

'They knew him years ago,' Langham pointed out, 'before the war. And thinking back, when we entered the library that night, Maria did say he was unrecognizable . . .'

They drank their coffee and discussed the case for the next few minutes. Langham was about to say, 'What doesn't make sense—' when the door opened and the big mackintoshed figure of Jeff Mallory entered the café. He ordered a coffee and joined them.

'As I was about to say,' Langham said as Mallory sat down, 'what doesn't make sense in all this is that Doctor Bryce identified the corpse as that of Maxwell Fenton.'

Mallory smiled. 'But it *does* make sense,' he said.

'In that case, enlighten me.'

'It'll make sense, that is, if I tell you that Venables was going through Doctor Bryce's accounts this morning and discovered that every month, for the past five years, Bryce has been paying twenty-five quid into Fenton's account.'

'You mean . . .?' Ralph began.

Mallory nodded. 'Fenton was blackmailing the doctor.'

'Blackmailing?' Langham repeated. 'Just a second . . . George Goudge mentioned something about Bryce treating one of Fenton's lovers way back, but it went wrong and she died. I wonder if this is what Fenton had over the doctor, and Bryce was paying him to keep mum?'

'OK,' Ralph said, 'so if Fenton was blackmailing the doctor, how does that tie in with—'

Mallory interrupted. 'So Fenton was blackmailing Bryce, twenty-five quid a month, but he decided to tap the doctor for a little more. Not cash, this time, but services rendered. He coerced Bryce into lying to the police surgeon and identifying the corpse as that of himself.'

Ralph shook his head. 'But why would the actor agree to come to the house of his ex-friend, pretend to be him, and then blow his brains out?'

Langham thought about it. 'How about this? Benedict agreed, when Fenton contacted the theatrical agency, because he wanted Fenton's forgiveness for whatever wrong he'd done the artist. Apparently, Benedict was desperate to patch things up with Fenton, according to Beckwith. Of course he'd agree to play the part. A piece of cake for an actor of Benedict's experience. Fenton would explain that he wanted to put the wind up a few old enemies, promised to pay the actor handsomely, and gave him the script we all heard that night—'

'And then Benedict willingly went and blew his brains out?' Ralph said, shaking his head.

'No, not willingly at all. *Unknowingly*,' Langham said. 'You see, that wasn't in the script. In the script, the gun was unloaded. Fenton probably told Benedict he wanted to scare his guests by suggesting he was going to kill himself. Perhaps he showed Benedict an unloaded gun, then switched it – with the result that the actor inadvertently killed himself. And the guests didn't recognize that it wasn't Maxwell Fenton because Benedict was made up to look just like him and to appear terminally ill.'

It went a long way, he thought, to answer his niggling feeling that Fenton's threats and his subsequent suicide had not added up.

'And the reason Fenton wanted Benedict dead,' Mallory said, 'was that he *hadn't* forgiven the actor for whatever they'd fallen out about. In fact, Benedict was just another one of his victims – the very first one.' He shook his head. 'Ingenious – how diabolically clever of Fenton to fake his own death in order to be free to kill the rest of the guests, starting with Bryce – who needed to be got out of the way in case he spilt the beans about the corpse's true identity.'

'Neat,' Langham said, 'very neat. However, there's just one snag.'

Mallory finished his coffee. 'Go on.'

'Why did Fenton contact the theatrical agency and use an alias? Why didn't he simply use his own name if he wanted to give the impression to Benedict that all was forgiven?'

Mallory frowned. 'It's certainly odd, but I don't think it undermines the case we've outlined. What I need to do now is get down to Essex and have the corpse examined. If you could give me Edgar Benedict's details, I'll rustle up his dental records. It's only just over two days since "Fenton" died, so he wouldn't have been buried yet.'

He stood and buttoned his raincoat.

Langham said, 'If we're right, and Fenton is still alive and responsible for the killings, what about the redhead?'

'As we mooted,' Mallory said, 'it's no more than a coincidence. She has nothing to do with any of this.'

Langham frowned. 'If so, then how did Fenton kill the Goudges? How the blazes did he manage to get in past the bobby on the door, and the concierge, and out again without being seen?'

Mallory shrugged. 'Perhaps he filched the back-door key from the concierge's office at some point, made a copy and used it yesterday to get in and out?'

Ralph nodded. 'That'd certainly work.'

'Good work,' Mallory said. 'I'll be in touch.'

Ralph finished his coffee and shook his head in amazement. 'That's what I like about this job, Don: never a dull moment. Who'd've thought?'

Langham stared into his empty coffee cup, a sick feeling in the pit of his stomach. He looked up at his friend. 'What I *don't* like about this job is the idea that there's someone out there who's gone to a hell of a lot of trouble planning the deaths of six – no, seven – innocent people.'

'What now?' Ralph asked as Langham rose to leave.

'Now I'm going back to Bermondsey. I'll stop at an off-licence to buy a few bottles of ale, some wine for Maria and Pamela, and we'll settle down for a quiet evening in front of the fire . . .'

A quiet evening was a nice idea, he reflected later, but it was not to be.

He arrived back at the Bermondsey terrace house laden with four bottles of Bass and an expensive French Merlot. The door was locked, and it was Maria who opened it and greeted him.

She looked relieved. 'Donald.'

'Sorry I'm late. I had to take a detour to find somewhere that was open. Bought these,' he went on as he kissed her cheek and stepped into the front room.

Pamela was sitting on the edge of an armchair, fretting and biting her nails.

He looked from the girl to Maria, standing silently beside the sitting-room door. 'What?' he said, his stomach turning.

Maria closed the door and leaned against it. 'Donald, Pamela noticed someone earlier.'

He dumped the bottles on the sofa. 'Noticed someone?'

'A woman,' Pamela said. 'She was watching the house. I saw her when I was upstairs, and when I came down here, she was still there, walking up and down the street, on the other side, and stopping occasionally to stare across.'

'Did you get a close look at the woman?'

'Pamela went out to confront her—' Maria began.

'What?' He ran a hand through his hair, exasperated, and slumped into an armchair.

'I wanted to know what she was up to, so I went out.' She shot an odd look at Maria, then went on. 'As soon as the woman saw me, she hurried off down the road. I followed, but . . .'

'Did you see her? Close up, I mean?'

Pamela shook her head. 'No. It was misty. She was always twenty yards away.'

'Can you describe her?'

She shrugged, hugging herself. 'She was smallish . . . in a raincoat and a beret.'

Langham stared at the girl, his pulse suddenly loud in his ears.

So much for the redhead having nothing to do with the murders. But how the hell, he wanted to know, had the woman known that Maria had taken refuge here?

He nodded, trying to order his thoughts. 'And what happened then? How far did you follow her?'

'Just around the corner, halfway along the street. She jumped into a car and drove off.'

'Did you get its registration?'

She shook her head. 'It was too far away.'

'Or notice its make or colour?'

She shook her head again, looking woebegone. 'No. I'm sorry. By this time she was fifty yards away, more. It was misty and getting dark. I just saw its red lights as it drove off.'

Langham nodded again, staring at the wall and going through what he had to do next.

'I take it you phoned the police?'

Maria nodded. 'I explained the situation, and they said they'd send someone round just as soon as they could. But that was just after three.'

'And they haven't shown up yet?'

She nodded.

He sat in silence for a time, brooding.

Maria said, 'Donald?'

He sighed and lifted his hands from the arm of the chair in a hopeless gesture. 'A small red-headed woman in a raincoat and beret was seen leaving the Goudges' mansion yesterday evening.'

He hesitated, staring across at the shocked women.

'The Goudges were killed between six and midnight. The woman, who had rented an apartment at the mansions, was seen leaving around nine o'clock last night.'

He recounted the events at the Tivoli Mansions that morning, and the various interviews he and Ralph had conducted that after-noon, finishing with a long, involved account of what Holly Beckwith had told them.

Maria stared at him. 'But how does this red-headed woman fit in with all this?'

'Your guess is as good as mine. What a bloody situation!' He saw the bottles on the sofa. 'I need a drink.'

Pamela gathered the bottles and carried them into the kitchen. He heard her prising the cap from one of the beers.

Maria called out, 'Could you also open the wine, Pamela? I need a drink, too, I think.' To Langham, she said, 'What now?'

'I'll get through to Scotland Yard and see what the situation is regarding police protection. And in the morning you're both coming with me to the office. I'm not leaving you here.'

Pamela returned with Langham's beer, the wine and two glasses.

The women sat drinking in silence while Langham telephoned the Yard. He spoke to a desk sergeant and explained the situation at length. The sergeant heard him out, then said he'd contact his supervisor and arrange for someone to get to the address as soon as possible. Langham requested that Detective Inspector Mallory be informed as soon as he returned to duty and rang off.

'We haven't eaten,' Pamela said a little later. 'Would you like something, Donald?'

'Don't cook. I'll be happy with a sandwich.'

'I have some potted beef and tomatoes.'

'Lovely. And if you could open another beer . . .'

While Pamela was in the kitchen, Maria sat on the arm of his chair and said in a small voice, 'Donald, how did . . .? The Goudges? How were they killed?'

He grimaced. Earlier, in his account of the events of the morning, he'd refrained from going into detail.

He shook his head. 'It doesn't matter.'

'It does!' she insisted. 'I'm in danger, Donald. Fenton and this woman . . . they want to kill me. How did the Goudges die?'

He looked at her, then reached out and took her hand. 'The killer drugged them and slit their throats. They would have been unconscious by then. Wouldn't have felt a thing.'

Maria closed her eyes.

Pamela emerged from the kitchen with a pile of sandwiches and they ate in silence, Langham swilling the food down with gulps of beer. He finished the second bottle and opened a third. So much for a quiet evening, he thought, enjoying a drink and discussing the imminent move to the country.

They were startled, later, by a hammering at the door, and Langham answered the summons to find a huge, lumbering walrus of a man on the doorstep. He introduced himself as Sergeant Sheppard, and his young partner as Constable Wilson, and told

Langham that Detective Inspector Mallory had been informed and
had apprised them of the situation.

Sergeant Sheppard assured him that a bobby would soon be
patrolling the alley to the rear of the house, and that he and Wilson
would be outside in their patrol car. Langham thanked them, asked
if they wanted a tea or coffee – which they declined – and locked
and bolted the door behind them as they returned to their car.

Before returning to the sitting room, he removed the revolver
from the pocket of his overcoat hanging in the hall and slipped it
into his jacket pocket.

They sat up drinking for another hour, before Pamela said
goodnight and went to bed. Soon afterwards, Maria said, 'I think
I will turn in, too, Donald.'

'I'll be up in a while. I think I'll ring Ralph.'

He did so, bringing his friend up to speed with the events of
the afternoon and arranging to meet him at the office in the
morning.

Then he sat in the darkness and drank the fourth bottle of beer,
his revolver on the chair arm beside him.

NINETEEN

Langham was woken at eight by the rattle of the letterbox.
Groaning, he turned over and tried to get back to sleep.

He came awake with a start and was surprised to see that
it was almost ten. He dressed quietly, so as not to rouse Maria,
splashed his face with cold water in the bathroom, then went
downstairs to make himself a cup of strong coffee.

An envelope lay on the welcome mat, and with an ominous
sense of dread he picked it up. It was addressed to Maria.

He slid a finger under the flap and withdrew the blank sympathy
card, identical to all the others, then checked the postmark: it had
been franked at Marylebone the previous day at six forty-five.

Fenton and his accomplice were playing games, and the thought
sickened him.

He slipped the envelope into his jacket pocket, moved to the
kitchen and filled the kettle.

Maria joined him a little later, hugging her dressing gown close to her chest.

'Coffee?' he asked.

She nodded.

He made some toast and they sat at the table in the sitting room and ate breakfast in silence.

At last Maria said, 'This is like a bad dream, Donald. I never thought that Fenton would . . .' She trailed off, shaking her head.

'I can understand someone committing murder in the heat of the moment, provoked by anger,' he said, 'but for Fenton and the woman to cold-bloodedly plan murders like this suggests . . .'

She looked up at him. 'Go on.'

'I keep coming back to that word. Insanity.'

But did that mean, he thought, that his accomplice was insane, too?

Nursing his coffee cup, he moved to the window. The unmarked police car stood directly before the house; Sheppard and Wilson had finished their shift in the early hours and had been replaced by another pair of officers.

He moved to the hall and from the pocket of his overcoat fetched one of the photographs he'd taken from Miss Wardley's boarding house, showing the guests assembled outside Winterfield back in the thirties.

He returned to the sitting room and passed Maria the photograph. She stared distastefully at the image of Maxwell Fenton with a hand on her shoulder. 'It is odd, but I cannot recall this day. And yet I only visited Winterfield a few times.'

'Do you happen to know who any of these people are?' he asked. 'I want to contact as many of Fenton's old cronies as possible, as well as his old flames.'

Besides Maxwell Fenton, Maria and Edgar Benedict, there were a dozen other guests pictured – seven men and five women. Maria remembered nine, but the identities of the remaining three escaped her. Langham made a note of the names.

Pamela, bleary-eyed from lack of sleep, yawned her way into the kitchen and made herself a plate of bread and dripping.

After breakfast Langham went outside and spoke to the plain-clothes men, informing them that he was taking the women with him to Earl's Court, and suggesting they remain in situ and keep an eye out for a young red-headed woman.

They left the house just after midday and drove to Earl's Court.

He sat at his desk and made his meticulous way through the first of a dozen telephone directories stacked in a precarious pile on the floor beside his chair, searching for the names of the men and women Maria had recognized in the photograph that morning.

Maria sat before the electric fire, reading a manuscript. Pamela was with Ralph in the outer office, going through the London phone books in search of Maxwell Fenton's old flames mentioned by Holly Beckwith the previous day.

Langham dialled the phone number of the third name on his list, an individual named Russell Graves, impatiently tapping his pencil against the phone book while he waited.

He had already drawn a blank with two names. The first was in none of the dozen London directories, and the second had failed to answer his call. Maria recalled that Russell Graves had been an architect, and Langham found Graves's number under Graves and Kemp, an architectural firm based in Chelsea.

He stared at the group photograph on the desk. Graves had been a small, sturdy, blond-haired young man, cheerily waving a tennis racket at the camera.

A secretary answered, and Langham asked to be put through to Russell Graves. A minute later he gave his name and explained his business.

'Maxwell Fenton?' a deep, fruity voice replied. 'My word, that name brings back memories.'

'When did you last meet Fenton, Mr Graves?'

'That'd be back before the war. Some shindig at his pile near Chelmsford. Why do you want to know? What's old Fenton gone and done?'

'I want to speak to Fenton in relation to an investigation,' Langham replied vaguely. 'How did you get on with the man?'

'Fenton was a fine fellow, Mr Langham. A generous host and the life of the party. Of course, that was back then. Heard since that the war did for him. On his uppers, he was sent to Treblinka as a war artist. What he saw there sent him round the bloody bend. There was a rumour, after the war, that he'd been clapped up in a loony bin.'

'Do you happen to know if he ever married?'

'Fenton?' Graves guffawed. 'Too fond of playing the field to get himself hitched.'

'Children?'

'Wouldn't be surprised if he had a dozen brats, the number of women he had trailing after him.'

'I'm interested in tracing one particular woman by the name of Prudence or Patience.'

'Ah, Prudence. Met her a couple of times down at Winterfield. She was a quiet little thing. I couldn't see what Fenton saw in the woman, but he was smitten.'

'Can you recall her surname?'

'Her surname?' Graves tootled a little tune as he thought. 'Sorry, old chap.'

'And her age when she knew Fenton?'

'I'd say she was in her early twenties. He liked them young, the old goat.'

'Do you happen to recall if she and Fenton had a child?'

'Not that I know of,' Graves said, 'but then she was the kind of girl who'd keep things like that quiet. She was "awfully-awfully", as I recall.'

'As for Fenton's friends at the time . . . Did he have people he was particularly close to?'

'He was one of those chaps who divided people. Some chaps hated him, and others wouldn't hear a word said against him. I recall a chap . . . an actor . . . Benedict. That's him: Edgar Benedict. They were as close as kidneys back then, before the bust-up.'

'What happened?'

'Something to do with money Fenton sank into funding the West End production of a play Benedict hoped to star in. Fenton got his fingers badly burned when the whole shebang went belly-up. Word was that Benedict knew it was a shonky deal to begin with and managed to get out with his own funds intact. Fenton never forgave him.'

Langham made a note of this. 'Do you know if others beside Fenton were involved? Friends of the artist, perhaps?'

'As I recall, Fenton was the sole backer, other than Benedict, to the tune of a thousand or two, so I've heard.'

Langham questioned Graves for a further five minutes but learned nothing more of substance. He thanked him and rang off.

Maria looked up from her manuscript with an enquiring glance, and Langham recounted his conversation with the architect.

The next couple of names on the list added nothing to his knowledge of the artist. The first, a sculptor called Hardwick, barely recalled Maxwell Fenton, had visited Winterfield on only one or two occasions, and finished by saying that he'd assumed the artist was dead. The second, a woman Maria had described as a chorus girl, called Fenton an unmitigated cad and slammed down the phone before Langham could ask her to expand on this.

The next number he phoned belonged to Constance Merriman, a tall, blonde, strikingly attractive woman standing next to Edgar Benedict in the Winterfield photograph. Maria said she had been a painter with a rising reputation before the war.

'The Merriman residence,' a deep, cultured contralto answered.

Langham introduced himself and explained that he was attempting to trace friends and acquaintances of the artist Maxwell Fenton.

'I was certainly no friend of the scoundrel,' Constance replied, 'though I suppose I might have fallen into the category of an acquaintance.'

'You didn't know him well?'

'Perish the thought. He was the friend of a friend. Fenton was an awful man.'

'In what way?'

'In the way he treated women. As if they were servants to be used and discarded. I went down to his place in the country only once, and what I saw there persuaded me never to go back.'

'If you could elucidate,' Langham coaxed.

Constance sighed. 'I was appalled by the degree of the man's ego. He demanded that he was the centre of attention and was constantly boasting of his exploits and the money he made. He treated people appallingly, especially women. I recall the girl he was chasing at the time . . .'

Langham's mouth felt suddenly parched. He considered the photograph, his glance sliding along the row of guests ranged outside Winterfield and settling on Maria and Maxwell Fenton, his hand on her shoulder . . .

'Go on.'

As the woman spoke, he glanced across at Maria. She pored over the manuscript, pencilling a comment in the margin.

'She was a young French girl, dark and sultry and quite gorgeous. Barely eighteen, I recall. Fenton was old enough to be her father.'

'And . . . how did he treat her?' he asked, his heart thudding. He glanced again at Maria; she was still absorbed in her work, oblivious.

'Like a possession,' came the reply. 'She was head over heels, quite taken that this famous artist should be showing her so much attention.'

He closed his eyes as he felt himself flushing. 'Do you think they were having an affair?'

The hesitation at the end of the line seemed to last for ever. 'I'm not sure about that, Mr Langham. It wasn't for lack of trying on Fenton's part, I can tell you. But the girl – I can't recall her name – was a bright young thing despite the fact that she was starstruck, and I think this, and her Catholic upbringing, served to make her see sense.'

'Do you know,' he asked, his voice sounding tremulous even to his own ears, 'if there was any substance in the rumour that back in the thirties he'd fathered a child?'

Constance replied, 'I heard the rumour, too. Some people were certain of it, as I recall.'

'Can you remember,' he asked, 'the name of the woman involved?'

There was a silence as she considered the question. He glanced at Maria. Her head was bowed over her work, and there was nothing at all to suggest that she had been alerted by anything he'd said.

The woman said, 'Yes. Yes, I can. Prudence. Pru. A bit of a church mouse, as I recall. A nondescript kind of girl.'

'Prudence,' Langham said, relieved. 'You don't happen to know her full name?'

'Let me think about that . . . I'm sure it was something like Forest, or Forster – at any rate, it began with an F, I'm certain.'

'That's extremely helpful,' Langham said, making a note of the surnames.

He asked her if she was still in contact with mutual acquaintances who might know anything more about Maxwell Fenton and his relationship with Prudence F., but she apologized and said that she had lost contact with 'that set' well before the outbreak of the war.

He thanked her and replaced the receiver, then mopped his face with a handkerchief.

Maria looked up and smiled. 'Success?'

Smiling, he rounded the desk and kissed her. 'I think so.' He told her about Prudence F., then asked if she would like a cup of tea.

They adjourned to the outer office, where a frustrated Ralph was up to his elbows in telephone directories, scraps of paper covered with his scribblings, and two grease-stained brown paper bags that had once contained eel pies.

Pamela sat crossed-legged on the floor, a hefty directory in her lap.

Ralph slammed the phone down as Langham sat on the corner of the desk and Maria put the kettle on. 'Not a ruddy thing, Don! Not a sausage!' He waved at his notes. 'Talked to four of the women Holly Beckwith mentioned, but none of them admitted to having his kid, or knew anything about anyone who might've.'

Langham smiled. 'I might have something,' he said, and told Ralph about Constance Merriman and Prudence F. 'Let's try Foster, Forster, Forest and every variation thereof. Of course, she might have married since then.'

'I'll make a start anyway,' Ralph said, scribbling on a scrap of paper.

Langham was drinking his tea, a minute later, when the phone shrilled. Ralph snatched up the receiver.

'Ryland and Langham Detective Agency, Ralph Ryland speaking. Jeff? Fine, fine. Just trawling through the phone book trying to trace Fenton's conquests. Come again?'

Ralph listened to what Mallory had to say, frowning. 'Well, one of us could. The other should stay with the girls. I'll hand you over to Don.' He passed Langham the receiver.

'Jeff?' Langham said.

'Ever attended an exhumation?' Mallory asked.

'An exhumation? But it's only three days since the death.'

'Yes, I thought it odd. But the coroner was happy with the police report, and Fenton's solicitors – there being no next of kin that they were aware of – arranged for a burial in unconsecrated council ground without any kind of religious service, so that hurried things along. The body's in the council site next to the church in Oldhurst. I have an exhumation order and Edgar Benedict's dental records to hand. I'm driving down now, if you'd care for a lift to save petrol.'

'Hold on a sec, would you? Just need to check something at this end.'

He lowered the receiver and said to Maria, 'That was Jeff. They have an exhumation order for Fenton's supposed corpse. He asked me if I wanted to attend—'

Maria said, 'You can go, Donald.'

'I'm not sure. I was going to book us into a hotel for the night. There's no way we're going back to Bermondsey.'

Ralph finished his tea and wiped his lips with the back of his hand. 'I know a nice little guest house in Greenwich – the Laurels. I'll take the ladies there.' He patted his jacket, where his revolver sat. 'And don't worry, Don – I've got this.'

Langham lifted the receiver. 'All set, Jeff. And no, I've never attended an exhumation.'

'I'll see you in ten minutes.'

He replaced the receiver and finished his tea.

'Rather you than me,' Ralph said. 'The corpse can't have been a pretty sight when you saw it three days ago. Gawd only knows what it's like now.'

'Please!' Pamela protested.

Langham retrieved his coat from the peg by the door, kissed Maria on the cheek, and left the office.

TWENTY

Jeff Mallory's racing-green Humber pulled up dead on time and Langham ducked into the passenger seat. An early twilight was descending, and the lights from shop fronts reflected in the rain-slicked tarmac as they drove from London.

Langham told the detective about the Prudence F. lead, and that Ralph was tearing his hair out over the phone books as they spoke.

'Good work. I'll have the team look into that. What gets me about Maxwell Fenton,' Mallory said, 'is how opinion of him is so divided. Some people think he was God's gift, while others revile him. Speaking to the legion who knew him, I'm surprised at how many people he fell out with.'

'He was an egotist, Jeff, who didn't need an excuse to feel animosity towards people he rubbed up against.'

'And I find this odd: that there are only seven people he hates sufficiently to want to kill. Why not more? His enemies number a couple of dozen at least, and they're only the people I've managed to hunt down. There must be many more.'

'And yet he's selected these seven for his own form of justice,' Langham said.

'Doctor Bryce, who might have been responsible for the death of Fenton's lover; Hermione Goudge, who criticized his work; George Goudge, who married the woman he supposedly loved; Holly Beckwith, who destroyed some of his paintings; Crispin Proudfoot, who stole his money; and Maria, who had the temerity to fight back and scarred him for life.'

'Not forgetting Edgar Benedict,' Langham said, and recounted what Constance Merriman had told him about Benedict's cheating in relation to the West End production.

Hunched over the wheel and peering into the slanting rain, Mallory shook his head. 'And these are sufficient reasons to kill people?'

As the question was rhetorical, Langham remained silent.

They left London in their wake and proceeded at a steady forty miles an hour into the country. Darkness descended rapidly, and the rain became torrential. The wipers beat a regular, metronomic rhythm, and the heat of the car lulled Langham to the edge of slumber.

Mallory was saying, 'And speaking of Fenton's health, mental and physical . . . I've arranged to meet with Doctor Bryce's partner at Oldhurst later today. I want to take a look at Fenton's medical records. I know there was a rumour that he was seriously ill – but was it any more than that?'

Langham recalled the bedroom at Winterfield, equipped with a hospital bed, oxygen tanks and medicines. 'It was all set up at the house to give the impression that he was on his last legs. And Edgar Benedict was certainly made up to appear grievously ill.'

'All part of the charade to put us off the scent?' Mallory said. 'We'll probably find that he's as fit as a fiddle.'

London gave way to the low hills of Essex, and the quiet road climbed and dipped through rolling countryside. A gibbous moon raced through the clouds, and as they approached the small market town of Oldhurst an hour after setting off, the rain eased and then stopped altogether.

Mallory found St Michael's Church on the edge of town, and the patch of unconsecrated land adjacent. It looked to Langham's unpractised eye like a farmer's unploughed meadow, until he made out half a dozen headstones in the moonlight.

A navy-blue police van was parked in a gravelled area next to the church, along with several police cars. As they walked over the tussocky field towards a screened-off area, Mallory explained that half a dozen officers had started digging at three o'clock when the exhumation order came through.

Langham followed the detective around the side of the screen. Half a dozen paraffin lamps, hanging from metal skewers, illuminated the scene with a ruddy light that brought to mind a painting by an old master. A silent group of men stood around the open grave, and Mallory pointed out a police dentist, a fingerprint expert and a local coroner. Two sweating officers in boiler suits had just finished digging, supervised by the detective sergeant Langham recognized as Venables.

Mallory conferred with the coroner, then nodded to the boiler-suited officers. Langham watched them climb into the grave – utilizing rough steps especially dug for the purpose – and with crowbars tip the coffin so that they could gain a handhold and lift it the rest of the way.

In due course the soil-encrusted coffin sat on a pair of scaffolding boards to one side of the grave, and Mallory give the signal for the officers to unscrew the lid.

Everyone edged a little closer to the coffin. An air of expectation hung over the gathering as the officers laboriously removed the screws. They lifted the lid, set it on its edge beside the coffin, then stood back.

The undertaker in charge of the corpse had bound the dead man's shattered skull with a length of bandage so that it resembled an outsized turban. The material covered the right eye, and Langham was surprised to see that the left eye was open and staring from the coffin as if in posthumous accusation.

The dentist knelt beside the corpse and, with the aid of a torch held by one of the boiler-suited officers, opened the dead man's jaw and inspected the revealed dental work.

At the same time the fingerprint specialist inked the forefinger of the corpse's right hand and took a print.

'I had forensics lift some dabs from Benedict's rooms in Forest

Hill,' Mallory explained. 'The dental comparison should prove conclusive, but just to be on the safe side . . .'

While the examination was going on, several people lit up cigarettes and smoked. Clouds periodically obscured the moon, giving the scene the appearance of an old black-and-white film – a horror film, Langham thought, in which all present are startled when the corpse comes to life and sits up in the coffin.

He moved away from the grave and Mallory joined him, lighting up a cigarette.

'I have a team over at Winterfield, going through the place,' Mallory said. 'I don't think for a minute that Fenton was stupid enough to leave any clues as to his present whereabouts, but you never know. This afternoon a team scoured the grounds, and they'll start again in the morning.'

'Looking for?'

Mallory drew on his cigarette. 'It struck me that the little charade with the guests and their subsequent murders might not be the only time he's indulged his homicidal tendencies. If so, then the grounds of Winterfield would be the obvious place to dispose of bodies.'

Langham was sceptical. 'Good luck, but I think you're barking up the wrong tree. Why would Fenton all of a sudden change his modus operandi – from casually killing his enemies and burying them in the grounds of his house, to carefully planning and carrying out these latest murders?' He shook his head. 'Mark my word, these are his first and only killings.'

Mallory grunted. 'I hope you're right, Don.'

Langham stared up at the moon racing through the clouds. 'I wonder where it all went wrong. He was feted in the thirties, regarded as a rising star in the art world. His canvases sold for hundreds.'

'From what I've heard, what he saw at Treblinka did for him. He was never the same after that.'

Langham shrugged. 'Hundreds of British personnel saw the aftermath of what happened at the death camps, and they didn't become killers.'

'He was an artist – a sensitive soul and all that.'

'I've no doubt that his experiences during the war might have contributed to the man he became,' Langham said, 'but there was something deeply flawed about him way before that, back in the early to mid-thirties. He couldn't take criticism or opposition. He treated men and women appallingly – especially women. And yet he had what many people would kill for.' He winced at his inadvertent choice of words. 'He had looks and a certain charm, bags of artistic talent, wealth – back in the thirties, that is – and men and women falling at his feet. And yet look what happened.'

Mallory nipped out his tab end and flicked it into the long grass. 'In all my years with the force,' he said, 'I'm constantly surprised by man's propensity to sow the seeds of his own psychological destruction. It's almost as if certain individuals, affected by their good fortune, react by subconsciously devising their compensatory downfall.'

Langham peered at his friend. 'You've been reading too much Freud, Jeff.'

Mallory laughed. 'All my cheap philosophizing will be scuppered if this chap turns out to be Fenton after all, hmm?'

On cue, Detective Sergeant Venables appeared from behind the canvas screen. 'They're ready when you are, sir.'

They returned to the graveside and approached the police dentist, who nodded and referred to his notes. 'It's Edgar Benedict all right,' he said. 'Evidence of a maxillary molar extraction, and we have three lower mandibular fillings.'

'Good work.' Mallory turned to the fingerprint specialist hovering behind the dentist. 'Yes?'

'The prints match those we took from Edgar Benedict's rooms, sir. The corpse is that of the actor.'

The process of reinterring the coffin began, and Mallory strode from the graveside and lit up another cigarette.

'What kind of monster are we dealing with, Don? To set up Benedict like that, to string Bryce up, slit the throats of the Goudges . . .'

'I wonder . . .' Langham began.

Mallory peered at him through a cloud of cigarette smoke. 'What?'

'That little charade the other night at Winterfield, with Benedict playing the part and putting the wind up the guests, and then blowing his brains out. It wouldn't surprise me in the least if Maxwell Fenton had been present, you know, watching everything from a place of concealment.'

'It'd certainly fit with the kind of man he seems to be,' Mallory

said. He looked at his watch. 'It's almost five thirty. I've arranged
to meet Bryce's colleague in five minutes. The surgery's just across
town.' He called Venables to accompany them in his own car, and
he and Langham returned to the Humber.

'I've been wondering,' Langham began as they drove along the
quiet high street of the market town, 'whether I should take Maria
and get out of London altogether until all this blows over. On the
other hand, that'd feel like running away. I want to nail Fenton
before he kills again.'

Mallory shrugged. 'Combine the two. Find Maria a quiet place
somewhere in the backwoods, and you continue working on the case.'

Langham nodded. 'Ralph's taking Maria and Pamela to a guest
house in Greenwich tonight, but it'd make sense to get Maria well
away from London. It'd be a weight off my mind.'

They pulled into the driveway of a detached Victorian villa that
served as the town's medical practice. A light burned behind the
bay window of a front room.

They were joined by Venables and met at the door by a tall,
gaunt, silver-haired man in his sixties who introduced himself as
Dr Frobisher.

'We spoke on the phone, Inspector. I have Maxwell Fenton's
medical records ready, as you requested.'

Mallory made the introductions, then followed Frobisher into
a spacious surgery with a large mahogany desk in front of the
window and an examination couch against the far wall.

'Terrible business all round, Inspector; first that Mr
Fenton should take such a ghastly way out, and then poor Doctor
Bryce.'

'Did you have occasion to treat Maxwell Fenton?' Mallory
asked.

'Only once or twice, when Doctor Bryce was indisposed,'
Frobisher said. He moved to the desk and picked up a fat buff
folder stuffed with papers.

Mallory took the folder and, before opening it, asked, 'And
what did you make of the artist?'

Frobisher leaned against the desk, crossing his long legs at the
ankles. 'As a person?'

Mallory nodded.

'I judged him to be embittered and self-piteous.' Frobisher gave
a grim smile. 'But then, in the circumstances—'

'The circumstances?'

The doctor indicated the folder. 'As you'll see.'

Mallory leafed to the back of the records, read the most up-to-date sheet, then looked up. 'So he *is* ill?'

'Was,' Frobisher corrected. 'He was suffering from acute myeloid leukaemia. It's my professional opinion that, rather than allow the disease to run its course, Fenton took the easy way out.'

Mallory speed-read the notes. 'He was diagnosed a year ago and given two years. When did you last see him?'

The doctor considered the question. 'Professionally, perhaps a month ago. I could check my records, if you like.'

'That's OK; no need,' Mallory said. 'When you saw him, how was he? Physically able, debilitated?'

'He was surprisingly robust, given his condition, but prone to tiredness.'

Langham asked, 'And how long would you have expected Fenton to have survived?'

'That's very difficult to say in the circumstances. He was in remission at the time, though there's no telling how long that might have lasted.'

'In your professional opinion, approximately?' Mallory pressed.

'I would say that he would have been expected to live for between six months and a year.'

'With increasing debilitation and lack of physical wherewithal, I take it?'

'Towards the end, the last few months, yes, that is so.'

'But for the first few months, he would continue to be, as you said, robust?'

'Notwithstanding the possibility that he would suffer a relapse, Inspector.'

'And medication?' Mallory asked. 'Was that self-administered?'

'We prescribed painkillers and Chlormethine, the latter to treat the disease. He was seen at Broomfield Hospital in Chelmsford every three months.'

Mallory pored over the artist's medical records. 'And when did Fenton receive his last prescription of these drugs?'

His frown increasing, Frobisher said, 'Let me see.'

He took the folder and flipped through the records. 'Here we are. Doctor Bryce prescribed him his usual dosage just over a month ago, and the medication would have lasted six weeks.'

'So, had he lived, he would have had sufficient medication to last him another two weeks?'

'That's correct, Inspector,' Frobisher said, looking even more mystified.

'And,' Mallory went on, 'we're speaking theoretically here: how long might he have continued to function, in reasonable physical health, without the medication – had he lived?'

Dr Frobisher blinked at the question. 'Why, that's quite impossible to say.'

'At a guess?'

The doctor's grimace indicated his displeasure at being pressed to speculate. 'At a guess, a few weeks. And then, without the drugs, I think his deterioration would have been rapid.'

Mallory smiled and handed him the folder. 'You've been extremely helpful, Doctor. We won't keep you any longer.'

Frowning, Frobisher watched the trio leave his surgery.

As they were crossing to the cars, Langham said, 'So if Frobisher's right, Fenton had enough medication to last him a fortnight.'

'Always assuming,' Mallory said, 'that he hasn't been able to source it from elsewhere. Which, knowing the man's cunning, wouldn't surprise me in the slightest.'

Venables hurried across to his car, from which the sound of a crackling voice could be heard on the two-way radio.

He reached in through the open window and spoke into the receiver.

Langham and Mallory joined him.

'That was Sergeant Welland,' Venables said, lowering the receiver. 'Holly Beckwith has been attacked.'

'Fatally?'

Venables shook his head. 'Too early to tell, sir. The medics are with her now.'

'Let's go,' Mallory said.

TWENTY-ONE

As Mallory raced back to London, ignoring both the speed limit and the occasional traffic light, Langham thought back a day to his meeting with Holly Beckwith. The fact that Maxwell Fenton – or his red-headed accomplice – had attacked her in order to right some perceived wrong committed more than twenty years ago filled him with rage.

It was not knowing her fate, he thought later as they tore through Romford, that was so excruciating. He was sure that she was as dead as Fenton's other hapless victims, a life cut needlessly short by the egotistical vengeance of a psychopath.

Fifty yards ahead, Venables led the way in his squad car, its rotating beacon filling the night with a lapis lazuli light.

'There'll be hell to pay,' Mallory muttered to himself as he hunched over the wheel and accelerated.

'What's that?'

'The incompetent fools who were supposed to be guarding Beckwith,' the South African said. 'What the hell were they doing? I spoke to them myself just yesterday. I told them what they were up against. They're experienced men. Two of my best. I can't see how they'd let this happen.'

'Fenton's ingenious if nothing else,' Langham said. 'He or the redhead must have followed Beckwith at some point.' He looked across at Mallory. 'The sooner I get Maria out of London, the better.'

'To our advantage,' the detective said, 'is the fact that they're going about this meticulously – literally by numbers. Beckwith was fourth on his list, and Proudfoot is next up. Maria was number six, right?'

Langham nodded. 'Scant consolation,' he muttered.

'It buys us a bit of time – for you to get Maria securely holed up somewhere and for us to ensure that Proudfoot is placed beyond Fenton's reach. So far Fenton and Co. have limited themselves to a murder a day. Let's hope they stick to that.'

He swore and rammed the heel of his hand against the horn, angered at a lorry dawdling along at twenty miles an hour. He accelerated, overtook the truck and settled back to an even fifty miles an hour when he caught up with Venables.

They reached Dalston and slowed down along Queensbridge Road, then turned right and drove on for half a mile. A police car and a taped cordon blocked off the next left turning. Mallory wound down the window and flashed his badge. A uniformed constable waved him through.

Along the quiet street of terraced houses, an ambulance, four police cars and a forensics van were drawn up outside a house in which every window was illuminated. A gaggle of curious neighbours pressed in on either side, kept at bay by more police tape and four overworked constables.

Mallory screeched to a halt and leapt out. He crossed to the gate of the house and spoke to a plainclothes officer, joined by Venables. Officers in blue boiler suits moved to and from the house. Langham felt his stomach turn as he climbed from the car.

'Donald!' a familiar voice called out to him.

Incredulous, he turned and saw Ralph's Morris Minor parked behind the forensics van. Maria jumped from the back of the car and ran across to him.

'Maria? What the—?'

She sobbed against his shoulder for a few moments, and then he held her at arm's length, staring at her tear-streaked face.

'Donald, it was terrible! Holly phoned us. Ralph had just driven us back to Pamela's place to pick up a few things. We were in the house when the phone rang. Holly . . . she was trying to contact you. She'd phoned the police, but they hadn't arrived. So she rang your office, but you weren't there. Then she remembered that you'd given her Pamela's number.'

Behind her, in the back of Ralph's car, he saw Pamela holding her head in her hands. Ralph was beside her, attempting to console the young woman.

'Holly was desperate,' Maria went on. 'There was someone trying to get into the house. The police . . . the men who were supposed to be protecting her' – she shook her head – 'they were unconscious or dead, and someone was trying to get in through the front door. She pleaded with me to help her, Donald! I promised we'd be there as soon as possible. I raced out and told Ralph and the police. There was no way we could just drive straight off to Greenwich, Donald, so he agreed to bring us here.' She gestured pathetically to the house. 'We got here just as soon as we could . . .'

She shook her head, stricken.

'The officers entered the house when we got here,' she went on. 'The front door was wide open. I followed, but one of the officers shouted at me to stay where I was.' She smiled at him through her tears. 'But I wasn't going to do that, was I? So I followed him in and . . . and in the front room . . . Oh, it was horrible! Poor, poor Holly . . .'

She broke down again.

He murmured comforting words that he knew to be no more than futile platitudes.

Ralph climbed from the back of his car and approached, nodding to Langham and touching Maria's elbow.

'I could take Maria and Pam to the guest house, Don,' he said.

'No,' Langham said, surprising himself. 'I've got a better idea. Call me paranoid, but I wouldn't put it past Fenton or the woman to follow you. Wait here a sec.'

He crossed to where Mallory was conferring with a forensics officer, cleared his idea with the detective, and returned to Ralph and Maria. He called over one of the officers assigned to protect the women and said, 'Detective Inspector Mallory's okayed this: you're to take my wife and Pamela out to Suffolk. The Grange Hotel, Abbotsford. There'll be plenty of empty rooms at this time of year. You'll stay there until told otherwise. Any expenses above and beyond what you can claim from the force, I'll cover. Understood?'

The officer nodded. 'I'll need to have a word with the boss,' he said, nodding towards Mallory.

'Off you go.'

He squeezed Maria's shoulder. 'You'll be safe in the country, and I'll phone you.'

The officer returned. 'All set. I'll ring through to the Grange and book a couple of rooms. Don't worry yourself, sir,' he said to Langham. 'They'll be in safe hands.'

The officer returned to the car, informed his driver, then spoke to Pamela.

Langham wiped a tear from Maria's cheek. 'This is for the best. I couldn't bear the thought of your remaining in London.'

'You take care, Donald. No heroics, do you hear me?'

He smiled. 'No heroics,' he promised.

Pamela moved from Ralph's car to the squad car, and Maria slipped into the back beside her. Langham lifted a hand in a forlorn wave as the car started up and made its way beneath the tape obligingly lifted by a constable.

He pointed to the house and said to Ralph, 'I'll have a quick word with Jeff. Have you been inside?'

Ralph grimaced. 'Poor kid didn't stand a chance.'

'Don't wait, Ralph. I'll take the Tube home.'

'Don't be daft. I'll drive you, and I won't take no for an answer. I'll be in the car.'

Langham crossed the road and joined Mallory at the gate. He waited until the detective had finished speaking to the forensics man, then asked, 'How the hell did this happen, Jeff?'

Mallory pointed to the back of the ambulance. In its lighted interior, Langham made out two plainclothes men being attended to by a pair of medics. The officers appeared punch-drunk.

'Fenton knocked them out?'

'Chloroform,' Mallory said. 'He – or his accomplice – obviously had the place under surveillance. When one of the men went into the house to use the bathroom, the chap in the car was approached by someone who tapped on the window. No sooner had the officer wound it down than he had a face full of chloroform. Out like a light. Then the killer stationed himself beside the door, and when the first officer came back out, he jumped him.'

'Was either of the men able to describe the assailant?'

Mallory shook his head. 'Hardly saw a thing. Just an arm and a chloroform pad.'

'Then the bastard went inside and . . .'

'Beckwith heard the scuffle when second officer was attacked. She had the nous to lock the door, run back to the sitting room and phone the police.'

'How did Fenton get in?'

Mallory indicated the front door, where a stained-glass window panel was missing. 'Simply smashed the glass and unfastened the Yale.'

He gestured for Langham to follow him up the garden path, and they crunched over the broken glass and entered the house.

A long corridor terminated in a kitchen at the back of the house. Halfway down, to the left, was a door leading to a sitting room.

From this, periodically, came the blue-white illumination of the police photographer's camera flash. Mallory indicated that they should wait until the photographer had finished. He leaned against the banisters and lit a cigarette.

Langham said, 'Beckwith was staying with someone—'

'That's right. Her friend was out for the night, visiting her parents. She got back about fifteen minutes ago.' He thumbed towards the road. 'She's in one of the cars, being consoled.'

Langham swore.

'We're having a job keeping this from getting out, Don. The press are sniffing around. The Super hit the bloody roof when I phoned him about Beckwith just now. It looks bad – crazed killers on the loose and innocents being slaughtered one by one. Christ, the hacks would have a field day.'

'Have you considered the possibility that it might be better out in the open?' Langham said. 'Then at least the public could be alerted to be on the lookout for Fenton and the redhead.'

'I discussed it with the Super last night,' Mallory said. 'He weighed the benefit of the public knowing who to look out for against the panic it might cause. He thought it wise to keep schtum. He called in a few editors today, explained the situation in the strictest confidence and promised them the full story when we nabbed the killers.'

The photographer emerged from the sitting room, grim-faced, and edged down the hallway. He was followed by a forensics officer who paused to report to Mallory. 'Multiple stab wounds to the chest and stomach. Surgeon says she died within minutes of the first incision. I'll give her this: she didn't give in without a fight.'

'Dabs?'

'Nothing. We've finished here – I'll have a report on your desk first thing.'

'The killer? If she fought . . .'

The officer said, 'He'll be covered in blood, that's for sure. No way of telling if she managed to inflict injuries. Her nails are clean, so she didn't scratch him.'

'What a sodding mess,' Mallory swore.

The officer nodded towards the front door. 'How are . . .?'

Mallory grunted. 'Abbott and Costello? Woozy with the chloroform. They'll live.'

'Go easy on them, boss.'

'Go easy? They were slack at best, incompetent at worst. Chap in the car should've been alert to someone coming up and tapping on the window – especially when his partner had nipped to the ruddy loo. And because of their incompetence . . .'

The officer made no comment and moved off down the hall.

Mallory gestured to the sitting room. 'Shall we?'

The state of the room testified to the officer's claim that Holly Beckwith had not died without a fight. A small table and a couple of easy chairs were overturned. A broken vase and a smashed glass ashtray suggested she'd used them as missiles. A rug was rucked up, a magazine rack tipped over and its contents spilled across the carpet.

Holly Beckwith was curled up in a corner at the back of the room, her stockinged legs folded beneath her. She wore a floral-print dress, the material of its fitted bodice saturated with blood. Her head rested against the wall, her eyes open and staring, her arms covering her stomach as if in a futile attempt to protect herself. The expression on her face was oddly peaceful, wholly at odds with the circumstances of her final seconds.

Langham took one look, then walked over to a sofa beside the window and sat down. He leaned forward and rubbed his tired eyes.

Mallory joined him and slumped into an armchair. 'What are you doing tomorrow?'

'We're going through the phone books in search of Prudence F. We need to find out everything we can about Fenton's friends and acquaintances – see if anyone knows anything about the redhead.'

'I have my team looking into that.'

Langham massaged his tired eyes. 'At some point I should talk to Crispin Proudfoot. He might have some idea about the people the artist knew five years ago. Will you inform the people you have protecting him that we'll be around?'

'Will do,' Mallory said. 'Christ, I'm tired. Up at five this morning, and I've yet to talk to the chumps who were detailed to stop this happening.'

'Haul them over the coals?'

Mallory shook his head. 'No, I'll have them roasted in hell. Except . . . that might've been me out there, Don. They'll be feeling bad enough. One lapse, and an innocent woman dies. It'll be on their consciences for a long time, so I suppose that's punishment enough.'

Langham climbed to his feet. 'I'll leave you to it, Jeff. I'll be in touch if we come up with anything.'

He left the house and crossed to Ralph's car. 'I'm dead beat, Ralph. It's been a long day.'

Ralph drove under the police cordon and along the quiet street.

They continued in silence for a while, and at last Ralph swore. Langham glanced across at him.

'Just thinking about yesterday,' Ralph said. 'Holly was lovely, wasn't she? A real beauty. I finished her cake.'

Langham nodded, feeling his throat constrict at the odd naivety of his friend's non sequitur.

They talked back and forth for the next ten minutes, moving on from the case and discussing football, politics, the petrol shortage. At one point Langham found himself asking, 'Remember Madagascar, Ralph?'

'As if it was yesterday.'

'Remember just after the skirmish at Diego Suarez, where we lost Macgregor? We ransacked that bar and got potted.'

Ralph laughed. 'Hell, that stuff was rotgut. My head the next day . . .'

'I remember sitting with you when the sun came up. We were still drinking, trying to make sense of a good man's death.' He shrugged to himself. 'I feel a bit like that now, Ralph. None of this makes much sense.'

They pulled up outside Langham's Kensington apartment. 'Fancy a nightcap?'

'Better not. Annie'll be wondering where I've got to.'

'See you in the morning, then.'

Ralph saluted. 'So long, Cap'n.'

Langham let himself into the flat. Instead of going straight to bed, he sat in the lounge under the orange glow of the standard lamp and reached for the telephone, then stopped. He wanted to talk to Maria, but she wouldn't yet have arrived at the hotel. He looked at his watch. It was just after eleven.

He sat back and considered the events of the day.

TWENTY-TWO

Langham spent a restless night and woke from confused dreams at seven the following morning. He drew himself a hot bath, shaved, then toasted a couple of slices of white bread, spreading them thickly with butter and Marmite.

It was the first time for months that he'd sat at the breakfast table without Maria. He missed her conversation, their inconsequential chatter about what they would do that day, about the thriller he was working on and the manuscripts Maria was reading for the agency.

At eight he took a bus to Earl's Court. A thick fog had descended during the night, reducing visibility to twenty yards. Figures appeared suddenly through the gloom like ghosts. The grey pall that hung over the city matched his mood.

He saw that Ralph had arrived before him: his Morris Minor was parked outside the Lyons' tearoom. Langham climbed the stairs to the first-floor office and found Ralph seated behind Pamela's desk, pen in hand, going through a phone book. He looked up as Langham entered.

'Couldn't sleep. Got in at seven.'

'Tea?' Langham filled the kettle and spooned three heaps into the stained teapot.

A few minutes later, he passed Ralph his chipped mug and sat on the corner of the desk.

'I'm jiggered,' Ralph said, taking a deep draft. He indicated a handwritten list of telephone numbers. 'Over fifty numbers – and what's the chances of coming up trumps? Like I said yesterday, Prudence F. might've married and changed her name.'

Ralph had extended his search from the London phone books to those covering Essex and Suffolk. Langham nodded to the piled directories. 'What's your logic?'

'Most of Fenton's acquaintances in the thirties were from London, Essex or thereabouts, so that's where I'm concentrating the search.' He passed Langham the list of telephone numbers. 'You might as well start here.'

Langham moved to the inner office, sat back in his chair and lodged his feet on the desk with the telephone in his lap.

For the next hour he worked his way down the list, scoring a thick line through each number as he drew a blank. He fell into a monotonous routine: 'Donald Langham speaking, of the Ryland and Langham Detective Agency. I'm awfully sorry to bother you, but I'm attempting to trace acquaintances of the artist Maxwell Fenton.'

When he did manage to get through, answers varied from 'Never heard of Maxwell Fenton' to 'Now, why would you be trying to trace these people, young man?' He was either given short shrift from people rushing to get to work or subjected to inconsequential chatter from lonely individuals with time on their hands.

It was a slow, painstaking process, and he couldn't shake the conviction that he was chasing the proverbial wild goose.

At nine thirty, with more than twenty numbers crossed off the list, he cradled the receiver and joined Ralph. 'This is flogging a dead horse.'

'I'll say.'

He moved to the window and stared out. He remembered speaking on the phone the day before to Constance Merriman, and his suspicions regarding Maria and Fenton . . . He recalled the portrait of her he'd seen at Winterfield, and the look in her eyes. It was the same expression that Maxwell Fenton had captured in his portrait of the younger Hermione Goudge, when they had been lovers.

He moved suddenly from the window, reversed a chair before the desk and sat down.

'What is it?' Ralph said, staring at Langham.

'Something that occurred to me yesterday, while I was quizzing those women about Fenton and the possibility that he'd fathered a child.'

'What about it?'

'The photo of the guests outside Winterfield.' He hesitated. 'The way Fenton had his hand on Maria's shoulder . . . What if Maria wasn't telling the truth?'

Ralph lowered his chipped mug. 'You mean about her and Fenton?'

'What if she *did* have a fling with him – at her age?'

'What did she say about it?'

Langham shrugged. 'She said they met a few times and Fenton painted her. She said she was flattered, a little in awe.'

'Did you ask her straight out if they'd . . .?'

'Not straight out. But while I was talking to Merriman, it struck me: what if they *had* had an affair, and what if Maria had had a child by Fenton? That'd be reason enough for her not having told me anything.'

Ralph swore. 'But you don't think she did have a kid?'

'No . . . But that doesn't mean they weren't lovers. And if she hasn't been honest with me . . .' The idea made him feel sick.

Ralph shrugged. 'How old was she back then?'

'Eighteen.'

'A kid,' Ralph said. 'As you said, she was dazzled by Fenton showing her so much attention. And so what if she did have an affair and now regrets it? It's understandable that she doesn't want to hurt you by raking it up.'

'Yes, but her not telling me would be somehow even more hurtful.'

Ralph looked thoughtful. At last, he said, 'If I were you, Don, I'd ask her. She loves you. She'll understand how you feel about it.'

'But if she *did* have a fling with him . . .' he said, trying to work out just how he would feel about it. Jealous, over an affair that had happened before the war when she was no more than a girl? He had to admit that, shallow though it might be, he would feel jealous.

Ralph said, 'I'll tell you something, Don. This happened donkey's years ago, back in the early thirties. Me and Annie, we'd been going steady for a couple of years. We were young, both in our late teens. I was head over heels, and I think she was with me. Well, *now* I know she was. Anyway, we had a tiff. More than that – a real, full-blown bust-up. And you know what's daft? I can't even remember what it was all about. I do remember I walked out and said I never wanted to see her again. So weeks passed and I felt sick – you know that feeling in the gut when you miss the girl you love something shocking, and you know you've been a bloody fool? And then I started hearing rumours she was seeing some other bloke – a little git from down Barking way, and boy was I sick!' He smiled at the recollection, sipped his tea and went on, 'To cut a long story short, we got back together and I was as happy as Larry. Annie swore she hadn't seen this lad from Barking, and we got wed six months later.'

'Where's all this leading?' Langham asked, smiling.

'I'm getting there, Don. So a couple of years down the line
. . . I don't know how it came up, but Annie wanted to tell me
something, but couldn't bring herself to. So I ask her straight out
what was bothering her. And she says, "You know that time we
split up, Ralph, and I said I hadn't had a fling with this other
bloke? Well, I did – but I swear it wasn't anything serious. Just
a rebound thing."' Ralph shrugged again. 'Can't say I wasn't cut
up about it, but I thought, well, I can get all shirty about it and
take the high ground, or I can grin and bear it and take it like a
man. It was water under the bridge, and we loved each other, so
why let myself get all het up about something that happened years
ago?'

'So you're telling me to ask Maria, and take it on the chin if
she admits to having an affair, right?'

'That's about the long and the short of it, Don.'

'And if she denies—'

Ralph interrupted. 'Then believe her, you bloody fool, and get
on with it.' He stood up and took his trilby from the hatstand.

'I'm going stir-crazy in here, Don. What say we tootle off and
pay a call on Mr Proudfoot?'

'I thought you were about to suggest a pint,' Langham said.

'When Fenton's behind bars,' Ralph said, 'I'll stand you a gallon.
Righty-ho. Your car or mine?'

'How's your tank?'

'Running on empty.'

'Then we'll take mine,' Langham said, and led the way down
the steps and into the enveloping fog.

He consulted his notebook before they set off. 'The Gables, Highlands
Rise, Muswell Hill.' He smiled. 'The poet of Muswell Hill. It sounds
like something from Chesterton.'

He drove slowly through the fog, heading north.

'Never met a poet before,' Ralph said. 'You read his stuff?'

Langham shook his head. 'Can't say I take to verse. Maria's
up on it, though.'

'You think he makes a decent living?'

'Doubt it. Few poets do. He'll turn out hackwork on the side
– reviews, articles. He might even read for publishers, do a little
copy-editing.'

'Nice work if you can get it.'

Langham shook his head. 'Soul-destroying, believe me. I've done it.'

'So what's he like, this Crispin? From what I saw of him the other morning, he looked a right—'

'Drip,' Langham finished. 'Yes, you said.' Langham accelerated through a set of traffic lights about to turn red. 'What's he like? Oddly enough, he conforms pretty much to the stereotype of your average *fin-de-siècle* poetaster – imagine an up-to-date version of Swinburne.'

'Sorry, guv, you've lost me.'

'In other words, he's effete, privileged, no doubt public-school educated – and probably never done a day's work in his life. And the poor chap's frightened to death. Which, in the circumstances, is quite understandable.'

'What're the chances we'll find him butchered?'

'You have a sick sense of humour, Mr Ryland.'

They came to Muswell Hill ten minutes later. Langham turned on to Highlands Rise and drove up a steep hill lined with respectable Victorian semi-detached villas.

They pulled up on the slope and parked behind an unmarked police car. Langham climbed out and showed his accreditation to the officer in the driving seat of the Wolseley.

'The boss said to expect you.' The officer indicated the tall, turreted mock-gothic pile set back in its own grounds and looking sepulchral in the fog.

'Proudfoot has the attic flat. You'll find Sergeant Wells in the grounds. We're taking it in turns to patrol the place.'

'Good man,' Langham said. 'We just want a quick word with the chap.'

The officer smiled. 'A quick word? If you can get in, you mean.'

'If we can get in?'

'You'll see,' the man said with the smug privilege of prior knowledge.

They made their way through a wrought-iron gate and down the front path.

Langham hammered on the front door, and it was two minutes before a tall, grey-haired woman answered and peered through her pince-nez at them. 'Yes? And who might *you* be?'

Her patronizing manner riled Ralph, who flapped his accreditation before her horsey face and snapped, 'Police.' He pushed past the woman before she had time to stand aside. 'Proudfoot at home?'

'If you are referring to Mr Crispin, then he has informed me that he will *not* be receiving callers.'

'We're not callers,' Ralph said, peering up a flight of gloomy steps. 'Like I sez, we're the Bill. Top floor, I understand?'

Ignoring the woman's feeble protests, Ralph led the way up three flights of steps, Langham smiling at his friend's brusque insolence when dealing with those he considered 'up themselves'.

They came to the third-floor landing and Langham knocked on the door.

Ralph leaned against the woodwork and lit up a Capstan. Langham knocked again, then moved closer to the door and called out, 'Crispin, it's Langham. I'd like a word.'

Still no sound issued from within. Ralph raised his ginger eyebrows. 'Maybe I was right and Fenton's already got at him.'

'If he has, then Jeff's not going to be pleased with the guard detail.'

He knelt and applied his eye to the keyhole, but a key inserted from the other side obscured the view.

He knocked again. 'Come on, Crispin. Open up. It's Langham.'

'I've got an awful feeling, Don.'

Langham nodded. He was beginning to share Ralph's premonition when a frightened, reedy falsetto sounded from behind the door. 'How do I know it's you?'

Ralph wiped his brow. 'The poet lives.'

Langham smiled. 'Crispin,' he said, 'we met the other day, outside the Tivoli Mansions. We had coffee in that café across the road and I gave you my number, remember?'

'There's someone with you. I heard you talking.'

Exasperated, Langham said. 'It's my partner, Ralph Ryland. We'd like a word. Come on, Crispin, open up. There's a good fellow.'

A silence ensued, followed by the sound of the key turning and a bolt being shot.

The door opened a reluctant inch and a pale grey eye focused on Langham. 'Come in. Quickly!'

Langham slipped inside, followed by Ralph, and Proudfoot lost no time in slamming the door, turning the key in the lock and shooting the bolt.

He looked terrible as he collapsed against the door, his normally pale face a shade whiter and his brow speckled with sweat. He wore a lemon-yellow silk shirt and a pale-green cravat beneath his non-existent chin, and looked as if he'd just stepped from the set of an Aldwych farce. Langham was alarmed to see a small pistol clutched in his right hand.

'You've no idea how terrible it's been!'

'I think I can guess,' Langham said.

He looked around the odd-shaped room, crammed in under the sloping eaves. It was sparsely furnished with a battered armchair, a coffee table and a bookshelf bearing slim poetry editions which he guessed Proudfoot had brought with him.

Ralph moved to the only window and peered out. 'I hope the rozzers realize someone could easily climb up here.'

This had the effect of raising a strangled cry from the poet. 'What?'

'I mean, look at it,' Ralph went on, pointing. Langham joined him and looked out. Grey tiles sloped from the dormer window to a flat roof, and a monkey puzzle tree extended its tortured limbs to within a few feet of the roof's guttering.

'Someone could easily shin up the tree, jump on to the roof, climb up the tiles – and in through the window. Bob's your uncle!'

Proudfoot joined them and wailed something unintelligible.

'Don't worry,' Langham said. 'I'm sure the officers are well aware of the risk. Anyway, I'll mention it on the way out.'

Ralph pointed to the gun in the poet's palsied hand. 'Is that thing loaded?'

'Of course. Do you think I'd be fool enough to protect myself with an empty weapon?'

'Then be a sport and put it down, OK, while we have a little chat.'

As if fearing a trick, Proudfoot glanced at Langham, who nodded. The poet collapsed into the armchair and slid the revolver on to the coffee table.

Ralph leaned against the wall and Langham found a squat, barrel-shaped pouffe and sat down.

Proudfoot looked from Ralph to Langham. 'You've come about Beckwith, haven't you?'

Langham stared at him. 'How do you know?'

The poet's face contorted into a rictus of agony. 'There! I knew it.'

Ralph stepped forward and leaned menacingly over the poet. 'How the hell do you know about the actress, chum?'

Proudfoot almost wept. 'Don't you see? And you're supposed to be detectives! Doctor Bryce was killed first, and the following day the Goudges joined him. The actress was destined to be next. Our invitation cards were numbered, as were the seats in the library. One, two, three, four. And four days have elapsed since Bryce's death! Beckwith is dead, and I'm next!'

Langham glanced at Ralph, unsure how much to divulge to the poet.

'Tell me!' Proudfoot cried. 'How did she die?'

'The killer overpowered the officers detailed to guard her.'

'Overpowered?'

'It won't happen again, Crispin. The police won't be caught a second time.' He hoped, for the young man's sake, that his calming words would prove correct.

'How . . . how did she die, Mr Langham?'

'That doesn't matter—'

'Tell me!'

'You heard what he said,' Ralph snapped. 'It doesn't matter. The poor woman's dead. Just leave it at that.'

Now Proudfoot did weep. He hung his head and wailed, 'But who's doing this?' He looked up. 'That night, Fenton threatened us before he killed himself. He's hired someone to carry out his wishes from beyond the grave, hasn't he? An assassin. A cruel, ruthless assassin! I'm right, aren't I?'

'Maxwell Fenton is the killer,' Langham said, silencing the distraught young man.

Proudfoot opened his mouth, but no words were forthcoming. He shook his head, incredulous, and at last found his voice. 'What?'

Ralph said, 'It wasn't Fenton who died that night. It was an actor he hired to play the part. Fenton's still alive.'

'Fenton?' It was almost a whisper, uttered with an almost pantomime expression of disbelief. 'That's impossible!'

'Wish it were, chum,' Ralph said. 'So in a way you're right. He *is* responsible, but not from beyond the grave. He's alive in the here and now.'

Langham rose from the pouffe and stood by the window. Down in the overgrown grounds, he made out a burly figure stalking around the house. The officer looked up, saw Langham and saluted. He returned the gesture.

He turned and said to Proudfoot, 'We'd like to ask you a few questions about Maxwell Fenton.'

Still attempting to process the news of Fenton's return from the dead, the poet nodded distractedly. 'Yes, of course.'

'You were the last person, of the six invited to Winterfield that night, to have known him. What, five years ago?'

'Something like that – before I left for Paris.'

'Do you know if he had a place in London at the time – a flat, or a hotel or guest house he preferred to stay at, or someone he stayed with?'

'I really don't know. Fenton did come up to the capital occasionally, on business, but for the most part he avoided the place like the plague.'

'Did he have friends in the capital, do you know?'

'At the time I knew him, he had few friends. He'd alienated people over the years, you see.'

'And yet he befriended you?'

Proudfoot gave an insipid smile. 'I suppose I was young, just twenty at the time. I wasn't of the generation who'd betrayed him – and he did profess to like my work.'

'What did you talk about?'

The poet waved a languid hand. 'The arts. Poetry. The degeneracy of modern art and the sad decline of culture under the Labour government after the war.'

Langham refrained from arguing. 'Do you know if Fenton had a lover at the time?'

'A lover?' Proudfoot blinked.

'I know he had women by the bushel-load in the thirties, but what about more recently?'

The poet shook his head. 'No, there was no one. He struck me as a very isolated, lonely figure.'

Langham nodded. 'Now, back in the thirties . . . Did he ever talk about those times?'

'Very little, and then only to bewail those he considered his enemies.'

'Did he mention a woman called Prudence? Her surname might have been Foster or Forster, or something similar.'

'No, he never mentioned old lovers. I'm sure I would have recalled his mentioning someone called Prudence.'

'Are you sure? You see, we believe that she might have been the mother of his child.'

He looked startled at this. 'Fenton had a child? Well, he said nothing about one to me.'

'We can't be absolutely sure. There were rumours, talk at the time. Did anything in his conversation about life in general suggest that he might be a father?'

Proudfoot smiled. 'We never spoke of anything like that,' he said. 'As I said, our conversation revolved around the arts, culture and, occasionally, politics.'

Langham looked across the room at Ralph and raised his eyebrows. 'Anything else, Ralph?'

'I think you've covered everything.' Ralph pointed to the armchair situated before the window. 'You don't use that, do you?'

The poet blinked at the object. 'Sometimes. Why?'

'Don't. Or if you do, move it away from the window. We don't want Fenton taking a pot shot at you, do we?'

Proudfoot gulped and said. 'Very well, yes. I'll certainly move it.'

Langham rose to his feet. He indicated the revolver on the table. 'Do you know how to use that thing, Crispin?'

'Ah, no. Not really. I borrowed it from a friend.'

'I hope you never do need to use it, but if you do, then there are one or two things to bear in mind.'

Proudfoot nodded, pathetically eager.

'Hold it in your shooting hand,' Langham said, 'with your non-shooting hand bracing your wrist, like this' – he demonstrated – 'and don't make the mistake of aiming for the subject's head. You might think it's the obvious target – but it's relatively small and easy to miss. Aim for the torso; it's a much larger target. If possible, wait until the subject is within feet of you – that is, presuming he too isn't armed – and fire off two shots in quick succession, then roll right or left, seeking cover, and take aim and fire again.'

He moved to the door.

The poet stared at the gun on the table as if it were a viper. 'Thank you. Yes, I'll remember that.' He smiled up at Langham. 'And I appreciate your coming here today.'

Langham opened the door and stepped from the room. 'We'll talk again soon,' he said.

Ralph tipped his hat at the poet and joined Langham on the landing as Proudfoot locked and bolted the door behind them.

They made their way down the three flights of stairs, ignored the landlady hovering in the hall and emerged into the fog.

Ralph laid a hand on Langham's arm. 'I don't like it, Don. The set-up here.'

'You don't think two men are enough?'

Ralph held up his hand and stuck out a thumb. 'First off, two aren't enough. Second, the front door was unlocked and anyone could get in. Third, Proudfoot might lock and bolt the door, but did you notice the door itself? Thin as matchwood. A chap with an axe would be in there in three blows. Or he'd simply put his shoulder through it. The place is a death trap.'

He gestured for Langham to follow him, then stepped off the path and through the undergrowth. They walked across to a low fence and Ralph peered over into the neighbouring garden. He shook his head. 'Anyone could sneak in there, wait till the patrolling rozzer has passed by, then make for the house. He could be up the tree, on the flat roof and into the attic in three minutes flat.'

They moved along the length of the fence to the back of the garden. Langham made out a dense spinney beyond. Ralph led the way to the monkey puzzle tree and looked up into its branches.

He clutched the lowest and tutted. 'Easy as pie,' he said. 'Even I could climb the ruddy thing.'

They made their way to the front of the house and down the path to the gate.

Ralph indicated the police car. 'Just a jiffy while I have a word in his shell-like,' he said, moving to the Wolseley and tapping on the window.

Langham returned to the Rover and watched Ralph and the officer in animated conversation. Ralph joined him a minute later.

'Told him it was a murder waiting to happen,' he said, 'and suggested he get on to Mallory and ask for reinforcements.' He peered through the fog at the house, frowning. 'I reckon they need at least four men to guard the place, Don.'

'Let's hope these two are a bit more savvy than the pair last night,' Langham said as he started the engine and set off back to Earl's Court.

Ralph had the bright idea of laying in a few bottles of Double Diamond from the off-licence on the corner when they returned.

While he was doing that, Langham bought four pork pies from the butcher's around the corner.

They spent the next two hours in the office, going through the list of names and telephone numbers and getting nowhere. Once, after hearing Ralph chatting for a minute or two, he called through the communicating door, 'What was that?'

Ralph laughed. 'An old biddy wanted to know if being a private detective was anything like a Raymond Chandler novel.'

'What did you say?'

'I told her it was more like a Dorothy L. Sayers – dull and boring.'

'Didn't know you read Sayers.'

'I don't, but Annie likes 'em. I tried one once, but give me a Western any day.'

Langham took ten minutes off, opened another beer and ate his second pie, then picked up the phone again. It was almost four o'clock and getting dark outside. He'd try another ten numbers and then call it a day.

As it happened, he struck lucky on the second call, a Prudence Forester from the village of Wilton near Great Dunmow in Essex.

'Donald Langham speaking,' he said, by now tired of the sound of his own voice, 'of the Ryland and Langham Detective Agency. I'm sorry to bother you, but I'm attempting to trace acquaintances of the artist Maxwell Fenton.'

He heard the catch in the woman's voice as she said in a refined Home Counties accent, 'I . . . I beg your pardon?'

He repeated his introduction.

The woman said, 'Maxwell?'

'That's right. I'm trying to trace the artist's old acquaintances.'

'And did you say that you're a private detective?'

Langham sat up. 'That's correct.' He took a gamble. 'I understand that you knew Maxwell Fenton?'

A silence, followed by, 'I . . . Yes, I did, but it was a long time ago . . .'

Yes!

'I wonder if we could speak in person?' he went on.

'What is this about, Mr Langham?'

'We're attempting to trace the whereabouts of Mr Fenton. If we could meet and discuss—'

'Very well, but . . . but not today. I'm very busy at the moment. But possibly tomorrow.'

Ralph appeared at the door, drawn by the prolonged conversation, a beer bottle in one hand and his eyebrows raised.

Langham gave a thumbs up sign. To the woman, he said,
'Tomorrow will be wonderful. I'll motor down in the morning and
see you around . . . say, eleven?'

'The afternoon would be more convenient.'

'The afternoon it is, then. Would one o'clock suit?'

'Very well, yes. I'll see you at one.' The line went dead as she
replaced the receiver.

'Bingo!' Langham said, copying the woman's address from the
phone book, then clinking beer bottles with Ralph.

'Good work,' Ralph said. 'How about a celebratory pint or two
round the Bull?'

'Lead on, my man.'

One or two pints led to five, and it was after ten o'clock when
Langham drove back to Kensington.

He sat in his armchair in the glow of the standard lamp, the
telephone cradled in his lap. He fumbled with his address book,
found the number of the Grange and dialled.

He wondered if he would be too late, and if everyone at the
hotel would be in bed. He wanted to hear the sound of Maria's
voice, ensure that she was settled in and comfortable, and tell her
all about his day.

He was about to give up and replace the receiver when a
peremptory voice said, 'Yes? The Grange.'

'I would like to speak to Maria Dupré, please. Donald Langham
here. I'm her husband.' He muffled a belch and hoped he didn't
sound too drunk.

'It is rather late, sir.'

He squinted at his wristwatch. 'It's just . . . just ten thirty. If
you could find my wife and tell her that I'd like a quick word.'

The woman drew a breath and a long silence ensued.

He stared through the open window. A streetlight glowed in the
darkness, illuminating the incessantly falling rain. He hoped
the woman hadn't had to rouse Maria from sleep. She wouldn't be
best pleased . . .

'Darling?' She sounded anxious.

'Maria. It's lovely to hear the sound of your voice.'

'Donald, you're drunk!'

'No, not drunk. Not really. Just . . . just a little tight.'

'Are you at home?' she asked. 'Have you been drinking all by yourself?'

'Yes and no. I'm at home, but I've just got back from the Bull after a session with Ralph. And you? Have you settled in? What are you doing?'

'Pamela and I have just finished a game of Scrabble. I'm about to go to bed.'

He told her about his day, the meeting with Crispin Proudfoot and the endless telephone calls culminating in the tracking down of one of Maxwell Fenton's old lovers.

'But are you all right, Maria? You and Pamela. Do you feel safe?' He stared at the bookcase across the room, his vision swimming.

'Very safe. The officers are the epitome of conscientiousness.'

'The epitome of . . .' He tried to repeat the phrase but failed. 'That's good. Very good.'

'They have a room at the end of the hall and will take it in turns to patrol the landing.'

'Have you been working, reading your . . .?'

'This morning I did nothing but read, Donald, and then this afternoon Pamela and I went for a walk up the hill behind the hotel to the folly. Do you remember the folly, darling? We had a picnic there that afternoon.'

'How could I forget? It was a beautiful day.'

The last sunny weekend, he recalled, of summer.

'I'm missing you, Donald.'

'And I'm missing you. But we'll soon have this ghastly business done and dusted, and just as soon as we have . . . I know, I'll come and stay. We'll have a break, a little holiday.'

'That sounds wonderful.'

'And I'll beat you at Scrabble,' he said optimistically.

'You'll try!' She laughed. 'You have been signally unsuccessful so far, my darling!'

They talked for a little longer, tiredness catching up with him, and when he yawned for the third time, Maria said, 'Off you go to bed, Donald. Sleep tight.'

He said goodnight and replaced the receiver.

He poured himself a nightcap, another large whisky, and at midnight dragged himself to bed.

TWENTY-THREE

The summons of the telephone bell woke him at seven.

He sat up, wondering at first what the sound was, then rolled out of bed and staggered into the sitting room. Bright winter sunlight cascaded through the bay window. He blinked at the dazzle and slumped into the armchair, holding his pounding head.

'Langham here. Speaking?' His first thought was that it might be Maria and that something was amiss.

He was relieved when he heard Mallory's baritone. 'Donald? You sound rough.'

'Just a little. Thick head. I'm fine.' He peered across the room at the wall clock. 'Why the blazes are you ringing at this ungodly hour?'

'I've been up since five,' Mallory said. 'Anyway, you were wrong.'

Langham blinked. 'Come again.'

'About Fenton's modus operandi. You doubted that we'd find anything at Winterfield.'

Langham swore.

'My team unearthed a corpse around nine last night,' Mallory went on, 'just after I'd knocked off. I'm heading down there now.'

'Do you know if it's male or female?'

'Male.'

'Any idea who it might be?'

'Not yet. There's a team down there as we speak, examining the remains.'

Langham rubbed his face and tried to marshal his thoughts. 'Look here, we're heading down that way later today.' He told Mallory about having located Prudence Forester. 'We could drop by Winterfield this morning and swap notes.'

'That sounds like an idea. See you there. Oh, there is one other thing. Will you thank Ralph for his suggestion yesterday, about the lack of security at Proudfoot's place?'

'I'll do that. You've drafted more men in?'

'I went to take a look-see last night, and I didn't like the set-up. As Ralph said, anyone could have got in there. And that flat roof was an open invitation. I considered getting a couple more officers to guard the house.'

'I sense a "but" coming.'

'But to be honest I didn't want to endanger my men. I decided to get Proudfoot out of there and take him up to the Grange. I reckoned everyone would be safer there, all round.'

The phrase 'all your eggs in one basket' suddenly occurred to Langham, but he dismissed the thought.

'Are you any closer to locating where Fenton might be holing up?' he asked.

'We've traced a London flat he rented for his occasional trips to the capital, but that was two years ago,' Mallory said. 'Right, duty calls.'

Langham thanked him and rang off, then got through to Ralph at home and arranged to meet him outside the office at eight thirty.

He made himself a quick coffee, decided against a slice of toast, then left the flat and drove to Earl's Court. He was sitting in his car outside the Lyons' tearoom thirty minutes later when Ralph climbed in beside him.

'Beautiful morning, Don. How's the old head?'

'Old. And thick.'

'What have I told you, mate?' Ralph said as Langham started up and pulled out into the flow of traffic. 'Always have a pot of strong tea after a session, before you turn in. But you didn't heed my wise words, did you?'

'I had a whisky instead. I didn't feel like sleeping.'

'A whisky? You're a glutton for punishment. No wonder you look like death warmed up. I'm surprised you didn't go for the hair of the dog.' He peered at Langham. 'You didn't, did you?'

'Well, when I saw the whisky bottle on the table this morning . . . I was tempted. But I fought the urge.'

'Good man. So what did Jeff say about this stiff they dug up at Winterfield?'

As they drove from London, Langham recounted the little that Mallory had reported earlier that morning.

'I'll tell you what,' Ralph said, 'I'm glad I didn't know this Fenton geezer back in the thirties. Odds on I'd've got on his wrong side and ended up in his little black book.'

'What I don't understand,' Langham said, 'is why, if Fenton was in the habit of murdering his enemies and burying them at Winterfield, he suddenly decided to change his method now and stage the little theatre the other night – then bump off his victims one by one with the help of the woman?'

Ralph shrugged. 'I dunno. P'raps he was getting a bit bored with simply killing his victims without warning, so he decided to ring the changes? He wanted the thrill of his victims *knowing* they were for the chop.'

'And as he was too ill to carry out the killings by himself, he roped in the redhead?'

'You've got it in one, Don.'

They drove on through open countryside basking in the unseasonal winter sunlight.

'Did Jeff know if any of Fenton's friends or acquaintances have been reported missing?' Ralph asked.

'He didn't say, but I'm sure he has his team looking into it. And Jeff asked me to thank you for tipping him off about the security at Muswell Hill. He took a gander himself yesterday and decided to move Proudfoot to the Grange.'

'Sounds like a sensible idea.' Ralph touched the rim of his trilby. 'Glad to be of service, Cap'n.'

They passed through Lower Malton and took the lane towards Winterfield, coming to the gate and turning into the long driveway. Storm clouds were massing in the east, threatening rain later. For the time being, bright sunlight illuminated the dew-wet rhododendrons and, when it came into view, the dour facade of the country house.

Jeff Mallory's Humber and three police cars stood before the building, and a uniformed constable was stationed at the front door. Langham crossed to him, showed his accreditation and said that Detective Inspector Mallory was expecting them.

'He's with his team in the grounds half a mile behind the house, sir. Follow the track, then turn right down the pathway.'

They walked around the house, crunching over the gravel, and took the rutted track that cut through a plantation of pines. In the distance, the blue forensics van was parked at the end of the pathway. They reached it and turned down the path, Langham batting away wet fronds of undergrowth.

They came to a clearing a hundred yards into the forest. On the far side, scaffolding boards had been laid out around the grave in a grid pattern, and the forensics team and a police photographer were at pains to use the boards as a walkway so as not to trample the surrounding ground. Two men in boiler suits knelt to examine the corpse.

With the sunlight streaming through the evergreens and birdsong in the air, it would have made an idyllic setting for a picnic. Then Langham caught a sudden, brief whiff of putrescence and grimaced.

Mallory saw them, lifted a hand in greeting and crossed the clearing.

Langham said, 'I assumed, when you said you were ordering the search, that if you found anything, it'd be from years back. But the corpse is more recent, isn't it?'

Mallory nodded. 'He's been dead a month, maybe two.'

'Any idea who it is?' Ralph asked.

Mallory gestured towards the grave. 'The dentist is doing some preliminary work, though the fingerprint chap doubts he can lift anything from the corpse.'

'How did he die?' Langham asked.

'A single gunshot to the head,' Mallory said.

He was interrupted by Detective Sergeant Venables, who turned from the grave and beckoned to Mallory.

'Half a minute,' Mallory said, joining his colleague. They conferred in lowered tones, the big South African nodding from time to time.

Then Langham heard Mallory exclaim incredulously, '*What?*'

Ralph said, 'What the hell?'

Mallory gestured for Langham and Ralph to join him. They crossed the clearing and stepped on to a scaffolding board, and Langham stared down at the corpse.

The man had been old, if his iron-grey hair was any indication. The flesh of his lean face had the silver-green sheen of putrescent meat, and maggots had made a home in the remains of his right eyeball. A neat bullet hole showed as a dark circle at his left temple.

'What is it, Jeff?' Langham murmured.

Mallory pointed to the corpse as the police photographer took a series of shots from various angles. 'I was pretty damned sure it was one of Fenton's old cronies,' he said. 'Another poor sod who'd fallen foul of his vengeance.'

'And it isn't?'

Mallory shook his head. 'Dental records confirm that the corpse is that of Maxwell Fenton.'

'Fenton?' Langham felt the odd urge to laugh at the improbability of the idea. 'There must be some mistake?'

Mallory shook his head. 'It's Fenton all right.'

Ralph said, 'And you say he's been dead for a month or two?'

Mallory nodded.

'But that means . . .' Langham began.

He saw a fallen tree trunk a few yards away, crossed to it and slumped down. Ralph and Mallory joined him.

Ralph lit a cigarette and pulled on it. Mallory knelt before Langham, his arms on his knees like a rugby prop forward posing for a team photograph.

Langham said, 'If Fenton's been dead for a month or more, then he can't have killed Bryce, the Goudges and Holly Beckwith – or arranged for Benedict to shoot himself.'

'And he can't have had anything to do with that piece of theatre here four nights ago,' Mallory said. 'Benedict was contacted, via the Kersh agency, just over two weeks ago.'

'So . . . let's get this straight,' Langham said. 'If he didn't set it up or kill these people, then who might be behind the murders? The redhead, right?' He looked from Ralph to Mallory. 'But why would she have a grudge against all these people, Fenton included, and why did she kill Fenton – if indeed she did?'

He'd been so convinced that Maxwell Fenton was behind the killings, out for sadistic revenge, that the sudden need to reassess everything he had assumed about the man was too much to take on board.

Ralph asked, 'Are we assuming that the same person – the redhead – killed Fenton *and* the others?'

'Isn't that a fair guess?' Mallory asked. 'Surely it's too coincidental otherwise.'

'Very well,' Langham said at last, 'how about this: we go back to our original hypothesis, for argument's sake. Fenton *did* plan that piece of theatre the other night – he *did* want the guests to die one by one. But he was too ill to go about it himself.'

Mallory looked sceptical. 'So he hired the woman, then shot himself, or had himself shot and buried by the redhead, who then goes on a murder spree?' He shook his head. 'Why would she willingly do that? And it isn't as if Fenton had the cash to pay her to go through with it. It's just too fantastic.'

'Maybe he didn't need to pay her,' Langham said.

Mallory frowned. 'What do you mean?'

'What if the woman had her own reasons for wanting these people dead, and killed Fenton to frame him?'

Ralph flicked his cigarette into the undergrowth and shook his head. 'There's a flaw in that argument, Don. Everyone who was a guest that night – including Edgar Benedict – had at some point angered Fenton: they've admitted as much themselves. So how likely is it that the redhead would bear grudges against the *same* group of people and want them all dead? It doesn't wash.'

'No, you're right,' Langham said. 'It's just too coincidental.'

Mallory gazed across at the activity around the grave in brooding silence.

'What now?' Langham asked.

'I'm staying here,' Mallory said. 'The team has been through the house from attic to cellar, but after finding Fenton . . . I should take another look. You?'

'We'll motor up to Great Dunmow and have a chat with this Prudence woman – she had an affair with Fenton back in the thirties, and might even have had his child, though apparently it died in infancy.'

'Do you know if she was in recent contact with Fenton?' Mallory asked.

'I don't, but I'll ask. She might be able to shed a bit more light on Fenton.'

'You don't think the woman herself might be . . .?' Mallory began.

'What? Our killer?'

'The redhead?' Ralph said.

Langham smiled. 'She was described as being young, in her twenties. This woman would be in her mid-forties now, even older.'

'Appearances can be deceptive,' Ralph said. 'I've seen stunning forty-year-olds who could be mistaken for girls.'

Mallory smiled. 'Maybe Fenton treated her so badly she has resented him ever since, took the opportunity to kill him – and then framed him by killing the guests one by one? But I seriously doubt it.'

He led the way from the grave and back through the forest. They said goodbye outside the house just as the storm clouds unleashed a sudden downpour. Mallory sprinted into the house and Langham and Ralph hurried across to the Rover.

Ralph looked at his watch. 'Half eleven, Don. We could drive up to Great Dunmow, find a quiet pub and have a spot of lunch. How's the petrol?'

Langham peered at the gauge. 'A quarter full. It should be enough to see us home.'

He started the engine and drove away from Winterfield, through the village of Lower Malton, and took the road north.

TWENTY-FOUR

Maria and Pamela ate a late breakfast in the great hall on their second morning at the Grange. The hall was vast, with a high vaulted ceiling crisscrossed by oaken beams, its walls hung with hunting prints and landscapes depicting the surrounding countryside. They sat at a big oak table before the window, warmed by the winter sunlight slanting through the tiny leaded panes.

Maria tried to forget about the events of two nights ago, but the image of Holly Beckwith curled up in the corner of the room, blood-soaked and defenceless, kept returning to haunt her.

She looked around the hall, at the dozen or so empty tables, and recalled the place as it had been in the summer when she and Donald had stayed here. The Grange had been full then, and they had spent an idyllic weekend walking through the nearby woods and along the riverbank. She smiled as she remembered what Donald had said the previous night: that when all this was over, they'd have a few days away from everything.

Pamela ploughed her way through a plate piled with bacon, sausages and fried eggs, but Maria could only nibble on a slice of toast.

'Where do you get such an appetite?' she asked. 'For a slim girl, you eat a lot.'

'Always have done,' Pamela laughed. 'My old dad always said you shouldn't start the day on an empty stomach.'

'Even at the best of times, I can take only a slice of toast and a cup of coffee.'

On cue, a waitress crossed the great hall from the kitchen,

bearing another pot of coffee. 'Here you are; I thought you'd like a fresh pot. Now can I get you anything else? More toast?'

'I think we have everything, thank you,' Maria said.

The girl hesitated, looking from Pamela to Maria. 'I was wondering . . . I hope you don't mind me asking?'

Maria smiled. 'Yes?'

'Well, me and cook, we was wondering – are you and Miss Pamela film stars?'

Maria's first impulse was to laugh. 'Film stars?' she said, shaking her head in bemusement.

'Only, you see, we had some actresses staying here last year – they were shooting an Ealing comedy over at Malthorpe Hall – and they had a couple of men with them who me and cook reckoned were bodyguards.' She nodded through the window to where Sergeant Sheppard was standing beside an ornamental flower urn in the drive, smoking a cigarette. 'And what with these two hanging around, all suspicious like, and the young chap spending all night on the landing upstairs, we was wondering . . .'

Maria was trying to think of a convincing cover story when Pamela said, 'We're location scouts, researching a few possible venues for a film.'

'A film at the Grange?' the waitress gasped.

'Well, possibly. We haven't decided yet. And Dennis – the young one – has terrible insomnia.'

'Wait till I tell cook!' the girl said, hurrying back to the kitchen.

Maria laughed. 'Quick thinking!'

'I couldn't honestly tell her the truth, could I?'

'It must look strange, you and I doing nothing all day but mooning around, and Dennis and Sergeant Sheppard patrolling the place.' She hesitated. 'I'm sorry about all this, Pamela – dragging you away from work.'

'What do you mean? This is work, isn't it? Remember, I asked Donald if I could be promoted, and here I am, protecting you.'

Maria smiled. 'Protecting?'

'The other night, in the back of his car, Ralph told me to guard you with my life.' She nodded defiantly. 'So I am.'

Maria smiled. 'That's very kind of you.'

Pamela finished her breakfast and Maria poured another coffee.

'Anyway, what do you think of Dennis?' Pamela asked a little hesitantly.

Maria tipped her head and regarded the young woman. The previous day she'd seen Pamela and the constable chatting in the ornamental garden, and in the evening, on the pretext of going outside for a cigarette, Pamela had spent half an hour in his company before turning in.

'I can't say I've spoken to him.' She smiled. 'But he is rather good-looking, isn't he?'

'I'll say, and do you know what?'

'Let me guess. He's asked you out to dinner?'

'Well, to the pictures when we get back to London.'

'What did you say?'

'*Ra-ther,*' Pamela said, affecting the posh tones that always made Maria laugh.

The young woman finished her coffee and said, 'Scrabble or a stroll?'

Maria had her manuscript to read but baulked at the thought of ploughing through another hundred pages of undergraduate angst. 'I need a little fresh air. Shall we walk up to the folly?'

'Let's,' Pamela said.

'Better clear it with Sergeant Sheppard,' Maria said as they left the great hall.

While Pamela fetched her coat, Maria crunched across the gravel to where the burly policeman was still smoking. He extinguished his cigarette in the flower urn on her approach and raised two fingers to his forehead in an oddly formal salute. 'Morning, ma'am. Enjoyed your breakfast?'

'The coffee certainly woke me up,' she said. 'Pamela and I were thinking of strolling up to the folly.'

'Very well, ma'am, but the same as yesterday, if you will. The folly and no further, and always keep the house in sight. I'll come round the back so I can see you at all times. And if you see anyone approaching who looks suspicious . . .'

'Back to the house lickety-split,' she finished.

Sergeant Sheppard saluted again. 'Okey-dokey, ma'am.'

Maria fetched her coat, hat and gloves from her room and met Pamela in the hallway.

They walked around the house and climbed the gravel path that wound through the rockery at the back of the building, then ascended the steep greensward rising to the high knoll that afforded a wonderful panorama of the surrounding countryside. On its crest stood a seventeenth-century folly, a semi-circular colonnaded stone building with a cupolaed roof.

Halfway up the incline, Maria turned to admire the winter landscape.

The countryside, a combination of woodland and farmland, rolled away in every direction. A low mist obscured the horizon, and in areas still sheltered from the mid-morning sunlight, the land was silvered with frost. There was not a breath of wind; smoke rose vertically from a handful of cottages and the occasional wood pigeon set up a throaty, muffled cooing.

Far below, Sergeant Sheppard appeared around the end of the hall, sat on a boulder in the rockery and lit up another cigarette.

Maria shivered and turned her collar up against the icy chill.

They reached the circular folly and sat on the cold stone seat, facing the Grange. At the far end of the long drive that snaked away from the building, an unmarked black police car stood by the gates. The young constable, Dennis, leaned against the bonnet and gazed down the lane.

Maria scanned the land falling away on either side, and the surrounding woodland beyond. Even if Maxwell Fenton and his accomplice had somehow learned of their whereabouts, she thought, they would find it difficult to approach the hall without being seen.

The odd thing was that despite the evidence of what Fenton had done to date, she did not feel threatened; it was as if she was inhabiting a dream in which the threat was nebulous and directed at someone else. She wondered if this was because she found it almost absurd that Fenton had magnified out of all proportion the slights committed against him. The Fenton she had known had been vain and egotistical, but he had not been insane: that had come later, and with it the desire to seek vengeance.

She thought of the actor, tricked into shooting himself, Dr Bryce and the Goudges and Holly Beckwith . . .

'Strange,' she said, more to herself.

'What is?' Pamela said, lighting a cigarette and inhaling deeply.

'I was thinking about Maxwell Fenton. The odd thing is I would like to meet him, or rather to confront him. I'm angry. I want to know if he is insane. Or if he is quite rational and genuinely thinks he has the God-given right to take the lives of innocent people.'

She shook her head. 'I don't know what would be worse, Pamela: to find that he is mad or sane.'

'Sane,' Pamela said upon reflection.

'Yes, you're probably right.'

Pamela pointed. 'We have company,' she said.

Maria jumped, surprising herself, then saw with relief that Pamela was pointing to a big car that had stopped by the gates to the Grange. Someone climbed from the driving seat and spoke to the constable stationed there, then returned to the car and drove up the winding drive to the house.

'Reinforcements?' Pamela said.

From this angle, they had a partial view of the gravel turning area to the left of the Grange. The car halted and the driver climbed out again, along with another man: they both had the brisk, no-nonsense air of policemen. The driver opened the saloon's back door and a third figure emerged. This one, by complete contrast, had a diminished, skulking aspect as he scuttled to the entrance of the house clutching a small bag to his chest.

'I wonder who . . .?' Pamela began.

'Crispin Proudfoot,' Maria said. 'Another one of Maxwell Fenton's potential victims.'

Pamela finished her cigarette and crushed the butt with the toe of her two-tone shoes. She peered at the policeman stationed by the distant gate.

'Do you think Dennis would like a bit of company?' she asked Maria with a grin.

Maria laughed. 'From a pretty young girl who thinks he's quite a dish? I think he just might.'

'Would you mind awfully if I abandoned you?'

'I really should be getting some reading done,' Maria said.

They left the folly and descended to the house, and Pamela continued along the drive with the purposeful stride of a young woman with only one thing on her mind. Maria collected the manuscript from her room and moved to the library, where a blazing log fire warmed three big sofas positioned around the hearth. She curled up and began reading.

She was surprised when a knock at the door brought her back to the real world. She looked at her wristwatch: an hour had passed in no time at all. She wondered if it might be the waitress, come to see if she would care for refreshments.

The door opened and Crispin Proudfoot inserted his diffident head. 'Oh, there you are, I was wondering . . . I hope you don't mind my interrupting. Sergeant Sheppard said you were here. If you're working, I can . . . Only it would be nice if we could talk, perhaps?'

He had the manner of a jerky, defective clockwork toy coupled with a chronic shyness that made Maria uneasy in his company. There was something at once pathetic and annoying in his diffidence, and she was torn between wanting to tell the young man to pull himself together and hugging him as if he were a needy child.

She smiled and indicated a sofa. 'Not at all. Please, join me.'

'That's awfully good of you.' He hurried across the room and seated himself on the edge of the cushion as if he might at any second leap up and sprint off.

'The police have obviously decided that there's safety in numbers,' Maria said, smiling.

He gave a sickly smile. His hands lay on his corduroy lap, his fingers trembling. He was not, Maria decided, an appealing individual, with his long fingernails, hatchet face, white eyelashes and spittle-flecked lips.

'I saw your husband yesterday. It's thanks to him, I think, that the police decided to move me here. The place I was renting in Muswell Hill . . . Well, Sergeant Sheppard said it was a death trap.'

Startling her, he leaned forward suddenly, almost as if he were about to leap into her lap. 'Donald . . . he told me that Fenton's behind all this. He's killing us all one by one, first poor Doctor Bryce, then the Goudges, and then—'

'Crispin, we're safe here; please believe me. Fenton cannot have traced us here, and we have excellent protection.'

The poet shook his head, almost appealing to her. 'But *are* we safe? Fenton traced the actress, Beckwith – he knew where she'd fled to! How can you be sure he doesn't know where we are?'

His lips trembled as he spoke, and he clutched and unclutched the material of his trousers, comically lifting the turn-ups to reveal lengths of sallow, ginger-haired shin.

'The police have the place surrounded,' she said, excusing her exaggeration. 'Even if by some miracle Fenton knew where we were, he couldn't possibly get through, believe me. And the police are working all hours to capture him. It's only a matter of time.'

A knock sounded at the door, and Proudfoot gave a whinny and almost shot from his chair.

The door opened and the waitress appeared. 'I thought I saw you come in here. All cosy, are we? Now, would you be wanting anything in the way of tea or coffee?'

Maria said that tea would be wonderful, but Proudfoot shook his head as if she were offering hemlock.

Later, Maria sipped her tea and wondered how she might put the young man at his ease.

TWENTY-FIVE

At the Wheatsheaf Arms in Witton, a couple of miles south of Great Dunmow, Langham and Ralph each enjoyed a pint and a ham-and-mustard sandwich.

At five to one Langham consulted his notebook. 'The Old Rectory, Duck Pond Lane.'

Ralph finished his beer. 'Don't think she's a vicar's wife, do you?'

Langham smiled. 'I very much doubt it. She has the same name as she had back in the thirties, when she was seeing Fenton. My guess is she never married. Maybe her experience with Fenton put her off men for life.'

Langham asked the publican for directions to Duck Pond Lane, and they returned to the car.

'How are we going to play this, Don?'

'We don't mention that Fenton is dead,' Langham said. 'We ask her about his friends and acquaintances, and if she's had any contact with him of late.'

'She doesn't live that far from Winterfield,' Ralph said. 'You never know, they might have got back together again.'

Langham grunted. 'More fool her, if so.'

They passed the church, turned left down Duck Pond Lane and drove on for fifty yards until they came to a substantial thatched cottage set back in an extensive lawned garden. A wrought-iron sign bearing the legend 'The Old Rectory' was screwed to the timber gatepost.

Langham pulled into the drive and climbed out.

Ralph rang the doorbell and it was answered almost instantly by a tall woman in her early fifties, her blonde hair turning to grey and swept back from a high forehead. She regarded them with slate-grey eyes and the kind of tight, reserved smile that polite gentlefolk reserve for guests whom they would rather not entertain.

As the nearby church bells tolled the hour, she said, 'Mr Langham, are private detectives always so punctual?'

He smiled. 'More through luck than good judgement, this time.'

He introduced Ralph, and she gestured for them to follow her along the hall to the rear of the house and into a conservatory heated by winter sunlight.

She indicated a pair of wicker seats. 'Would you care for tea?'

Langham was about to decline, saying that they wouldn't keep her long, but Ralph said, 'Don't mind if I do. Mine's white with three.'

'Just black for me, please,' Langham said.

She left the room, and Ralph said, 'Nice place. Wonder how she came by a pile like this?'

'Notice the Bible on the table in the hall, Ralph? And the crucifix on the wall? For a second, I wondered if you're right and she *is* married to a vicar.'

'And kept her own name?' Ralph sounded dubious.

She returned with a tea-tray and sat opposite them on a wicker sofa. She poured three cups of tea and sat back with a china cup held in both hands before her chest, regarding her guests dispassionately.

Langham said, 'I'm sorry to intrude on your time like this—'

She interrupted. 'You mentioned you were attempting to trace Maxwell Fenton, Mr Langham. I take it that you've tried looking for him at Winterfield?'

He nodded. 'Without much luck, I'm afraid.'

'What is this about? Is Maxwell in trouble?'

'We'd like to speak to him regarding an investigation,' he said. 'Were you in contact with Mr Fenton recently?'

She shook her head. 'No. No, I wasn't.'

'When was the last time you did see him?'

She looked past him and stared at the vale falling away behind the house, a slight frown creasing her high forehead. She smiled distantly. 'That would be a long time ago, gentlemen.'

'Before the war?'

'Yes, long before the war.'

'So you wouldn't be able to tell me much at all about his recent activity? His current friends, acquaintances, lovers? You haven't happened to hear anything on the grapevine, so to speak?'

She shook her head. 'I'm sorry, no. Our contact ceased more than twenty-five years ago, and we certainly have no friends or acquaintances in common.' She sipped her tea, looking from Langham to Ralph and back again.

Ralph finished his tea with a gulp, replaced the cup on the saucer, then said, 'We understand you and Fenton were close, back then?'

'I knew Maxwell Fenton in the thirties, yes.'

'You were lovers?' Ralph asked.

Langham could tell, from the sudden set of her jaw, that she resented the question.

'Gentlemen, I would really like to know what this is all about—'

'As Don said,' Ralph interrupted, 'we'd like to trace Fenton regarding an ongoing investigation.'

'And how can anything I have to say about what happened way before the war have any bearing on your enquiries?'

Ralph smiled. 'That's for us to work out.'

Sensing her barely restrained exasperation, Langham said, 'We're working on a murder enquiry. A number of murders, in fact. We believe that the person responsible might be an acquaintance of Maxwell Fenton.'

'Murder?' Her eyes widened fractionally and she set her tea cup aside. 'But is Maxwell in danger?'

Langham hesitated. 'It's too early to say, yet. But everything we can learn about Maxwell Fenton might assist us in tracing him and bringing the killer to justice.'

Her right hand tightened around a small, wadded handkerchief. 'It was all so long ago,' she murmured.

'You probably can't recall that much from back then,' Langham said, 'but if you could answer a few questions . . .'

She shook her head, and at first Langham thought it was in refusal. Then she said, 'You're quite wrong, Mr Langham. I can recall the time as if it were just yesterday. You see, it was the happiest time of my life.'

Langham exchanged a surprised look with Ralph. 'It was?'

'You don't often meet a man like Maxwell Fenton, gentlemen.

And when you do, well . . .' She smiled, and the expression trans-
formed her face. 'You grasp it with both hands, don't you?'

Ralph asked, 'You loved Fenton?'

'I was deeply in love with him. He was the kindest, most loving
man I had ever known.'

Langham tried not to show his surprise. 'Just when was this?'
he asked.

'It was nineteen thirty,' she said. 'I was twenty-five, and Maxwell
was in his forties. He was at the very start of his most successful
period: he was selling his work, staging important exhibitions in
the big London galleries, enjoying critical acclaim. I loved him
so much, and I revelled in his success, in his love for me.'

'But you didn't marry him?' Ralph said.

Her eyes clouded. She looked down at her fists clenched in her
lap. 'That was impossible,' she murmured.

'Impossible?' Langham echoed.

'I was married already, you see.'

'Ah,' Langham said.

'I was married to a man called Archie Forester, and a greater
contrast to Maxwell Fenton you could not imagine. I married
young, Mr Langham, and regretted doing so from almost the very
first day. Archie was an insecure, domineering bully, a businessman
who worked in the city. Oh, he was successful in his field, and
wealthy . . . but shallow, *vindictive*. He kept me tied to the house,
monitored my every movement.'

'How did you meet Maxwell Fenton?' Ralph asked.

She smiled as if at the recollection of that very first meeting.
'Archie allowed me to go to painting classes – we were living in
London at the time – and Maxwell was a tutor there. We were
attracted to each other immediately, and . . .' She shrugged. 'And
we embarked upon the most wonderful, intense love affair.
Embarked? I make it sound like an ocean voyage, don't I? "Swept
up" would be a better phrase. We were swept up in a beautiful,
headlong affair. It changed my life, gentlemen; it made me realize,
after five years of servitude, what real life could be like.'

'What happened?' Ralph asked. 'Hubby found out?'

'He did, but not immediately. What happened to end the affair
was that I fell pregnant.'

Ralph leaned forward. 'And Maxwell was the father?'

She nodded. 'He was.'

Langham recalled what Hermione Goudge had mentioned about one of Maxwell Fenton's lovers losing her baby in infancy.

'And when he found out about the kid, Fenton left you?' Ralph said.

She twisted the handkerchief in agitated fingers. 'You must understand that Maxwell was a free spirit. He made it clear, at the start of the affair, that he didn't want me to leave my husband, that he didn't want conventional domestic ties. I accepted that; I was so happy at having found someone like Maxwell, in contrast to Archie, that I would have accepted anything, any condition Maxwell might have placed on our relationship.' She smiled sadly. 'Call me a fool, if you like.'

'I'm sorry,' Langham said. 'It must have been—'

'It was hell, Mr Langham, and then my husband found out. He suspected something and hired a detective . . . And when he discovered I'd been unfaithful to him and was having Maxwell's child – or rather children, as I was pregnant with twins – Archie demanded that I have the pregnancy terminated.'

So Hermione Goudge had been wrong, Langham thought: Prudence Forester had not lost her child in infancy.

'I refused, of course. I was not killing my babies to assuage my husband's jealousy. But when I told Maxwell I was having his children, he simply walked away, left me. I found myself suddenly all alone without a penny to my name – without Maxwell and tied to a vindictive husband. I told Archie that I would stay with him, but that I would not end the pregnancy. Instead, I would have the twins adopted. He agreed to this with ill grace. He thought that by allowing me to have the children adopted he could keep me. Well, in a way he was right; he did have me – physically, though never in spirit.'

'I'm so sorry,' Langham said. 'And the children?'

'A boy and a girl, and it broke my heart when I gave them up for adoption. They were taken into an orphanage in London.' She smiled, on the verge of tears now. 'I can see you asking why I didn't stick to my guns, tell Archie to go to hell, leave him and keep my son and daughter. But I was young and naive, and I would have had nothing, nothing at all – no house, no money, and certainly no social standing. This was back in the thirties, at the height of the depression.'

'So you stayed with your husband,' Ralph said.

'For better and for worse, richer and poorer.'

'And your children?' Ralph asked.

'When the children were four years old, I was informed that my daughter . . . that she had died. Encephalitis. My son was in a home in London. It was my hope that he would be adopted by a kind, loving family, but . . .'

Langham leaned forward. 'What happened?'

She shook her head, almost flinching at the recollection. 'He was ill for the first few years of his life. He barely survived, and he was five by the time he was well enough to be taken into foster care. He needed a lot of medical attention, and he never found the adoptive parents I wished for him. He was returned to the orphanage and remained there.'

Ralph asked, 'Did you ever see him during this time?'

She shook her head. 'No, that wasn't allowed.'

'And I take it Maxwell likewise wasn't allowed to see his son?' Langham asked.

'He wasn't,' she replied. 'Not that he was in the slightest bit interested in doing so.'

That, Langham thought, sounded more like the Maxwell Fenton he had come to know.

She smiled from Ralph to Langham. 'But happily my son survived, gentlemen. Not only survived, but prospered. When he was twenty-one, he was allowed to access his records and, with my consent to the authorities, he arranged that we should meet.'

Langham nodded. 'And?'

'One moment, please.' She stood and moved from the conservatory.

Ralph ran a hand through his thinning hair. 'Don, you don't think . . .?'

Langham found that his mouth was very dry as he said, 'I don't know.'

Prudence Forester returned, smiling. She was holding a slim booklet and a small black-and-white photograph. She passed Langham the photo, which showed a boy and girl seated side by side; they were perhaps three years old.

'My daughter, Hilary, had the most wonderful head of red hair, Mr Langham, though obviously you can't make that out in the photograph.'

Hilary, Langham thought . . .

She passed him the booklet. 'My son discovered literature, gentlemen. He changed his name and became a poet.'

His heart pounding, Langham stared down at the booklet in his hands: *Etude: Twenty-One Poems* by Crispin Proudfoot.

He looked up at the woman. 'When did you last see your son?'

'Why, just two weeks ago.'

'Do you know if he was in contact with his father?'

Prudence nodded. 'He's been a regular visitor at Winterfield over the course of the past year.'

'The past year?' Ralph repeated. 'He wasn't living in Paris?'

The woman looked bemused. 'But he's never lived in Paris. He often stays with Maxwell at Winterfield, though he doesn't tell me much about the relationship he has with his father. Is something wrong?'

Langham stood. He moved past the woman and stared through the glass. Ralph was at his side, gripping his arm. 'Proudfoot . . .' Ralph murmured. 'But why the hell would he shoot his own father?'

Langham felt ill. 'Or kill the others? Christ, Ralph, he's in Suffolk with . . .'

Ralph clutched his arm. 'I'll get through to the hotel, speak to Mallory's man.' He turned to Prudence. 'Do you have a telephone?' he snapped.

She indicated the door. 'In the hall, but . . .'

Ralph shot through the doorway and into the house.

'Mr Langham, is something . . .?'

Langham stared at her, his vision swimming. 'We must go. Thank you so much for your time.'

He pushed past her, hurried down the hall, and edged past Ralph who was speaking urgently into the receiver.

He ran out to the car and started the engine. As soon as Ralph emerged from the house at a sprint and dived into the passenger seat, Langham accelerated from the drive and turned down the lane.

'Got through to a receptionist at the hotel,' Ralph said. 'She said the detectives were somewhere outside. I told her to find them, quick sharp, with the message that Proudfoot was the killer. Then I phoned the Yard and told the desk sergeant about Proudfoot. He said he'll alert the constabulary at Bury St Edmunds right away. They'll have someone there in twenty minutes.'

'It won't be in time,' Langham said, hunching over the wheel. 'They won't be armed.'

'But Mallory's men at the Grange should be,' Ralph said.

'Should be – but I'm pretty damned sure they aren't.' Langham cursed. 'And Proudfoot's been there all day. He's had time to . . . and you saw what he did to the others.'

'Don, it'll be fine. Jeff has his best men up there, and if the worst comes to the worst, Pamela has my revolver.'

Langham glanced at him. 'What?'

'In the car the other night, when you were consoling Maria – I told Pamela to protect Maria and gave her my revolver.'

'Even so . . .' Langham began, his mind racing.

'Don, it'll be fine, OK? Everything'll be fine. Look, do you want me to drive?'

'You?' Langham shook his head. 'No, I . . .' He needed to be in control, needed to be doing something.

They sped through the village and turned on to the main road. He accelerated, hit forty, then fifty, and overtook three dawdling cars in quick succession.

'North on the A131, right?'

'That'd be quickest.'

He overtook another car. He tried to calculate how long it might take them to reach Abbotsford. Twenty minutes? Twenty-five at the most? The police would arrive just before them, but what if Proudfoot had already . . .?

There was no need to speed, he told himself. But something pressed him to do so. What if the police could do nothing, unarmed as they were? What if they had confronted Proudfoot, but he'd already . . .

He swerved around a coal lorry. The road ahead, rising to the near horizon, was clear of traffic. Langham put his foot down and hit sixty.

He thought back to his meetings with Crispin Proudfoot.

When he had seen the young man outside the Tivoli Mansions, on his way – or so he said – to see Hermione Goudge about the sympathy card he'd received . . .

'Christ, Ralph! What a fool . . .'

'Don?'

'The other day, when I saw Proudfoot outside the Tivoli . . . and what he told me in the café . . . What a stupid, blind fool I've been!'

'Don, you couldn't have—'

'But I could! That's just it. Listen, when I saw him that morning – he was in a blue funk about the card he said he'd just received. I asked him how he had the card when he'd moved into the Muswell Hill place the day before – and he said he'd had to pop back to his old flat for something. Hell – why didn't I realize I'd inadvertently caught him out, and that he was lying?'

'You weren't to know that, Don.'

'And another thing – in the café he told me he'd stolen two hundred pounds from Fenton's desk at Winterfield five years ago, but why didn't I cotton on to the fact that Fenton wouldn't have had that kind of cash lying around in a drawer? He was impoverished. I should have realized that, seen that Proudfoot was lying.'

'That morning when we saw him outside the Tivoli,' Ralph said. 'You think he was going to kill the Goudges there and then?'

Langham thought about it. 'I reckon so, but he changed tack when he saw that I'd seen him in the street. He gave me the sob story about his being on the hit list. I'll grant him this, he was convincing. He even showed me the sympathy card – he probably had a stack of them for future use.'

'So he went back to the Tivoli later that day? But how the hell did he get in?'

'How else? Jeff said he didn't post a guard on the place until four. My guess is he went back before then and simply walked in and said he was visiting a resident, if he was asked.'

'And he killed the Goudges sometime after six o'clock . . . but how did he get out of the place, with the bobby on the door as he was?'

Langham glanced at Ralph. 'The redhead!' he said. 'The concierge and the constable both reported seeing the woman leave at nine. Bloody hell, could it have been Proudfoot, dressed up as his dead sister?'

'Proudfoot? You're kidding!'

'Why not? The redhead was described as small, plain . . .'

'I s'pose it's possible,' Ralph allowed.

They drove on in silence for a while.

'Proudfoot being the killer clears up why Edgar Benedict was contacted via the agency by someone calling himself Mr Smith,' Langham said. 'Fenton was dead by that time, two weeks ago, so Proudfoot used the alias when he called the agency.'

'But why did he kill his old man?' Ralph asked.

'A mercy killing?' Langham suggested. 'To end his suffering?'

They came to a junction and the car in front slowed down. Langham braked, swearing, 'Come on, come on!'

They set off again and Langham put his foot down, swerved around the car, and left it in his wake.

'If the rozzers see us now!' Ralph said.

'I'm stopping for no one. They can chase us into Suffolk and then slap me with a ticket! Hell.'

'What?'

He felt like weeping. 'Yesterday, at Muswell Hill. Remember, I gave Proudfoot that little lesson on how to fire his revolver?'

Ralph murmured, 'You weren't to know.'

'And if he uses it against Maria . . .'

'He won't. The cops'll get there first. And anyway, Pamela's armed, isn't she? She's a bright girl, Don. Proudfoot's a drip. She'll have him on toast.'

'He's a drip who evaded the cops and killed four innocent people – five, including Benedict. He's a wily bastard. Christ, if I get my hands on him, I swear, Ralph, I'll tear him limb from limb.'

'And I'll help you.'

They bypassed Braintree and drove north, and Langham was relieved to see that the road ahead was sparsely populated with traffic: just a handful of cars and the occasional lorry.

He thanked his lucky stars that soon he and Maria would be moving into the country. He recalled her delight at finding the cottage at Ingoldby-over-Water and her gaiety that afternoon as they explored the village.

But if Proudfoot had his way . . .

The sickness in his stomach was matched by the ache in his back as he crouched forward over the wheel. He was too tense; but how could he possibly relax?

He nodded towards the glove compartment. 'The gazetteer. Page forty.'

Ralph pulled the booklet from under the dash and flipped through the pages. 'Got it.'

'The Grange is this side of Abbotsford, on the B1066. But when we come off this road, what's the number of the road?'

Ralph found the relevant road and gave the number.

'Shout when we're getting near.' Langham licked his lips. 'How far from Abbotsford are we?'

'Five miles, a little more. We're nearly there, Don.'

It was the uncertainty that was the torture, the not knowing one way or the other. Maria was either fine now or . . .

He winced at the alternative.

The traffic was light. The sun was still out. On any other occasion, he would have enjoyed the sight of the rolling country, the farms and villages nestling in the vales and folds.

'OK,' Ralph said. 'Take the next turn left, about a quarter of a mile away. We're almost there. Two or three miles off . . .'

He slowed down, turned left along the secondary road, then accelerated, speeding along the dipping and rising lane and around tight bends. There was no other traffic on the narrow lane; he just hoped they wouldn't come across a tractor or truck trundling in the opposite direction.

He felt the weight of the revolver in his overcoat pocket and thought about what they might find at the Grange.

It was all over, one way or another.

Maria was alive.

Or dead.

And the hell was that he didn't know.

He accelerated up a long, straight stretch of road that climbed the gradient of the swelling hillside. They crested the rise and he stared down on the patchwork vista of Suffolk farmland far below. His heart leapt.

'There!' he said, pointing.

The village of Abbotsford, a collection of stone cottages and a Saxon church, nestled in a vale perhaps a mile away. Before the village, standing in splendid isolation, was the Grange.

Langham swerved right down a narrow, twisting lane, and after a minute the engine spluttered. He swore as the car stalled.

'Don?'

'The petrol, Ralph! For Christ's sake!'

The car slowed, moving in spasmodic jerks. Langham gripped the wheel. He felt like screaming in rage and frustration. Instead, he steered the Rover into the side of the lane and leapt out, Ralph in close pursuit.

He set off along the lane at a sprint.

TWENTY-SIX

After lunch in the great hall, Maria took her manuscript to the library and read for an hour. Pamela had retired to her room, dreamy-eyed from spending an hour with Dennis.

Maria looked up as a tap at the door interrupted her reading. She set the manuscript aside with a sigh, regretting telling Crispin Proudfoot that she would be there all afternoon if he needed someone to talk to.

He appeared at the door, fidgeting like a marionette, then strode across to the fire and stood above her.

'It's no good,' he began.

She sighed. 'Sit down, Crispin, and we'll talk.'

'No. I can't sit down. I can't stand being cooped up. You've no idea what it was like, sitting there in that place in Muswell Hill, just waiting. And it's the same here. I was in my room, pacing back and forth, back and forth, helpless . . . Just waiting. I feel like a condemned man.'

'Now, that's just defeatist talk, Crispin. Do sit down and tell me what you're reading at the moment.'

He stood before the fire, cracking his knuckles and looking desperate.

'I need to go out. I need to get some fresh air. Do you think that would be safe? I mean, would the police allow it? I don't suppose you'd care to . . .?'

She sighed again and climbed to her feet. 'We can go for a stroll up the hill to the folly. The police will be fine with that, just as long as we don't stray too far.'

He nodded, gulping so that his Adam's apple bobbed; he looked pathetically grateful. 'That's kind of you. I feel so *imprisoned* in here. I need to get out.'

She arranged to meet him in the hallway in two minutes and fetched her coat, hat and gloves from her room.

As she was passing Pamela's room, the girl emerged. 'I thought I heard you. Going out?'

Maria rolled her eyes. 'Crispin is in a blue funk. I'm taking him for a walk up to the folly.'

'I'll join you.'

'There's really no need, Pamela.'

'In that case I'll go and ask the waitress for a cuppa. I might wander up later.'

They walked down the great staircase together and said goodbye in the hallway. Crispin Proudfoot was examining a framed parchment hanging on the wall beside the entrance. He was garbed in a ridiculously oversized tweed greatcoat and silk scarf, and smiled pathetically when she appeared.

Outside, Maria found one of the officers, who had just relieved Sheppard and Wilson. She told him where they were going, then led Proudfoot around the house and up the hill.

'You don't know how grateful I am to have someone to talk to,' he said.

'You don't have to be, you know? It's nice for me, too.'

'Is it really? I mean . . . Well, you seem to be taking all this in your stride.'

She paused halfway up the hill and turned to admire the view. The frost of that morning had been burned off by the winter sun; a hazy steam rose from the land. The sky was clear, and it would be bitter and frosty again in the morning.

'I don't know,' she said at last. 'Things like this affect everyone differently. People have various strategies to cope with stress.'

'Strategies?' Proudfoot whinnied. 'I'm afraid I can't cope with stress. I fear I go to pieces. How do *you* cope?'

She set off again, hiking up the incline. She wondered suddenly what Donald might be doing; she desperately wanted to see him again, and soon.

'I try to take a realistic view, Crispin,' she said. 'I look at the facts. We are far from London and there's no way Fenton can guess our whereabouts. We're protected by professionals, and the police are working hard to bring him to justice.'

'But do you think all that is enough?'

She sighed, a little exasperated with his defeatism. 'Of course I do, and you should, too. It's no good giving in to despair.'

He shook his head, staring at the grass as they walked. 'I suppose,' he said at last, 'that we're all products of our upbringings, aren't we?'

'Perhaps we are,' she allowed.

'We're influenced by what happened to us as we grew up.'

'To an extent, yes.'

'And if we had good, strong people around to guide us . . .'

She wondered where this might be leading.

The poet said, 'Did you have a good, strong person around to guide you through your youth?'

She nodded as they reached the crest of the hill, flushed with the exertion. 'I had my father. My mother died when I was very young, and in fact I don't remember her at all. A series of nannies brought me up, but my father was always there, and yes, he was strong and loving.'

'Loving,' he said wistfully, as if unfamiliar with the word.

Maria indicated the stone folly, and they crossed to it and sat down.

'Is your father still alive?'

'He is, and he's in London.'

'Do you see him often?'

'Every other week, as it happens. He's the French cultural attaché, though he's due to retire next year.'

'That must be nice. Having him so close, I mean.'

'It is,' she said. 'And you?'

'I beg your . . .?' he began; he had been staring into the distance, and now he brought his focus back to her, and smiled. 'Oh, my father. No, my father is dead, now.'

'I'm sorry,' she murmured.

'I hardly knew him,' he went on quietly. 'You see, I was brought up in an orphanage.'

She shook her head, found herself saying, 'I'm sorry,' again, and realizing how inadequate the words were.

'My mother couldn't keep me,' Proudfoot said. 'She was married, and had had an affair, and her husband wouldn't allow her to keep her children. She had twins, but was forced to put my sister and me up for adoption.'

She nearly said, 'I'm sorry,' for a third time, but instead said, 'That must have been terrible.'

'We were put in an orphanage, but my sister was taken away when I was four. I was heartbroken.'

'I can imagine. How terrible.'

'It was. Terrible; you don't know how terrible . . .'

'But your father?'

The poet shrugged forlornly. 'My father was a great man, a truly great man. He wanted to keep us, he really did. But he wasn't allowed to. He told me that: he said that because of what had happened to him, the authorities wouldn't let him have custody of his children.'

Maria shook her head. 'So . . . you knew your father? You met him?'

'I met him for the first time last year. I traced my mother and asked her about my father. I wanted to meet him, you see; I wanted to know what kind of man he was.'

'It's good that you did meet him, before . . .' She trailed off, watching the poet as he stared into the distance, his pale grey eyes liquid with unshed tears.

'I discovered that he was a good man, a great man.' He stopped, swallowed, and pressed his thumb and forefinger into his eyes, wiping away the tears. 'But he was very ill. He was dying. Can you appreciate the irony? At last I had found my father, only to discover that he had only months to live.'

'At least,' she murmured, 'you did meet him before the end, and found that he was a good man.'

'Oh, yes,' he said. 'At least I did do that. And I am so very glad that I did.'

A silence came between them. She felt uncomfortable witnessing the young man's distress. She stared down at the house, at the police car stationed by the gate. She expected to see the officer down below, behind the house, watching them as the conscientious Sergeant Sheppard had done, but there was no sign of the young man.

'I . . . I asked him why he'd been unable to look after my sister and me when we were young,' Proudfoot went on. 'I wasn't accusing him; I was curious. I wanted there to be a good reason, you see, not just . . . not just apathy or indifference on his part. I wanted him to have had a valid reason for his being unable to take us from the orphanage and love us.'

'And was there?'

'Oh, there certainly was,' he said. 'He told me that the authorities wouldn't allow him to take my sister and me because he was deemed unsuitable.'

Maria looked at the young man. 'Unsuitable . . . in what way?'

'You see, over the years he *had* tried to take us in. He told me that he had first tried when we were just babies, and again when we were three. And then my sister was taken away. But my father said that he tried, again and again. He wanted to take me in, be a loving father to me. But the authorities just wouldn't have it.'

'You said they found him unsuitable?' she said.

He smiled at her, tears glistening in his eyes. He lifted a bony finger to his narrow forehead and tapped his temple. 'Up here. They said he was . . . unstable, unbalanced.'

'He told you that?'

'This summer, when I came to know him a little more. He was an artist, you see, and you know how some people – people in authority, who don't really understand creative types – you know how they regard artists?'

Maria shook her head, trying to find suitable words of sympathy, but failing.

'And do you know what he told me?' he asked.

She shook her head again. 'No. Go on.'

'He told me *why* he had become unstable.'

He slipped his hands into the pockets of his greatcoat and sat back against the grey stone parapet, staring at her.

'And why was that, Crispin?'

He said, 'I think it was Sartre who said that hell is other people, wasn't it? Well, people were certainly hell in my father's case. You see, other people made his life hell. Certain people. Enemies. Terrible people who cheated him, lied to him, denied him love, hurt him.'

'And your father told you this?'

'He did. He told me before he died.'

A chill stole upon her suddenly, a cold that had nothing to do with the weather. She sat very still, unable to move, oddly detached from the scene as if she could not possibly be part of what was happening here.

She said in little more than a whisper, 'Who was your father, Crispin?'

His watery eyes fixed on her. 'I think you know,' he murmured, smiling at her. 'He was Maxwell Fenton.' Then he added, quickly, 'Don't move!'

She wanted to move; she wanted to stand up and run, to get as far away from the poet as she could, but she was frozen to the seat, paralysed with fear and disbelief as she stared at the young man.

She tried to discern any emotion in his face as he regarded her: hatred, rage, satisfaction that he had her where he wanted her. But she could detect none of these things, simply a cold, staring vacancy which she found even more terrifying.

He went on. 'I found my father at last, and he told me he was dying. Then he told me about his life, why he had not been allowed to rescue me . . .' He almost choked on a sob, then gathered himself. 'Do you have any idea what that was like? Learning that I'd had a father who had wanted to love me, but had been prevented from doing so by the actions of other people?'

Maria had the sudden urge to say that Fenton had lied to his son, that the artist was not the aggrieved victim he had claimed to be; that he was a manipulating egotist who had abandoned his children to the orphanage without a second thought.

She kept quiet, knowing full well that the wrong word now, the wrong move, would only hasten her end.

'He told me all about the people who had failed him down the years,' the poet said. 'He told me about the actor, Edgar Benedict, and how he'd cheated my father out of thousands, and Doctor Bryce, whose incompetence had led to the death of someone my father had loved dearly, and my father could never forgive him for that. Then there were the Goudges, George and Hermione. My father was in love with Hermione, at one time, and then George stole her from him, and later Hermione turned against him and traduced his reputation. And Holly Beckwith, the actress who destroyed some of my father's finest paintings just before he was due to have an exhibition in London . . .'

He stopped, then smiled at Maria. 'And then,' he went on, 'there was you. Of all the people who had turned against him down the years,' the poet said, 'he saved his greatest rancour for you. Because it was you who struck the blow – the literal blow – that most affected him. He was never the same, after that, you know. He suffered headaches, blackouts, fits of depression and melancholia. And it was *this*,' Proudfoot seethed, 'that turned the authorities against him and told him he was unsuitable to take me from the orphanage.'

Maria licked her lips and found her voice. 'So . . . you and your father killed these people?'

Proudfoot shook his head, surprising her. 'Not my father, no. He knew nothing about it. Oh, speaking to me over the course of his final weeks, as I nursed him, he expressed the desire to see you all rot in hell. He truly wanted to see you dead, but at that point he hardly had the strength to kill himself, never mind the people who had tormented him.'

From his coat pocket Proudfoot pulled a revolver and clutched it in his thin white hand. He looked up from the weapon resting on his lap and smiled at Maria.

'My father begged me to put an end to his suffering. I nursed him at Winterfield over the course of the last few months, but there came a time when the drugs, the painkillers, were ineffective, and my father wanted nothing but to die. He begged me to kill him, *begged* me. So I bought a gun – this gun.' He shook his head, openly weeping now. 'Can you imagine what that was like for me? Can you? I had at long last found my father, only to discover that he was dying, and was pleading with me to end his life!'

She was frozen with indecision. She could dive at him now, while he was racked with grief and distracted; but at the same time she knew that if she failed to wrest the gun from his grip, if he lifted it and fired . . .

Then the moment was over as the poet gathered himself, gripped the weapon even tighter and said, 'So I agreed. I said I would end his suffering – and, oh, the joy that suffused his face at that moment, the relief. I felt truly honoured then to be his son, to be able to do his bidding. And that morning, one month ago, we went on his favourite walk through the woods, and we sat down on a fallen tree trunk and talked for the very last time. Then I took the revolver'– he lifted the weapon from his lap, staring at it – 'and my father closed his eyes, and I put the gun to his temple and told him that I loved him, and then I pulled the trigger . . .'

Maria was aware of the silence as the poet stopped speaking; even the birdsong had ceased. She was suddenly aware, also, of the intense cold that surrounded them.

To her left, far below behind the house, she saw movement. She turned her head minimally and with a mixture of relief and dread saw that Pamela was making her way slowly through the rockery towards the sloping greensward. The girl saw Maria and raised an arm in greeting.

Maria sat, frozen, unable to respond – not knowing whether to acknowledge the girl, and so alert Proudfoot to her presence, or to stay very still. Did her very inaction endanger Pamela? But if she called out for the girl to run, then she would be endangering herself.

She must keep him talking. If he were distracted, he might not notice Pamela's approach . . .

She said, 'And then, after killing your father, you decided to avenge him, kill the people he claimed had turned against him?'

'I buried my father in the forest he so loved,' said the poet. 'But do you know something . . . I had no intention at the time of killing you and all the others. That only came later, as I grieved for my father, and I came to realize that while it had been so hard to kill the man I loved, it would be so easy to kill those people I now hated. So easy morally, of course – I would be doing the world a service, after all – but how to go about these executions?'

She glanced beyond the poet. Pamela was a hundred yards away and climbing steadily, her eyes on the grass.

'I wanted these people to know *why* they were going to die. I wanted them to dwell on the wrong they had caused my father, and to regret their sins. But how might I do that?'

Maria licked her lips, her heart pounding. Donald had ascribed insanity to Maxwell Fenton, but it was his son who was truly insane.

'Then it came to me in a euphoric flash of inspiration. I would invite you all to Winterfield, and have that fine actor Edgar Benedict play the part of my father, and confront you with your sins and issue his threats – and then conclude the evening by killing himself!'

His grip tightened on the gun. 'So I hired Edgar Benedict to play the part of Maxwell Fenton. I told him that Max was ill and hospitalized, but would forgive Benedict all his misdemeanours once the little charade was over. And the actor was so pathetically grateful at the thought—'

Maria said, 'You gave him a loaded gun, without his knowledge?'

Proudfoot smiled. 'He deserved nothing else for what he did to my father!'

Maria shook her head. 'And Doctor Bryce was complicit in all this?'

'He had little option, after all. My father told me all about how Bryce's incompetence in treating a woman during the war had led to her death. My father, in his magnanimity, did not declare him to the authorities at the time. However, I used this knowledge to gain his assistance.'

'He told the police that Benedict was Maxwell Fenton?' Maria said. 'But you had him where you wanted the poor man – why kill him?'

Proudfoot gave a sickly smile. 'He drank – he drank to excess – and he was far from comfortable acceding to my little game, so how could I trust him to keep his silence in future?'

'So you cold-bloodedly staged his suicide.'

'He was responsible for the death of my father's lover!' he spat, as if this justified his actions.

Maria glanced beyond the young man.

Pamela had almost reached the crest of the hill by now, hands in pocket, head down.

'I couldn't do it all alone, of course,' Proudfoot went on. 'I had help.'

'Help?' Maria said, shaking her head. 'Who . . .?'

'Who else,' he said, 'but my sister?'

The red-headed woman, she thought.

She said, 'You found her, and she agreed to . . .?'

'Found her? She was never really very far away. She was always with me, you see, in here.' He raised a finger and tapped the side of his head. 'In here, talking to me all the time, guiding me, encouraging . . .'

He was, she thought, truly insane.

He looked up, tears spilling from his eyes. 'And together, Maria, we did it. One by one, we killed my father's tormentors.'

Pamela came around the folly and stopped dead in her tracks, staring at the revolver gripped in the young man's hand. He looked up when he saw her, and smiled.

'And you are?'

The young woman froze. She clutched the cheap red handbag hanging from her shoulder, her face white as she stared from Maria to the poet.

She murmured her name.

'Well, Pamela, you're just in time.'

Maria glanced down at the Grange. There was no sign of the officers.

Proudfoot saw the direction of her glance and peered down at the house.

'Stand up,' he said to Maria.

She rose to her feet, aware that she was shaking. She expected him to raise the revolver and shoot her, but the weapon remained on his lap, gripped in his cold, raw, bony hand.

Pamela said, 'The police . . . they're joining us at any minute. If I were you, Mr Proudfoot, I'd put the gun down—'

'Be quiet,' Proudfoot said, smiling. 'I had no intention of shooting Maria here; it was not at all what we had planned. And if the police are really coming . . . Shall we go for a little walk?' He gestured with the gun. 'Maria, join Pamela and walk down the hill, away from the house.'

Maria stepped away from the folly and stood next to Pamela, who reached out instinctively and gripped her hand.

'Now move,' Proudfoot said, 'down the hillside towards the copse in the valley. Walk, don't run, or we will be forced to shoot you in the back. We shall be right behind you, all the way.'

They set off. Maria prayed that one of the officers might be watching, and, seeing them disappear from sight, would decide to follow.

But she knew it was a forlorn hope.

If only the conscientious Sergeant Sheppard had still been on duty . . .

Squeezing Maria's hand, Pamela called out to the poet, 'Where are we going?'

'Beyond the Devil's Bridge,' Proudfoot replied. 'Did you read about the bridge, back at the Grange? There's a piece about it in a frame beside the door. How appropriate, we thought.'

Pamela murmured to Maria, '*We?*'

Maria could not bring herself to formulate a coherent reply.

They continued down the hillside, towards the line of denuded trees. A bitterly cold wind sprang up, blowing along the valley and freezing Maria as she walked.

'Follow the path through the trees,' Proudfoot said.

They left the grass and moved through the woodland, the ground still frozen underfoot. Somewhere nearby, a magpie cawed, the sound ugly in the stillness of the afternoon. She heard the chuckling of a small stream before she saw its silver sparkle beyond the undergrowth.

As they walked, Maria considered her options and came to a decision.

In an undertone, she said, 'I'm going to rush at him, before he
. . .' She paused. 'When we're facing him again, I'll squeeze your
hand. Drop to the ground and I'll rush him—'

'No!' Pamela hissed. 'No, don't do anything. Leave it to—'

Behind them, Proudfoot snarled, 'Quiet!'

They reached the stream and Maria made out, ten yards to their
right, a small, humpbacked stone bridge spanning the water.

'Towards the bridge,' Proudfoot said.

They walked on until the poet called out for them to stop.

'There's a local legend,' Proudfoot said, 'all about the Devil's
Bridge. Four hundred years ago, the lord of the manor was one
Percival Dearborn, an evil man and a fornicator. One day, as he was
walking through his estate, he came to the bridge and halted. On
the far side of the stream was the Devil who was playing a small
golden flute, and the Devil beckoned him and said that if he crossed
the bridge, he could take the flute, for it was magical and would
bring great wealth to those who possessed it. Dearborn crossed the
bridge and reached out for the flute, and the Devil smote the man
dead, then laughed and danced away with Dearborn's soul, playing
a merry tune on his flute. And from that day to this, locals have it
that anyone who crosses the bridge and does not retrace their steps
back across it shall die a painful death.'

Pamela hissed, 'He's mad!'

Maria could only bring herself to nod and squeeze the girl's
hand.

Proudfoot said, 'When we read about the Devil's Bridge, Maria,
we knew – we knew that we should come here. Now cross the bridge.'

Maria stepped forward, her feet pushing through a litter of elm
and sycamore leaves, and as she reached the highpoint of the small
bridge, she heard the first of the sirens. Her heart kicked with
hope. The siren sounded, muffled by the surrounding hills but
growing louder; it was joined by a second, seemingly coming from
the opposite direction, closing in . . .

They crossed the bridge and came to a small clearing in the
trees on the far side of the stream.

Proudfoot seemed unperturbed by the approaching sirens. 'Now
turn around slowly,' he commanded.

They did so, still hand in hand, and faced the young man.

Proudfoot stood before the bridge, clutching the revolver in both
hands, aiming it directly at Maria's chest.

The sirens shrilled in the freezing winter air. One cut out, while the other wailed on, drawing ever closer.

'When we spoke with your husband yesterday, Maria,' Proudfoot said, 'he was kind enough to instruct us how to use the revolver. Until then, you see, we had intended to dispatch you as we had Holly Beckwith – with a carving knife. But how ironic, we thought, to employ the revolver that Mr Langham had so kindly shown us how to use.'

'You're sick!' Pamela cried out.

The second siren stopped suddenly, and the silence in its aftermath was profound. A breathless quiet hung in the air, broken not even by birdsong.

'We had intended to kill only Maria,' Proudfoot said, 'but as you have aligned yourself with evil, Pamela' – he shrugged – 'then we shall have to kill you, too.'

'I'll dive at him,' Maria began.

'You won't!' Pamela hissed in a tone that brooked no argument.

Was she imagining it, or could she hear distant shouts – men's voices calling repeatedly through the cold afternoon? If he heard the voices, Proudfoot gave no sign of heeding them. She peered past the poet and through the trees, but saw no one. She almost wept with despair.

He said, 'Do you regret now what you did to my father, all those years ago, Maria?'

She stared at him, at the thin, desperate face above the shaking hands. If she dived at the poet, would he be quick enough to adjust his aim and hit her before she reached him?

'Well?' Proudfoot barked.

'You don't understand what he tried to do to me!' she began.

She heard a sudden cry and peered through the trees. High above them, on the crest of the hill beside the distant folly, she made out the tiny dark figure of a man, and beside him a smaller figure, and beyond them others in uniform.

Donald and Ralph? Her heart surged at the thought.

She dropped her gaze to the poet.

With his left hand he dug into the pocket of his greatcoat. He pulled something out, something startlingly ginger in the grey of the surrounding terrain – and reached up and placed it, askew, on his head. The effect of the ginger wig atop his pale, twitching face was part comical, part shocking, and for some strange reason made Maria want to weep.

He reached into his pocket for something else; as he felt for it, his expression became suddenly desperate.

'Where is it?' he cried. 'We . . . we *always* use it. Every time!' He reached up with his left hand and touched his lips. 'Crimson, the colour of blood. We always . . .'

Pamela stepped forward, staring at the young man. 'Lipstick? You . . . you can use mine, if you like?'

Beyond Proudfoot, through the trees, Maria saw Donald and Ralph running down the hillside, and heard their voices calling out in desperation.

Proudfoot raised his weapon and aimed at Maria, and with his left hand reached out to the approaching girl.

Pamela took another step towards the poet, opening her handbag and reaching into it as she did so.

Proudfoot held out a hand, weeping now, his expression pathetic and at the same time desperately grateful as Pamela pulled something from the handbag and directed it at the young man.

Maria saw the shocked expression on his face as he registered what Pamela was holding – then she heard the shattering explosion as the girl pulled the trigger of the revolver she gripped in her right hand.

Proudfoot cried out and fired his own weapon, and Maria heard the bullet thud into the bole of a tree behind her. Proudfoot fell to the ground, clutching his right shoulder and sobbing with pain, the ginger wig hanging grotesquely from his head. Pamela strode towards him and stamped on his gun hand, then kicked the revolver into the undergrowth.

Maria looked up. Her vision swimming, she made out half a dozen men running through the trees on the far side of the stream. One of them was Donald, and she would never forget the look of stunned relief on his face as he came towards her.

Walking very slowly now, Maria stepped across the Devil's Bridge and into his arms.

EPILOGUE

Langham kicked his heels in the hallway, reading about Lord Dearborn and the Devil's Bridge while he waited for Maria to fetch her coat. It was a spine-tingling tale, all the more so after what Maria had told him about Crispin Proudfoot's desire to carry out her murder at the bridge.

What, he asked himself, if Proudfoot had never read about Lord Dearborn and his meeting with the Devil? Would the poet have elected to shoot Maria at the folly before Pamela arrived at the scene? The notion made him feel sick.

He considered Proudfoot and how the young man would have the rest of his life, confined to a mental institution, to dwell on his crimes. The previous day Mallory had brought him up to speed with the case: the poet's defence lawyers were to plead insanity, and the inspector was sure that they would win the day.

He heard the click of a door closing and Maria's footsteps on the ancient, creaking floorboards of the gallery. She appeared at the top of the staircase and the sight of her took his breath away, radiant in her bright red raincoat and cloche hat.

He recalled sprinting down the hillside two days earlier, sickened at the sight of Proudfoot aiming his weapon at Maria. He had fumbled with his own revolver, all too aware that he was not within range of the killer.

Then he had heard a gunshot, quickly followed by a second, and expected to see Maria fall to the ground.

Instead, Proudfoot had fallen, and it had seemed incredible to Langham that both Maria and Pamela had survived.

'All set?' Maria said, tapping down the steps.

'Are you sure . . .?' he began.

'Donald, I told you. I want to do this. I need to . . .'

'Lay the ghost.'

'Ah, *oui*. Lay the ghost. I want my memories of the Grange to be pleasant ones, of you and me here – not of Proudfoot and what he tried to do.'

'Come on, then.' He proffered his arm and she took it.

They left the house and walked up the hill to the folly.

It was a brilliantly bright, cold winter's day, ten days before Christmas. On Saturday they were due to have a second viewing of Yew Tree Cottage, and they had decided to stay at the Grange for a few days until then. At first, Langham had been unsure that remaining here was a good idea, but Maria would have none of it when he suggested they return to London. She wished to lay the ghost.

They came to the folly and halted, taking in the view.

The land on every side was very still, sealed silver with lingering frost and hazy. In the distance he made out a solitary tractor, drawing black parallel lines through a field of stubble. Rooks took off from woodland at the foot of the valley, cawing as they rose en masse.

They sat side by side in the folly and Maria gripped his hand.

She said quietly, 'Now I know how Ralph feels, Donald.'

He looked at her, frowning. 'Ralph?'

'Yes,' she said. 'He is tied to you.'

Langham opened his mouth in a silent '*Ah*' of comprehension.

'When someone saves your life,' she said, 'something happens between you. It is not a debt – nothing as simplistic as that. It is a kind of gratitude that goes beyond words and ties you to that person.' She smiled. 'I cannot even begin to describe what I feel for the girl. Had Pamela not done what she did, had she not been given the gun by Ralph' – she shook her head – 'I would be dead, Donald.'

He gripped her hand. 'The very thought . . .' he murmured.

'And I am glad that she did not kill Proudfoot,' she said.

Langham nodded. 'Me, too.'

She stared down at his hand in hers, then said, 'He tried to make me feel guilty. Proudfoot said that what I did to Fenton, that my hitting him over the head . . . that that was the start of his troubles—'

'What utter rubbish!'

'I know it is. That's what I was about to say. Maxwell Fenton was as he was long before I met him. What he told his son about me and all the others . . . He was lying in order to make Proudfoot think better of him. And look what it led to – the deaths of five innocent people.'

'And all along I thought Fenton the insane one.'

'Oh,' she said, staring off into the distance, 'how I wish I had never met Maxwell Fenton!'

She jumped up suddenly, startling him, and strode off a few yards. She stopped, staring down at the Grange, her back to him. She hung her head, and only then – by the movements of her shoulders – did he realize that she was crying.

He jumped to his feet. 'Maria?'

She turned, staring at him with tears streaming down her cheeks. 'I lied, Donald!'

He reached out for her, tried to pull her to him, but she resisted. She shook her head. 'I lied!' she said, staring at him.

'Lied? I don't . . . About what?'

She pressed her knuckles to her lips, half turned and stared into the distance.

'You'll hate me, Donald, but I *must* tell you. I lied to you, because . . . because I didn't want you to know, in case you would think less of me. But I must tell you the truth, and if you hate me for that, and want to . . . to leave—'

He reached out, took her by the shoulders and gently shook her. He smiled, oddly relieved at her words. 'I love you, Maria, and what you did when you were eighteen, a mere girl . . .' He shook his head. 'How could what you did then – manipulated as you were by a scheming egotist – how could that stop me loving the person you are *now*?'

She stared at him with wide eyes. 'You know?'

'I think I suspected when I saw Fenton's portrait of Hermione Goudge at her apartment. There was something in her eyes, a certain look . . . And it was the same look as you had in your eyes in the painting I saw at Winterfield.'

Maria shook her head, staring at him, her expression frozen with fear.

He reached out and stroked her cheek. 'So what if you were smitten with him and had an affair?' He shrugged. 'You were eighteen, Maria, a child, and you shouldn't suffer for what you did then – or what he did to you.'

'Oh!' She gave a sob and embraced him. 'I thought you'd hate me – hate me for what I did then, and for lying to you now.'

He stroked a strand of hair from her forehead. 'Two days ago, down at the bridge when I saw that you were unharmed . . . I'd expected the worst – all the way to the Grange, I feared you were already dead. And what I felt for you as I came over the bridge . . .' He held her at arm's length and stared into her eyes, squeezing her shoulders. 'I understand why you didn't tell me what happened all those years ago, and believe me when I say that it doesn't matter one jot, all right?'

She rested her head on his shoulder and wept with relief.

Later, they walked arm in arm down the hill and through the woods to the Devil's Bridge.

They crossed the bridge and turned, and Langham stood in silence as Maria stared across to where Crispin Proudfoot had confronted her and Pamela.

He watched her. She compressed her lips, her eyes hard as she relived the moment. Then she nodded to herself and, in silence, she took his hand and they made their way back across the Devil's Bridge to the Grange.

.